Praise for Quite Perfectly Dead

"The scenes Geri Newell Gillen told from the killer's POV left me with a chill. Well done. *Quite Perfectly Dead* is a story written with a confident style, offering some unexpected twists that find PI Joe Cameron on the edge of a murder investigation that starts out at a Las Vegas poker tournament and shadows him to his home in Montreal." — *Dietrich Kalteis, Author of Triggerfish*

"The premise of the book is entirely believable, and it held my interest throughout, moving at a great pace. I felt immersed in the characters' lives, and although this is a mystery, the motion of the book is driven by the well-developed characters. A very enjoyable read, I found myself looking for excuses to get back to it whenever I had to put it down." — *Gerry Fostaty, Whistler Independent Book Awards Finalist*

"Laid-back detective Joe Cameron takes us on a rambling, funny, food-conscious tour through the underbellies (and restaurants) of two cities known for their casinos and night life—Montreal and Las Vegas. Joe's cross-border adventures on the trail of a serial poker killer will leave readers hungering for a sequel from the mischievously talented Ms. Gillen." — *Ann Diamond, Winner of the QSPELL Hugh MacLennan Award for Fiction*

"Gillen cleverly whipsaws the reader from Las Vegas to Montreal (both nicely evoked), and back again, in her fast-paced debut novel introducing likable PI Joe Cameron. I'd follow Joe anywhere. I eagerly await his next case." — *David Whellams, Author of The Verdict on Each Man Dead*

QUITE PERFECTLY DEAD

Cards and Crime
in Vegas and Montréal

A Novel by

Geri Newell Gillen

Deux Voiliers Publishing Aylmer, Quebec

First Edition

Copyright © 2016 by Geri Newell Gillen

All rights reserved.

Published in Canada by

Deux Voiliers Publishing, Aylmer, Quebec.

www.deuxvoilierspublishing.com

Library and Archives Canada Cataloguing in Publication

Newell Gillen, Geri, author
    Quite perfectly dead / Geri Newell Gillen.

ISBN 978-1-928049-45-6 (paperback)

    I. Title.

PS8627.E8643Q58 2016   C813'.6   C2016-906149-3

Cover Design – Ian Thomas Shaw

Cover Art – Grant Munro

Title Page Art – Grant Munro

Dedication

For Patrick, my very own pub-loving, poker-playing, Celtic-supporting Glaswegian. Stop worrying. I'm not planning your murder.

Life is like a game of cards. The hand you are dealt is
determinism; the way you play it is free will.
- Jawaharlal Nehru

1

I woke up smiling for the first time ever in my memory. I was lying on my left side in the immense king-size bed, duvet up to my chin, my head nestled into the feather pillow, facing the panoramic floor-to-ceiling windows.

The heavy drapes were open to their fullest, and I looked out at the striking skyline of Las Vegas and the faint mauve outline of the Spring Mountain range in the distance. The sky had taken on that unearthly early morning glow that only seems to happen here in the desert just before the sun rises.

I inspected my surroundings. The just-short-of-tasteful art on the wall. The bedroom furniture. Simple. A bit on the modern trendy side perhaps, but it worked in this space. Nothing was too terribly gaudy. I had to admit, this hotel suite was more than suitable.

The clock radio, that I had set last night, had switched on and was playing in the background. Dvorak's Bagatelles. It was rare to hear that piece played on the radio. So serene and soothing. And most certainly unexpected in a barren uncultured place like Vegas.

I played the scene from last night over and over again in my mind like a cherished old classic film. I had been a bit concerned that something might go wrong. That it might be more difficult than I had imagined. How silly of me. I felt slightly foolish for entertaining any doubts about my abilities to see this through. It was clear now that this was the beginning of something extraordinary.

There had been no mess. No struggle. No scream. Totally seamless. What an achievement. He was dead. And I had never felt more alive in my life.

2

THE PREVIOUS NIGHT

He heard the knock on the door as he was rummaging through the bar fridge for something to calm his nerves. *Who the hell could it be?* He vividly remembered putting the Do Not Disturb sign on the door handle outside. *If that's the maid I'll be giving the hotel management a goddamn earful later. No, that's impossible. It's nearly eleven at night.* He figured maybe it could be a hotel guest in a nearby room, or security reacting to his noisy outburst from earlier.

He contemplated not answering at all. No one could know for sure if he was there. He'd been quiet for the last few minutes after his initial eruption upon arrival back in his hotel room. He tiptoed to the door and looked through the peephole but only saw the door across the hall. He pressed his ear against the door. Silence. He backed away and sat on the edge of the bed.

If it was some poker player I'd made "friends" with in the casino, coming to give me sympathy about my big loss, I'd show them where they could put their damn patronising pity. Christ, more bloody knocking. To hell with it, may as well answer the damn door. I'm in the mood for a battle.

He stood up and stalked over to the door, opening it quickly with his left hand and reaching around with his right hand to grab hold of the privacy sign, ready to wave it in the face of the intruder.

"Ryan, I'm so very sorry."

What the hell? She was gorgeous, standing in the hallway outside his room. She was wearing black satin capris that looked painted on her body, a red halter top barely covering her breasts, big Jackie Onassis sunglasses, and a flying saucer of a yellow sun hat. A black straw beach bag was slung over her shoulder. The outfit was topped off with silky white gloves, like his Gramma used to wear to go to church. His brain raced for a suitable greeting but he just stood fidgeting with the Do Not Disturb sign in his hand.

"Ryan, don't talk. Let me explain." She leaned against the door jamb and removed her sunglasses. Her eyes were a muddle of grey and blue. The colour of a winter sky. "I saw what you went through downstairs in the poker game. Who could blame you for losing your cool? I decided to follow you up here to help you unwind."

She bent down and set the straw bag on the floor, giving him a clear view of her breasts. "Let you blow off steam. I even brought up a few cold beers from the bar. Trust me. I'm here to be your friend. One night only." She let out a giggle like a teenager at the mall. "I only ask one thing in return. Call me Lady MacBet. That's my on-line poker name. She's my wild impulsive side. She's who I want you to meet. Humour me and you won't live to regret it."

Never taking her eyes off him, she confidently slid the cardboard sign from his hand, and replaced it on the door handle. He backed slowly into the room as the heavy door swung shut, with this pin-up of a woman following, step by step. Ryan's mind transitioned from rage to lust. He wasn't convinced that he was reading her signals right. This was unknown territory. But he also realized there was only one way to find out.

"Sweet Ryan. I have some naughty plans. Are you up for it?"

His heart was pounding and his blood was rushing, and it sure wasn't travelling to his head. He barely managed to say yes, his voice cracking like a twelve year old boy hitting puberty.

She walked past him into the bathroom, and came back out with the hotel's fluffy white bathrobe draped over her arm.

"Get out of your clothes and into this," she said, handing him the robe. She turned and went back into the bathroom. While he was undressing he heard the clink of the metal tub stopper being lowered followed by the gushing noise of the water flowing into the tub. He sat down on the edge of the bed drying his clammy hands on the bathrobe.

What he couldn't hear was the unscrewing of a small vial. And he couldn't see the blissful smile on her face as she poured the liquid into a can of beer, swirling and mixing the two together.

"Are you decent?" she called from the bathroom.

"Yes Ma'am," he replied, embarrassed that he was still using his puberty voice, and silently praying that he wouldn't be decent for very much longer.

She walked into the room and offered him the beer. "Sit down on the loveseat, and drink that down. The tub is filling up quickly". She stroked his cheek with her gloved fingers, sending a shiver of pleasure from his head to his groin. His mouth felt as dry as the Vegas desert, and the welcome beer glided down his throat.

She winked before spinning back around and returning to the bathroom, explaining as she left, "I've got some preparations to make in here so that this will be an evening neither of us will ever forget. You drink up, and then we'll begin."

After a few minutes, the water stopped running into the tub, and she called out to him. He was light-headed and desperate to feel her touch again.

"Have you finished your beer?"

He guzzled the last few sips. She walked out of the bathroom, still dressed, much to his disappointment. She stood in front of him silently, taking the empty can from his hand and placing it on the nightstand. She still had those cute little gloves on but they were slightly moist now. She pulled him up from the loveseat and led him silently into the bathroom, which had been transformed. The light had been dimmed, and there were two lit candles, one on the vanity and the other on the inside rim of the tub.

"Take that robe off now and get into the tub. I can hardly wait to show you what we're going to do."

He felt a bit wobbly but lowered himself into the water, anticipating more orders to come. He lay back as she reached over and took the large bath towel from the door hook, folding it into a pillow shape and positioning it under his head. He watched her from the tub as she stood up and stared down at him. She turned to look in the mirror and tuck some stray wisps of hair behind her ears.

Every movement she made was excruciatingly languid and sensual. She lowered the lid of the toilet seat, and sat down beside the tub, never taking her eyes off him.

"Are you alright, Ryan?"

He gave a little nod, expecting her to strip for him. Instead she leaned over, put her hands on his two cheeks, and straightened his head so that he was staring at the ceiling.

"Be patient, Ryan. Relax." She left the room. He worried that if he got any more relaxed than this he would fall asleep. He could hear her moving about the hotel room, softly humming to herself. She called and asked if he wanted her to come back. He tried to answer but couldn't speak. He heard the click of her heels on the bathroom tiles. He tried to turn to see her but his head had become as heavy as a bowling ball.

She knelt down on the floor and lowered her face to his so that he could stare into those beautiful, bottomless eyes of hers. She was so close to him that he could smell her lemony hair. She placed her fingers on his forehead and asked him again if he was feeling okay. He couldn't feel her touch. He thought his lips parted slightly, but he couldn't talk. He realised at that moment that he could barely even breathe.

"Ryan? Can you talk? Nod if you understand me."

He attempted to move his head but was uncertain if he had. He was getting so confused. He tried to swallow. He needed to tell her that he had to get out of the tub. The heat must be getting to him. But he wasn't even sure how to speak anymore.

"Trust me, sweet boy. I'm here to help you."

He heard her rustling in the straw bag. She lifted one of his arms out of the water. *Why can't I feel anything?* She held his left arm up where he could see it, placed a straight edged razor in his right hand, and, wrapping her fingers around his hand, she lowered both of his arms and the knife into the water. *Why the fuck can't I pull my arm away?* He felt a faint stinging when the razor broke the skin just above his wrist, and slid down a few inches in a straight line. He felt nothing by the time she repeated the slice on his other arm.

She was searching again in the infinite pit of her beach bag.

"You understand now, don't you? Thrilling, isn't it?" She put one of her Sunday school hands on his left cheek and the other under his chin, leaning in close. She was wrong. He didn't understand at all. She whispered goodnight and slowly pushed down on the top of his head until he was looking up at her through an inch of water. She took her hands away, but he couldn't raise his head out of the water.

Water was flooding into his nostrils and gushing down his throat. His throat constricted and his lungs were on the brink of exploding. She blew him a kiss, and continued staring at him, adjusting her sun hat. Her eyes twinkled with happiness but he'd never seen a creepier smile. He realized that smile was the last fucking thing he was ever going to see. He stared up at her until she disappeared through the reddening haze of the water.

3

It was another sweltering and humid day in Montréal. The air conditioner was chugging and spluttering in its feeble attempt to lower the temperature in Joe's office. Joe feared it was fighting a losing battle and he'd have to find a new one soon, which was never easy in the middle of a heat wave. He had arrived at work an hour earlier, dressed as casually as possible in black cotton shorts and a T-shirt bearing the logo of the Montréal Impact, the only pro soccer team in town. He had become a staunch supporter over the last few years. The stadium was an easy Metro ride away from downtown, where he lived and worked, and made for a good night out.

Joe had started up his storefront private investigation agency after taking early retirement from the police force. He was 47 years old and felt every year of it. He was what most people would call average looking. An average height of nearly six feet. An average build that rarely deviated by more than five pounds. His hair, which had been average brown all his life, was beginning to acquire silver highlights. The only feature that really stood out on Joe were his eyes. They were anything but average. They looked like exotic brown opals—deep brown with gold striations—that twinkled, typically with either amusement or concern. Combined with the comforting tones of his Scottish brogue, people generally felt relaxed around him.

The office was a large two room space on the ground floor of a beautiful old greystone home, typical of western downtown, on Rue de la Montagne. There were very few actual homes left in the area. Most of the grand old buildings had morphed into offices, bars, restaurants, and beauty spas.

His agency was tucked between two bars. Not the trendy kind, like the bars above Saint-Catherine street, but the comfortable kind, where you could sit and talk to the locals without shouting over the thumpedy-thump of the latest pandemonium blaring through the sound system. Some would say these were the seedier bars and they would be dead right. But he'd never been accused of shying away from seedy. These grungy little pubs reminded him of his favourite watering holes back home. Pubs for the working man—that's where he felt most at ease. Where everybody knew who everybody else was. Where you could spill a drink or fall off a bar stool without too much embarrassment.

You had to be looking for the agency to know it was there. He had installed a small brass plaque on the outside wall next to the doorbell that read "Cameron Investigations." There were four engraved thistles, one at each corner of the plaque, a nod to his homeland.

His desk was tucked into the bay window of what would have been a living room a hundred years ago. In front of his desk he had placed a comfy chair and a vintage rosewood coffee table. The second room had probably been a dining room in its youth, and could be closed off by a sliding door with frosted glass panels, but it usually stayed open. That room was Chantal's territory: her cluttered desk, three oak filing cabinets and a small teak conference table. There was also an old brass tea cart that held the coffee machine, kettle, teapot and an array of cups and cutlery.

His secretary Chantal Meauville—or Personal Assistant as she preferred to be called—was off on a two week holiday, so today he was working alone. He had hired her a few months after start-up. She was nearly thirty years old and quite a character. Just being around her cheered him up on a bumpy day. She had graduated from the École des Beaux-arts de Montréal in her early twenties but had never been able to follow her dream of being an artist. Joe had commissioned a piece from her for the office. The canvas was the size of a small car and depicted an old roll-top writing desk piled high with dusty books, papers, inkwell, a beat-up hunting cap and a vase of dead flowers. Her technique was sort of Kahlo meets Dali. It was signed and titled "L'écrivain Mort". The dead writer. It was a bit creepy but he treasured it.

Chantal had eventually given up on ever achieving fame and fortune through her art and became a barmaid next door at the Lounge. After she was laid off from there, Joe had taken her on. He had taught her enough to keep her busy and useful. He felt very fatherly towards her. He believed she felt a similar connection, as her father had died when she was a teenager and her mother and brother both lived hundreds of miles away in the northern Québec community of Radisson. Furthermore she had a tendency to act like a bossy teenage daughter most of the time. She was completely bilingual and barely had a French accent, although her vocabulary was often as creative as her art.

There was an adjoining windowless alcove, that had been turned into a simple washroom: a toilet and wash basin. He had installed some metal shelving above the cistern to hold extra rolls of toilet paper, cleaning supplies and some everyday medicinal products:

Aspirin, Antacids, and pouches of Resolve, the British miracle hangover cure. Resolve was one of the few things he missed from Glasgow and stocked up on whenever he flew back for a visit. Chocolate was the other, but the Cadbury stash was back in his condo. The only renovation he had made when moving into the office space a few years ago was to have the maple floors sanded and glossed to a crystalline finish.

Above his office there was a cozy French Bistro that he only went to when he was trying to impress high-paying clients. Linen napkins—he couldn't deal with them. Unfold one with a flourish at the side of his chair and then let it float down to his lap? Unfold it covertly in his lap and press it to his thighs? Unfold it nonchalantly and then refold it into a perfect triangle so that he could slip a corner of it up now and then to dab his lips? Or just stuff it into his collar to catch the inevitable sauces and baguette crumbs that would otherwise adorn his shirt? Too many decisions when there was a perfectly good Chinese fast-food joint, an Indian takeaway, and a pub, all within an easy stroll. Paper napkins—that was real life— with a printed logo if the place was posh.

Being between contracts at the moment, he had brought his personal laptop into the office to play a little on-line poker to pass the time. Chantal would have his head if she caught him playing computer games rather than working on the shambles that was the filing system or sending late notice bills out to clients. He poured another cup of coffee, retrieved the biscuit tin from his bottom desk drawer, and fired up the computer. Before he could even log on to the poker site he heard a tentative knock on the outer door.

"Come on in!" he yelled, while folding down the laptop screen. The door swung inward to reveal a young woman, eyes seriously bloodshot, dressed in worn out faded jeans that were allowing one of her knees to escape, and a pale blue, slightly stained, T-shirt. He estimated her to be in her mid-twenties. Her hair was short, chipmunk brown, and didn't look like it had seen a comb that morning, although that may well have been the style she was aiming for. He was never sure anymore. Joe thought she looked sweet and innocent and reminded him of his young sister, who was still in Glasgow. He felt an immediate bond.

"Are you Mr. Cameron? Mr. Joseph Cameron?"

He hadn't been called Mister for a while, and was instantly charmed. "Call me Joe, hen. What can I help you with?"

"I need help, and I don't know what to do. I googled Private Investigators."

He sat quietly, pondering how the word "google" usually sounded fun and slightly kinky, yet out of her mouth, it had a desperate ring. He tried to encourage her to continue with his imitation of a slow wise nod. She stood silently rocking back and forth, fidgeting with the strap of her backpack.

"Let's start with your name, and then tell me what's happened to make you think you need my help." He reached over and turned on the digital recorder that sat on the corner of his desk.

That's all the motivation it took to set her off like a rabbit at a dog track. "I'm Kelly Harper. It's my brother, Ryan. He went to Las Vegas a few days ago and the police called me and he won a ticket on-line to play in a poker tournament and he's dead and the cop said he killed himself and he was in a bathtub..."

Joe's two hands rose in the air like a traffic cop. "Whoa. Hold on, Kelly." He stood up and walked around his desk to where she stood with tears streaming down her face. He held out a box of tissues, which she grabbed and clung on to like a lifesaver.

"Sit down and we'll go through this together, bit by bit, alright?" he said.

She pulled out a tissue, wiped her cheeks, and plopped into the nearby leather club chair while Joe lugged his chair around from the business side of the desk to sit beside her.

"Take a breath, hen, and tell me everything you know—everything that happened since your brother left for Vegas. I might stop you now and then to clarify something, but otherwise, just go slow and steady."

She began again. She had received a phone call from the Vegas police the day before, from a detective by the name of Rebecca Newcross. Newcross had informed her that her brother, Ryan, had been found dead in his hotel room the previous morning and, following their investigation, the coroner had declared the death a suicide.

"Where was your brother living?" Joe asked.

"We share an apartment in Ville Saint-Laurent. Ever since he split up with his wife. Neither of us make much money, so it made sense, you know?"

"How old are you, Kelly?"

"I'm 26. Ryan is..." She covered her mouth with a hand as if she'd been caught swearing in church. "Two years older than me." She stared down at the wad of Kleenex in her hand.

"Why don't you tell me about the trip to Vegas?"

"My brother plays on-line poker. A lot. He won an entry into a live tournament in Las Vegas and flew down there five days ago."

"And then you got the phone call from this detective yesterday that he committed suicide. You don't believe he would have done that?"

"There's no way in the world he would! No way. Look, he had a gambling problem a few years back. He lost a lot of money, his marriage broke up, and he hit pretty damn close to rock bottom. Then we got a place together and, on his own, he decided to get help. He joined Gamblers Anonymous and even began seeing a therapist for anger management. He does still gamble, but for very small amounts." Kelly's voice started to crack. She bent forward and buried her face in the palms of her hands, tufts of soggy Kleenex poking out between all her fingers.

Joe put his hand on one of her wobbling shoulders and rubbed it gently. He didn't speak until she sat up straight again. "Do you know the name of the website he used or the tournament he was playing poker in?"

Kelly looked at him and nodded. She seemed so much younger than her 26 years. "Buckingham Poker is the website he won the entry ticket with. They sponsored Ryan and a couple dozen other players to go to Vegas. They're all staying at the hotel where the tournament is—The Poker Palace."

"Okay, Kelly. What is it that you want me to do?"

"I can't fly. I'm terrified of flying. So I'm hoping I have enough money to get someone like you to go there and find out why they're not investigating any further. Someone who knows the questions to ask and who to ask them to. Shit. They don't even know Ryan." She looked down at the floor, took a deep breath, and then stared back at Joe. "Just because it looks like suicide doesn't always mean it is, am I right?" A new batch of tears started to pool.

"It would cost you less to hire someone down in Las Vegas," Joe said in nearly a whisper.

"I get that. Aside from the fact that I want someone I can talk to, face to face, I have something I want you to do for me. I want someone to fly back with his body. You know?" She took a deep, shaky breath, and her voice quivered. "So he isn't alone on the plane. Can you give me an idea how much you're gonna charge me though?"

He went back behind his desk and scribbled out an estimate; airfare, two nights' hotel, meals, a few taxis. He looked over at Kelly. She was shredding the water-logged Kleenex into confetti and tapping her feet like an Irish dancer—vigorously but not as intricately. He decided—seeing as how he hadn't been to Vegas in a couple of years—that he could charge her half the airfare and have a mini-holiday. While he was there—as long as he made a few bets—he could get drinks for free, so she wouldn't have to cover his bar tab. It wasn't going to be a strenuous job and it wasn't as if he even needed the money. This business was more of a hobby for him. He erased a few more expenses and recalculated.

Joe turned the pad of paper around and slid it across the desk. For the first time since Kelly had walked through his door,she smiled.

4

Joe boarded the plane at Trudeau Airport, a few miles from downtown Montréal, at 8:00 a.m. the day following Kelly Harper's visit to his office. It was a direct flight to Las Vegas, and would get him in around 11:00 a.m., due to the three hour time difference. Once they reached cruising speed, he knew that he had about five hours flying time ahead of him and set up a mini-office on the pull-down tray table so that he could review his notes and paperwork.

He had pried a few more details about Ryan from Kelly. Then he had brought her to a notary who he dealt with occasionally to arrange authorization to ask questions, on Kelly's behalf, to anyone willing to talk to him. He had obtained the required paperwork for getting Ryan's body from the morgue and onto the return flight.

His plan was to stay in Vegas for two nights, so he only had a carry-on with two pairs of shorts, a couple of T-shirts, underwear, toiletries and, of course, aspirin. He had booked a room at the Poker Palace, where Ryan had stayed. It was a medium-sized casino hotel in downtown Vegas wedged between two larger well-known hotels. The Palace was his main link with Ryan—the tournament had been held there—and there should still be people around who had met or seen the young man. The added bonus was that the Las Vegas

Metropolitan Police station was nearby, so he could easily get around on foot, avoiding the heavy downtown traffic.

He had arranged, by email, to phone the detective who had contacted Kelly when he arrived. Detective Newcross had agreed to meet with him sometime in the afternoon.

After an hour of writing up a list of people to talk with, and questions to ask them, he tossed his notebook and pen into his carry-on bag, raised the tray table, put the seat back, and cat-napped till he heard the announcement to prepare for landing.

*

Staring down at Las Vegas from the air, he couldn't get over the size of it since he had first holidayed here with his ex-wife, Anna, in the early nineties. He could distinguish the T-shape of Vegas; the Strip hotels and resorts running from north to south along the Boulevard, and the smaller older casino hotels which ran east to west through the downtown core on Fremont Street. But the sprawling homes and condos stretching out from the city's hub nearly covered the valley's basin floor, enclosed by treeless mountains. Just a few years ago, in the good old days of Elvis, Liberace, and the Rat Pack, you only had to carry a dead body a few hundred yards from the casino to find a good desert grave. Now you'd have to drive for at least an hour. Joe wondered how many decayed bodies were revealed when the foundations were dug for all these homes and schools.

The change in Vegas disappointed him. It didn't have anywhere near the cachet it had before the criminal element was swept away. Approaching the tarmac, he could see the white Janet planes, with their single red stripe, and the black copters lined up in the remote section of the airport that carried Air Force personnel, base workers, and the occasional Extraterrestrial back and forth to Area 51. Civilians didn't know why the military called their Area 51 planes Janet, but Joe's theory was that the first E.T. they found was a female and so they created the portmanteau of Jane and E.T., thus reserving the name Jane and John Doe solely for the use of unknown human folk.

Not far from the Janets, he spotted the pink choppers which transported anyone looking for a bit of adult legal pleasure to one of the many brothels in the nearby town of Pahrump, outside the city limits of Clark County. It was still cheaper than a copter ride to the Grand Canyon and—in his opinion—would make for a more interesting excursion.

The plane landed smoothly and he quickly reached the door of the airport where the shuttles, limos, and taxis idled. He decided against the cheaper shuttle that would take hours to reach downtown as it dropped tourists at hotels along the way. A taxi would be more expensive, but they could circumvent the busy Strip by taking Highway 15, east of Las Vegas Boulevard, all the way downtown.

He stood in the short line at the taxi rank, baking in the 120 degree dry sauna he had just entered. He only had a few minutes to wait before it was his turn and slid into the back seat with his luggage. Joe sat back and enjoyed the air conditioning while the tiny TV, embedded in the back of the front seat, advertised shows and events around town. At the reservation desk of the Poker Palace Hotel within a half hour, he was pleased to discover he could check in to his room early.

By the time he dropped his bag near the closet, it was closing in on noon. He picked up the phone on the bedside table to call Detective Newcross.

"Las Vegas Metro. Homicide Division," a curt female voice answered.

"This is Joe Cameron. Can I speak to Detective Newcross? She's expecting my call." Without any acknowledgement, there was a click, two rings, and a different female voice answered.

"Newcross," she said.

"Detective Newcross? Joe Cameron, from Montréal. I emailed you yesterday regarding a case you were called out on. Ryan Harper?"

Her voice was friendly, yet business-like. "Of course Mr. Cameron. You've arrived safe and sound in our little town?"

"Just checked into the hotel and wondering what time we can meet today. I have a number of questions to ask you, on behalf of his sister."

"It's not unusual for a suicide victim's family to have difficulty dealing with the whole thing. I can meet you and go over the case events but I don't know how much help that'll be. However, after your email yesterday I was able to contact someone to facilitate the transfer of the body through airport security." She spoke very softly and Joe could hear the background racket of the police station. Phones ringing and voices shouting back and forth across desktops. It was the same in every station he'd ever been in.

"I appreciate it. I'll come over whenever it's convenient for you but the sooner the better, really," Joe said.

"I understand, but I have a fairly busy day. I'm getting off my shift in a few hours, and I can give you some time then. I have to drop off some paperwork at the City Hall on my way home, and there's a small neighbourhood pub across the street from it, on Stewart Avenue, just north of Fremont. Would you mind meeting there?"

He couldn't think of anything better than a cold beer right now. Well, nothing better except possibly a cold beer while flying in a pink helicopter to Pahrump.

They agreed to meet at 5:00 p.m. Before he hung up he asked what she was wearing. He got the impression that she was holding back a laugh as she told him she would be in jeans, a white t-shirt, and had a red back-pack.

Over his few years of being a PI, Joe had never relished interviewing detectives, or any police and legal personnel for that matter, probably based on the fact that he used to be a cop himself. Many of them thought PI's were the scum of the earth, and that they only existed to meddle with investigations and make their lives more difficult. Granted, Joe felt that was certainly a perk now, but not his main raison d'être. He didn't get that usual impression of disdain on the phone with Newcross though. He sat on the edge of the bed pondering what to do for two hours, and decided it was worthwhile to make an effort in his appearance, as he was, for all intents and purposes, meeting a woman in a bar.

After showering and towel drying his hair, Joe emptied out his toiletry bag onto the bathroom counter. He had shaved that morning and wouldn't see any growth for another day. He brushed his teeth and intently began to floss. He had a full set of perfect teeth and was proud of it. It wasn't an easy accomplishment when deep-fried Mars Bars were one of the major food groups of his youth. He was no Sean Connery but his Anna had continuously assured him that he had a strong, kind face. The sort of face a person could immediately trust. All in all, he was comfortable enough with himself. At least the physical part.

He dressed in bottle green cargo shorts and a pale brown T-shirt, threw an old Expo's Baseball cap on his head for protection against the desert sun, and went down to the casino floor.

*

Joe reached the hotel lobby and found a shortcut, through a narrow video-poker bar, that led directly into the poker room. The fifth day of the Southern Nevada Poker Tournament was in full swing. The room was separated from the main casino by a glass wall but the muffled clang of slot machines could still be heard. The poker room itself was a bedlam of noise: the flutter and swoosh of cards being shuffled and dealt, the clacking plunk of clay poker chips being rifled, stacked, and thrown into the pot. It was like a bizarre gambling symphony, a background accompaniment to hundreds of people calling out their bets and declarations to their opponents and dealers.

Kiosks, desks, and tables were set up along the entire length of the back wall, all of them displaying identifying banners or posters. Joe scanned the room for the Buckingham Online Poker group, who had sponsored Ryan Harper's trip and entry fee to the tournament.

He saw their banner—which promoted their site as being UK-based—and snaked through the network of poker tables. The modest fold-up table was manned by a casually dressed thirty-something couple. They were deep in conversation with each other and Joe could distinctly make out a Belfast accent and a London one. He looked at their name badges; the expected "Hi, my name is..." stick-on paper rectangle, although slightly posher because the perimeter was adorned with alternating hearts, diamonds, clubs, and spades. One was Peter Surrey, an overweight and older version of Harry Potter. He had a vintage Beatle haircut, round wire-rim eyeglasses and the vestiges of a baby face. Surrey's partner was Veronica Eastgate. She had a powerful build, a military style haircut on top of a sharply angular face, and a few Celtic cross and knot tattoos on her arms. They were dressed identically in jeans and red T-shirts printed with their company's logo: Buckingham Poker – London England – Keep Calm and Gamble.

Joe looked through their brochure and media package while they continued talking to each other about the previous evening's cocktail event. There was also a pile of branded merchandise on display on the tabletop, in case anyone needed an emergency hoodie, keychain, or sunglasses. There was a pause in their conversation and they looked over at Joe.

"Can I help you, mate?" said the Beatle haircut, in a tone that implied he'd rather not.

"Yes, you can. I'm investigating the recent death of Ryan Harper," Joe said, extending his hand to Veronica, and then Peter. "Detective Cameron." He saw no need to tell them that he wasn't a member of the Las Vegas police force.

They both looked much more attentive. "There was a detective here a couple days ago, mate. A woman. We told her everything we knew about the guy, which isn't all that much," said Peter, owner of the London accent. Veronica of Ireland bent down and removed some Buckingham baseball caps from a cardboard box and busied herself arranging them in a neat row beside the keychains.

"Well, some of the questions are well worth going over again due to further information that's come to light. Can you both spare a few minutes, somewhere quiet, to talk?"

"I'm due a break soon anyhow, so we could chat in the poker bar. Ronnie can take her break after that. It'll be dead quiet in there until the tournament breaks in twenty minutes." Peter said, sliding through the small space between the table and the wall.

Joe loved the fact that everyone suggested bar meetings. Damn civilised. They headed off; Joe armed with notepad, pen and his small list of questions. He could only hope that their answers would lead to more. Even if all the evidence pointed to suicide, talking to the last people who saw Ryan Harper alive was the least he could do for Kelly.

They sat at the bar and ordered two beers. Joe had the foresight to stick a dollar in the video poker machine that was built into the countertop so that he wouldn't have to pay for the drinks. He opened up his pad, asking Peter to tell him absolutely everything he knew about Ryan Harper.

"Ryan wasn't friends with anyone on the Buckingham site, at least not to our knowledge. We're a relatively new and small group. We have a website forum attached to the site which is quite unique to the on-line poker industry. Players can post and reply to comments. They tend to be mostly poker related, but some players also arrange personal meet-ups and tournaments at brick and mortar poker rooms." He was getting more animated, warming to the topic. "There's also a section to gripe and complain about bad beats. That's the section Ryan was most active on. He was constantly complaining that other players were 'cheats' and 'retards'. It was never his fault when he lost a game."

Joe continued sipping on his beer, nodding encouragingly to this flow of information. "Ryan's what we call a keyboard warrior in the chat-box during a game. The chat-box is like an instant messaging box which makes it easy to chat with the people you're playing a poker game with."

"Actually, Peter, I'm an on-line player myself, so I'm aware of the chat boxes."

"Fair enough, mate. You probably know the type then. A real wanker. He loses a hand of poker, and starts calling the winner nasty names. And when he wins a hand, he's God's gift and rubs the losers' nose in it. He flipped out when he got knocked out of the game here the other day."

Joe had often crossed paths and comments with players like that. Bad losers and lousy winners. "Had you noticed any change in him recently, online?"

"He was a lot less active on the site over the last year. He'd also reduced the stakes he was originally playing at. Maybe there'd been a slight improvement in his demeanour, but it's hard to say for sure. I don't like to speak ill of the dead…" He looked at Joe as if he was waiting for permission to continue. Joe smiled and nodded. "I can tell you I don't know anyone who liked the bloke, but I also don't know anyone on the site who would feel strongly enough about him, one way or the other, to want him dead." Peter added that he'd already offered full access to the Buckingham website so that Ryan's activity could be studied. Joe remembered that he had led Peter to believe he was a Vegas detective and was apprehensive of correcting the misconception, in case he clammed up.

"Can you tell me about the incident in the poker room when he got knocked out of the tournament?"

"I was on a break, so didn't get to see it. Ronnie was there, so she can fill you in." He stole a quick glance at his watch while taking the last sip of beer.

"Okay, then. Thanks for your openness, Peter. I'll just wait here if you want to go back and send her in for me."

While Joe waited for Veronica he played with the buttons of the bar-top poker machine. By the time she arrived, he had turned his $1.00 into $3.25, and was pretty chuffed. He ordered another round of beers, while Veronica repeated what Peter had said nearly word for word. The only addition to the story was the quarrel when Ryan lost the tournament.

"Ryan got knocked out of the tournament. He had been doing quite well in it, and was nearly in the money. He bet all his money on a bluff, and the bet was called, and won, by a young woman who only had one pair. Ryan started name-calling and swearing like a sea-dog. Casino Security reached him in a matter of seconds and pulled him aside to have words. When they released him, he returned to the table to apologize."

"What were you doing there?" Joe asked.

"I had arrived at the table to watch the play of the cards when Ryan's all-in bet was called. Our registration table was really close to the poker table he was playing at, so we heard him bet all his chips."

"I suppose that would be quite a coup for Buckingham to have one of their sponsored players go the distance."

"Normally it would be. But Ryan wasn't exactly the type of person we'd want repping the company, to be honest." She looked disconcerted and took a large gulp of beer, spilling a drop on her t-shirt. "I'm sorry. That was a horrible thing to say after what's happened."

"That's alright, lass. I understand what you mean. What happened then?"

"After he said sorry to the players and dealer, I brought him in here to the bar. We had a beer together and he calmed down."

"What did you two chat about?"

She squinted up at the ceiling and scrunched her nose as if she was inspecting a plate of rotting food. "This and that. A bit about poker in general. We talked about Vegas mostly. It's the first time here for both of us. After one beer, he shook my hand, and muttered something along the lines of 'Thanks for the beer, lady. See you around'."

"Did you get the feeling he was going somewhere after here?"

"I doubt it. He looked pretty beat. He'd been playing half the day and all evening, you know? I sat here watching him go, to finish my beer, and I saw him reach the hotel elevator. He looked pretty damn drained. If I'd thought for a second that he was crazy depressed, I wouldn't have let him leave. He just seemed tired." She closed her eyes and crumpled her nose again. "But I'm no doctor."

"I'm sure there's nothing you could have done," Joe said. He certainly didn't want these two to feel any blame for Ryan's suicide. "Just one more thing. This forum website that you run— where the players chat with each other—can I get onto it and look at what Ryan posted, and who he talked to?"

"Sure. Just go on to our website, create a player name, and then log into the forum. You don't have to deposit any money to participate in the forum."

"What was Ryan's player name?"

"TexasHarp. When you join up, you can do a player search on his name, and then see his posting history. If you have any questions just shoot me off a private message on the site. My site name is BuckinghamVer. Keep in mind though, if anyone on the site posts anything extremely offensive, the post gets removed by one of the moderators, so you won't see the worst of it online."

"Okay, well, cheers for this, Veronica."

"No problem. We'll be around for another week, and we're both staying in this hotel, if you need anything else." She rose from the bar stool and waved a goodbye to the bartender.

"One more thing," Joe called, as she was making her way back to the large tournament room. "Do you have the name of the woman who Ryan had the argument with when he lost?"

"Vanessa something or other. Honestly don't remember, but the woman copper who was here the other day took her name and interviewed her as well while we were here, so you'll have that information back at the station, I guess," she answered and continued out the door of the bar.

Joe cashed out his meagre winnings from the poker machine, and left it on top of the bar as a tip.

5

Joe began the walk to the pub. He calculated that it would take about half an hour to get there, if he went directly, but he could probably stretch that to an hour if he strolled down Fremont to see the sights. That would leave him some time to have a cold pint while he waited for Newcross, and maybe order a bite to eat. He hadn't had lunch. For that matter, he didn't recall having breakfast either. He jigged and jagged through the labyrinth of clanging slot machines to the main casino door which slid silently open automatically as he approached. Fremont Street was unaffected by the desert sun. He stood on the pedestrian street under the video-animated roof—known as the Fremont Experience.

It was still early in the day, but you could tell the outdoor partying would start up soon. Mingling with the clatter of slot machines and cries of hawkers, enticing people into casinos, were the clang and whir of hammers and drills being used to construct stages where local bands would entertain the drunks later in the evening. By the time he came back, downtown would be hopping.

He strolled towards the Plaza hotel at the end of Fremont, passing all the great casinos in what he felt was the true Heart of Vegas. Although Bugsy popularised Vegas with the California crowd, and ultimately changed the town forever, downtown was, and always would be, in Joe's estimation, the real Vegas. Outside what used to be the Pioneer Club, he stopped briefly to look up and give a nostalgic wave to Vegas Vic, the 40-foot neon cowboy perched atop what was now one more mass-market, made-in-China, souvenir shop. He missed the good old days when Vic used to wave to all the gamblers walking down Fremont, calling out "Howdy Pardner" in his booming drawl every 15 minutes, while smoke would lazily drift up from the giant cigarette dangling from his mouth.

He passed the Fremont, the 4 Queens, the Nugget, and Binion's, the real home of poker. Then he arrived at the mother of them all, the Golden Gate, the first casino ever built in Vegas, back in the early 1900's. With a silent prayer to the gambling gods, he turned right on Main Street, and two huge blocks later he reached Stewart Avenue and took a right towards the city hall. The Las Vegas racetrack was nearby, but Joe had never been there. He much preferred sitting in the air-conditioned sports-book of a casino, placing bets on horses and dogs all over the country at the same time, whilst scantily clad young women served him free drinks.

He could see the top of the city hall building a few blocks away, and the Red Lion Pub, where they were meeting, was supposed to be just past that.

He got half way down the block, and stopped dead. He couldn't believe his eyes. The old Court building had been turned into a museum—the Mob Museum. Bloody hell, only in Vegas would you come upon a museum devoted to the greatest criminals in the world. And only in Vegas would they so fittingly choose the old Federal Court building where the idolized mobsters tried to avoid spending any of their time at any cost. He hoped he could squeeze some time in tomorrow to take the tour.

He finally saw the sign for the pub up ahead, about a half-block away. The Rampant Red Lion himself, upright and glorious, on a shield-shaped gold background. He wondered if Detective Newcross had detected, and taken into account, the faint remnants of his Scottish brogue, and chosen this pub accordingly. Regardless, he thought the display of his country's standard could bring a tear to a glass eye.

The pub displayed Scotland's lion, but were calling it an Irish pub. Nevertheless, it gave him hope that he would be able to quench his thirst with something more interesting than a girlie American beer.

He opened the door, standing in the entrance of the pub, allowing his eyes to adjust to the dim interior after the blazing sun, swallowing up his surroundings. He was instantly satisfied that it didn't appear to be a typical North American Irish pub; walls plastered with artsy framed photographs of pub doorways, harps, and four leaf clovers.

Directly in front of him, taking up nearly a third of the room, was a worn mahogany bar with a dull and scuffed brass railing to balance a foot on. The floor was crimson red linoleum. A few old posters hung on the walls, most of which were tattered and yellowed from years of smoke, advertising various pub events: football games, karaoke, trivia nights. On one wall hung a burgundy coloured jersey, with the logo of Hearts, a team from Edinburgh. On another wall he spotted the pale blue jersey of Manchester City, a Premier team from the north of England. Fair enough then. They weren't attempting to be loyal to any one country.

He turned to check the wall behind him and held back the urge to genuflect and cross himself. The green and white hoops of his beloved Glasgow Celtic. Nothing could make him feel more at home and comfortable. He turned back to the bar. Two blackboards hung, side by side, on the wall. One had a list of food served during the day, the other had a posting of upcoming televised "Soccer" games. He could forgive them calling it soccer to differentiate real football from American football, because his Celtic's jersey was on their wall. He was willing to cut them a lot of slack for that.

Even the stink of the place was dead on: barley, whisky, something greasy wafting from the direction of the double doors beside the end of the bar, all rounded off with the shadowy odours of bleach and piss. He walked towards a booth beside the only window in the place, delighted to feel his shoes stickily pulling away from the floor with each step. "This place is bloody perfect", he thought, while sinking into the black spring-less leatherette bench.

A waitress sauntered over to the table, with a pad of paper in one hand, and a glass of ice water in the other. She was wearing tight black jeans, black and white high top sneakers, and a black T-shirt that had the Red Lion Pub logo stitched onto it. Her salt and pepper hair was tied up in a loose bun, and a pencil was tucked precariously behind her ear. She could have been a showgirl, maybe 30 or 40 years ago. Her eyes still had that sexy twinkle that, back in her prime, probably knocked men to their knees.

"What can I getcha to knock that dust outta your mouth, Honey?"

"A pint of Guinness would be perfect, thanks". He pointed to the taps, even though she probably knew where they were.

"You got it, Hon, and if you hanker for something to eat, the specials are on the blackboard." She turned away and headed towards the bar, apparently not seeing the need to connect pencil to paper. He was able to read the flip side of her T-shirt. "Pubs are the best sunblock in Vegas".

It was close to five o'clock, and he was starving, but continued to sip patiently on his pint while he waited for Detective Newcross, on the off-chance that she might want to order some food as well.

He looked around at his fellow patrons. In one corner there were three old geezers, not talking to each other, and looking extremely comfortable not to be doing so. An elderly lady, eerily resembling his Auntie Margaret Rose, was sitting in a booth alone, knitting up a storm, with her balls of yarn laid out in that typical old-auntie system on the table in front of her. There was one middle-aged gentleman sitting at the bar engrossed in the daily racing form. None of them acknowledged Joe's presence.

He didn't have long to wait for Newcross. In walked a pair of pale jeans, topped with a white t-shirt. Joe waved over to her, a bit more energetically than he'd waved to Vegas Vic earlier. He was rewarded with her friendly smile and a girl-guide type of salute. She was a couple inches shorter than Joe, maybe 5'8, slender but strong looking. Her shoulder-length blond hair was dead-straight. She looked like the traditional girl next door, freckles and all. Her brilliant blue eyes were penetrating, as if she could read minds. He thought she was probably in her mid-thirties.

She gave a wave to his old Auntie in the booth, and a salute— military style— to the Three Musketeers in the corner. She slid in to the booth across from Joe, as the waitress came over with a large pint of a reddish beer, which looked like Kilkenny, setting it down in front of her.

"Thanks Meg, 'preciate it." She was a regular. "Rebecca Newcross, but just call me Becky," she said, holding her hand out over the table for a quick firm shake.

"Pleased to meet you, Becky. Joseph Patrick Cameron, and feel free to call me Joe."

She took a long swallow from the glass, never taking her eyes off him. The drink left a thin line of foam on her upper lip.

"Becky, do you mind if I order something to eat? Haven't eaten all day. You want something?"

She took another much smaller sip and glanced at the menu-blackboard. "It would save me going for a take-out on my way home."

He asked what she recommended from the Specials, and she told him her favourite was the home-made steak pie with Guinness gravy and mashed potatoes. He could see nothing wrong with a main course that included beer in it. She called their order over to Meg and removed a file folder from her backpack.

"Joe, let's get down to it. I understand the sister has concerns about her brother's suicide. That isn't at all unusual. The family rarely accepts suicide judgements."

"I understand that, and appreciate you taking the time to go over the investigation with me."

"Harper checked into the hotel, alone, four days before his death —three nights prior to the start of the event—to take part in the Southern Nevada Poker Tournament. He'd won the trip and tourney entry ticket on-line with Buckingham Poker. I spoke with the organizers, who told me that Harper pretty much kept to himself. He attended only an hour or so of the welcome cocktail party on the night prior to the first day of the tournament. They weren't aware of him spending any time with any of the other on-line winners."

"Becky, I actually stopped and spoke with the organizers earlier when I was walking past the poker room. Veronica Eastgate and Peter Surrey."

"That's them. Eastgate and Surrey. Then you're already aware that Ryan didn't get along with other players on-line?"

"He sounded like a bit of a loose cannon and a piss-poor loser," Joe said.

"He didn't cultivate friends on the poker site, the way some others do. Also, there was an incident in the poker room when Ryan was knocked out of the tournament, and he was visibly distraught. I believe the organizers labelled him 'totally tilted.'"

"Right. One of them mentioned that he got really steamed at losing."

"Yep." She opened her file and looked down at her notes. "Eastgate sat with him at the bar after his tantrum. By the time Ryan finished his beer he appeared a lot calmer, and left. She felt bad Ryan was upset, but didn't think there was much more she could do for him. She was basically relieved that he was leaving the poker room."

"I'll tell you, the reason I'm here is that the sister says there is no way Harper would do himself in. He'd been excited, and was feeling like his life was turning around. He was living with his sister. He had admitted some time ago that he had a gambling problem, and was getting help for it. She said that things had never looked better for him. His work had allowed him to change one of his vacation weeks in order to come here. He had even phoned her to say he loved Vegas, was getting an early night before the tournament, and would call her after the game the following day. She never heard from him again."

Becky stared keenly at him, and replied "Doesn't it strike you odd that someone who has admitted he has a gambling problem comes to Vegas to play in a poker tournament?"

"Basically, I'm in agreement with you, of course. This is probably not the best environment for the boy. But the way the sister explained it to me was that Harper had addressed his problem. It wasn't so much about gambling as an anger issue. He was getting help."

"Well, he sure showed his temper that night," she said.

"So, what happened when he left the bar? Nothing to indicate foul play?"

"Joe, are you not aware that we found a suicide note? I told the sister about it."

"She never said a thing about a note."

"Must not have registered with her. The body was lying submerged in a tub, both wrists slit, razor still in one hand. There was also an empty bottle of pills—Remeron—prescribed for severe depression. The prescription had been filled out a week earlier for 30 pills. We presume he took them to sedate himself prior to getting into the bath. We took blood samples for the pathologist to run toxicology, but that's purely for confirmation of the overdose. We're running a fingerprint check on the note, but the handwriting matches his Buckingham entry form. It's pretty cut and dried. We've seen it over and over in this town. No sign of force. No sign of a struggle in the hotel room. No indication of anyone else having been in the room with him at all that evening. His wallet was on the bureau with hundreds of dollars in it."

"Got it. The sister probably had a lot of trouble taking it all in when you phoned her."

Their food arrived, and they dug in. Joe's fork excavated a small chunk of steak from the Stout gravy, scooped the tender little morsel onto the tines, and continued on to plough into the hill of creamy mashed potatoes. He let his fork linger in a pool of the dark gravy for a few seconds, while he broke off a small piece of puff pastry crust, lying at the side of the plate, and then, carefully balancing it on top of his creation, managed to get it up and into his mouth without dropping any of it. The flavours mingled and burst on his tongue. He paused a few times during the meal to take a sip of his creamy Guinness. When he finally put his knife and fork down, and looked over at Becky, she was staring back at him with a wide grin.

"You look like you haven't eaten in days." Her meal was only half finished.

"I haven't tasted a gravy like this since I was a young pup in Glasgow. I apologize if I've been rude here. Are you gonna finish that?"

She chuckled—a soft warm sound—and wisely pulled her plate closer to her body. "Not a chance, pal. I thought you might like this place when I heard your accent on the phone. I come here a lot, it's about halfway between the station and home. I can get a great meal, a couple beers, and I'm close enough to walk home. Speaking of which, why don't you go up to the bar, and order us a couple more?"

Seemed like a fair request to Joe, but he knew in his heart that she was really just trying to keep him away from her steak pie. He went up to Meg, ordered another round and watched as she expertly poured the Guinness, along with Becky's red beer, which did indeed turn out to be a Kilkenny. He brought the drinks back to the table, and sat down.

"Joe, while I finish eating, tell me what made you move from Glasgow to Montréal?"

"To make a long story fairly short, I graduated from the University of Edinburgh with a Linguistics degree and, to nobody's surprise, I couldn't get a job. Then I decided to train for, and eventually join, the police force in Glasgow. My Da had been a cop so it felt like a natural choice for me. After a few years of breaking up bar-fights and arresting post-football game drunks, I met a young Canadian lass who was holidaying in Scotland." Joe stopped to take a few gulps of beer. Rebecca continued eating, nodding once in a while, but her eyes were concentrated on his.

"We kept in touch, and eventually she couldn't bear to be apart from me any longer, and convinced me to marry her and get into the force in Montréal. I had a fair command of French from Uni. Combined with the fact that Anna's father was a Captain at one of the stations, I was able to get into a training program and then a job in Montréal."

Rebecca set her utensils into the middle of the plate, dabbed her mouth with a napkin, and pushed the plate towards the edge of the table. "But you aren't in the force any longer. Why not?"

"After a few years I was assigned to a squad dedicated to organized crime. I was injured in a gang-related incident, left the force, and set up the PI practice. It's too long a story." He was amazed how much he had opened up to this stranger. "I luckily have a great relationship with a few of the cops that are still around. That can be very helpful." He looked around for Meg, but didn't see her. All the other patrons were still in their same positions. It was like a wax-museum bar.

"What sort of injury did you have that took you off the streets?" Her eyes were hypnotic and strong, and never left his face.

"I think that's enough about me for now," Joe said, squirming a bit which made the leatherette squeak.

"I'm interested, Joe. Honest."

"Well, if we're being honest, it's not a part of my life I'm particularly proud of, and I'd rather not ruin a perfectly fine day by talking about it."

"Fair play. I won't pester you about it." She swirled her ruby red beer around in her glass. "So what made you set up a Detective Agency?"

"A lot of people, with my wife at the head of the line, were always telling me that I was a right proper Dick, so it seemed like the natural thing to do. I set up the agency out of our house for a while, but when I began to get clients on a regular basis, I rented a small office downtown. We had a really happy marriage for a few years, but then it sort of fizzled away and we agreed to part ways. It was rough going for a while, but now she's one of my best friends and we see each other a fair bit. She's a smart, insightful woman, and helps me a lot with my cases, giving me her take on some of my investigations. Speaking of which, is there anything more that you can tell me about Harper's death?" Joe sat back in the booth, exhausted and slightly embarrassed about being so candid.

"There's really not much to tell." She opened the thin file again and removed a photocopy of a short hand-written note. "Like I said, we should get the results of the toxicology report in a few days from the pathologist. We'll officially close the case then. But there's no problem with you taking the body back to Montréal tomorrow. I've written down the morgue details so that you can make the final arrangements for transport. I can't give you the actual police report, but here's a copy of Ryan's note." She slid the note across the table.

I'm sorry because I hurt so many people. I didn't mean to and I can't handle it anymore. I love you sis. Don't feel bad. Ryan

Joe read while she continued talking.

"Like I said, we had the handwriting compared against his Buckingham Poker entry form. If you or the sister have any other questions, call me. I really have to get home now." She slipped out of the booth, dragging her backpack along the seat, and stood.

"I can't thank you enough. I'm sure this'll put my client's mind to rest." She pulled her wallet from the backpack and Joe waved it away. "It's the least I can do." Rebecca smiled, gave a general wave to the wax figures around the room, and left. Joe drained his glass and tossed enough cash down on the table to pay the tab that Meg had conveniently slipped beside his glass when she'd taken the plates away.

Joe arrived back at the hotel at 7:30 p.m. He sat at the main bar, in the centre of the casino, watching the action, wishing he had enough energy to go and play some poker, but the time difference, combined with all the occupational drinks he had consumed throughout the day, was catching up on him. He took the elevator up to his room, collapsed on the bed, and slept till morning.

6

Joe woke up with the sunlight beating through the window, phoned Kelly Harper and gently explained there was no doubt about her brother's death being a suicide. She accepted his findings in a resigned manner but a shaky voice. He told her to arrange for a mortician to meet the plane in the morning and dictated the Customs information and flight details required.

After filling up at the casino's breakfast buffet, Joe went back up to his room to pack. The red light was blinking on his phone. There was a voicemail from Becky saying that the preliminary toxicology report had come back from the pathologist confirming that Ryan Harper had traces of two drugs in his system—Remeron and Ketamine.

Joe had to check out of the hotel, but was able to leave his travel bag with the valet. He was booked tonight on the red-eye flight back home, giving him nearly a full day to do as he pleased, as soon as he finalized the arrangements with the morgue to get the body onto the plane. It was adjacent to the Met police station, so he retraced his walk of the day before and continued past the Red Lion pub. True to her word, Becky had started the ball rolling for the paperwork, so Joe merely had to prove his identity, give the flight information, and sign a few papers, before he was assured the body would be on his flight.

He walked back to Stewart Street, and into the Mob Museum in the original courthouse building. There was a wonderful irony about that, considering the Mob members were prosecuted in the same building where now they were being honoured. There was a sweet nostalgia for that era of Nevada history before Vegas transformed into the Disneyesque wonderland of erupting volcanoes, musical fountains, and pirate-ship battles that it had become. The Mob had kept the violence down, as well as the prices. Oscar Goodwin, one of the most famous Mob attorneys, was Mayor of Vegas for the maximum three terms. When he had to step down, his wife was voted into office to replace him.

The photography exhibit struck a perfect balance between gruesome dead bodies and innocent childhood photos of future mobsters. It was an interactive, hands-on type of museum, and Joe spent a few minutes shooting virtual hoodlums, and the odd innocent bystander, on a Vegas backdrop screen with a simulated machine gun.

Joe entered the main courtroom, which had remained unchanged since the good old days. The curators had incorporated an exhibit —a projection screen lowered from the ceiling behind the judge's chair—presenting genuine footage of some famous Mob trials that had been held in that actual room. Sitting in the court pews, it was easy to time-travel back to witness the court case firsthand. He concluded his visit at the museum gift shop, where he bought a souvenir T-shirt. *In Godfather We Trust.*

He walked down the steps of the building and realized he would love to spend a couple more hours with Becky. He pulled her business card from his wallet and punched in the number.

"Homicide." The male voice had a robust southern drawl.

"Could you put me through to Detective Newcross please?"

"Sorry, she's out for the rest of the day. Do you want to speak with someone else, or leave a voicemail for her?"

"Voicemail would be fine, thanks."

A few clicks later, and he heard Becky's charming voice; "Newcross here. For an emergency, please press zero now. Otherwise please leave a message and I'll get back to you as soon as possible."

"Becky, Joe Cameron here. I just wanted to thank you for the preparation you did at the morgue for me, and for all the help yesterday. I guess that's it. Thanks again." He closed his phone.

He strolled back to Fremont Street and stopped at a café for tea and a slice of banana bread. As he opened his wallet to pay, he took Becky's card from his pocket to slide it in the billfold and noticed she had handwritten another phone number on the back of the card. He sat down at a small round table with his tray. He pressed in what he assumed was her mobile number. After three rings, it went to voicemail as well.

"Becky, Joe Cameron again. Just wanted to thank you for all your help. I checked out of my hotel, but I'm not leaving till 11:00 p.m. tonight. If you're not doing anything around 6:00 p.m., I'll be at the Red Lion for dinner before I leave for the airport. That's it. Thanks. Bye now."

More than a little disappointed, Joe left the café and went to Binion's Casino, the mecca of poker where all the greats had played. He walked through the casino, and found the poker room through an archway and down four stairs from the main floor of the casino. It was a luxurious and handsome room. It wasn't large—12 poker tables—and had the perfect atmosphere of restrained sophistication. Subdued spot-lighting from the ceiling, and a low-hanging lamp directing a milky glow over each table. On every wall, framed black-and-whites of all the winners from the Binion's World Series of Poker hung elegantly at eye level.

The poker manager approached him.

"Would you like seating at one of our cash tables, Sir, or are you here for the afternoon tournament?" he spoke softly but with the haughtiness of an English butler.

"The cash tables. What sort of limits are they playing?"

"At the moment, Sir, we're dealing $1-$3, $5-10, and $25-$50. We have seating available at a $1-$3 No Limit Hold'em table. Maximum buy-in is $200. Would that suit you, Sir?"

A bit put off that the man assumed he was a low limit player, Joe nodded his agreement. "That'll be fine".

"Perfect, Sir. Just buy your chips at the casino cage, and you can sit at Seat Four on Table Three." He pointed with one hand to the bank teller-like area situated near the entrance of the poker room. With his other hand he indicated the table on Joe's left.

Joe bought $200 worth of chips and took his seat. There were six other people at the table, not including the dealer. Three barely-past-puberty men, all wearing sun-glasses. Joe guessed they were together as they were chatting amicably and drinking Red Bull straight from the can. There was one woman, perhaps mid-forties who looked tired and hung over and played incessantly with her chip stack with one hand, while sipping from what looked to be a glass of orange juice, but could well have had a shot of vodka in it. There were no rules in Vegas as to what hour was acceptable to begin drinking. Lastly, there were two older gentlemen who appeared to be comfortable regulars in the poker room. The dealer called them both by name when it was their turn to play.

Joe played for two hours, and then, in a flourish, lost all his chips to one of the old gents, in what he had thought was a "sure thing".

He was about to re-buy another $200, when he realized it was nearly six o'clock, the hour he had told Becky he would be at the pub.

He picked up his travel bag from the valet, and sprinted to the Red Lion. He arrived there at 6:15 p.m., sweating like a pig near a sausage factory. There was no Becky to be seen.

"A Guinness, young man?" Meg called over from the bar before the door had even swung shut behind him.

"Yes, thanks. Has Becky been in today?"

"Not seen her since yesterday, here with you. You want food as well?" She poured his beer slowly from the taps.

"Sure." He looked over at the blackboard. "Fish 'n Chips sounds good. Thanks."

He walked over and sat in the same place as the previous day so that he could look out the window in case she passed by. His old Auntie was again, or still, in the same booth and appeared not to have moved a muscle. Although whatever she was knitting had grown about a foot in length. There were no other patrons.

After his meal and two pints, Joe gave up waiting and asked Meg to call for a taxi to take him to the airport.

The plane departed bang on time and he tumbled quickly into a fidgety sleep, arriving in Montréal at the break of dawn.

7

VEGAS MONACO CASINO RESORT HOTEL

My hands shaking with excitement, I fumbled in my bag for my key card.

It glided into the card slot, and the green light blinked, inviting me to push open the door to my hotel suite.

I retrieved the bottle of Mumm Brut Champagne which I had picked up earlier in the day from the casino's wine shop.

I deserved a little celebration for my accomplishment tonight. Removing the cork—not spilling a drop—I poured a full glass. Carrying it over to the table by the window, I sank into the butterscotch-coloured leather wingback chair, and took a lovely bubbly sip, staring out at the neon lights along Las Vegas Boulevard. My entire body tingled with satisfaction.

This one, John Graves, was even better than Ryan. His on-line poker name was Mr. Blue. I quite liked that name. Oh, and what a perfect setting! Outside in the cooling desert night air. A mere few blocks away from us were thousands of people in downtown Vegas, but they were all too mesmerized by the lure of winning and losing money. They were my audience, but they couldn't see the show.

I opened the small box of Godiva truffles on the table. A perfect complement to my champagne.

I would never forget his eyes as he stared up at me. This delicious memory was now burnt into my soul. He was quite perfectly dead. That was the one unfortunate problem with Ryan. I hadn't been able to see his eyes well enough with all the blood in the water. But this time was different. I watched the life slowly creep out of him. I watched his increasing comprehension of what I was doing for him. I could hardly wait to find another one.

I could get quite used to this.

8

THREE HOURS EARLIER

John Graves walked purposefully, but slowly, south along Bruce Street away from the bustle of downtown. He had stopped off at home and changed out of his scruffy shorts and t-shirt into chinos and a loud Hawaiian short-sleeved shirt. He liberally sprayed his face and neck with aftershave. He hadn't had occasion to use any for a while but had come across some punk selling knock-offs behind the Golden Nugget a few days earlier and bought a bottle.

He had no idea what was in store for him but he knew he wanted to look casually stylish. It was still hot outside, even though it was past midnight. The farther he got away from Fremont, with its flashing lights and lively crowd, the more he could feel a delicate cool desert breeze. It was quite a desolate area, as he passed small strip-malls occupied mostly by tattoo parlours and pawn shops.

She might be drop-dead gorgeous and slightly drunk. His favourite sort of woman. He only got a teasing glimpse of her face earlier in the evening when she leaned over and whispered to him— at the poker table during the tournament— that she was "one of his fans" from the Buckingham Poker site, and to meet her down the road in the bar of the Paradise casino at 1:00 a.m. By the time he

48

turned in his seat and looked up, all he could see was the figure of a woman walking away in skin tight clothes and a big floppy hat. But he knew that departing figure on the poker floor was a figure he definitely wanted to meet again. If, from the front, she turned out to be a dog, he could dream up an excuse to leave. Nothing lost but the price of a drink at the Paradise.

As he approached the Paradise casino, he felt a bit let down. It was a dump compared to all the other casinos he had passed to get here. There didn't seem to be a hotel attached to it, which was a bad sign for the fantasies that had been running through his head for the past two hours.

He arrived at the side door of the casino. It wasn't an automatic sliding door like most of the others. He had to pull it open the old fashioned way and it was like yanking on a suction cup. When it eventually broke seal, and opened towards him, a blast of wintry cold air conditioning smacked him in the face. He would never get used to that in Vegas, no matter how long he lived here. He wished he'd thought about that and brought a jacket. Goosebumps were not sexy.

There were four steps leading up to the casino floor. It was a small dingy place, the thick carpeting a muddle of oranges, reds, and browns. A lot of bad shit could happen on that carpet, and no one would ever know. It was the smell that really got to him though. A mixture of metal, stale cigarettes, sickly sweet piña coladas, and sweat. The other casinos must spend a fortune on air fresheners, but not this one. Young kids, not much older than teenagers, were wandering around aimlessly with yard-long glasses full of neon-coloured drinks that looked disgusting.

He could see the bar near the middle of the casino floor, on a round raised platform, in front of the Blackjack tables. It didn't look busy and it would be easy to spot her if she hadn't changed her outfit.

As he climbed the two steps up into the bar area, he could see that there were two elderly ladies sitting at the bar, playing video poker, their fingers moving across the screens as quickly as his young nephew texted his pals. There were at least a dozen square wooden tables scattered around the bar floor, and a few banquettes around the perimeter. It was shadowy and smoky and he could barely make out faces. There was a young couple at one of the tables staring like zombies towards the gaming floor, a group of giggling girls in one of the booths, and an elderly man at another table, head nestled into his crossed arms, fast asleep in a golden pool of beer.

In the gloom of the bar, he saw a woman stand up and wave in his direction. Walking towards her his smile grew with every step. She looked like a pin-up girl from the 1950's. Ten years ago, after graduating from high school, he had worked as an apprentice mechanic in a service station in Brooklyn, New York. They had an old calendar hanging on the greasy wall that this woman could have walked out from. She was wearing dark purple shorts that couldn't have been tighter. Her shoulders were totally exposed in a sleeveless black silk blouse. The neckline fell loosely halfway down her breasts. She was wearing wine-coloured straw sandals, a droopy straw hat and black satin gloves, which closed at the wrist with a pearl button. She looked like a million bucks. Maybe two million.

He tried to look nonchalant, desperately fighting back the toothy grin that always took over his face when he felt self-conscious. As he got within a few yards of her, she took a few steps towards him and stretched out her arm, her satin fingers enticing him to hold them.

"You're the only decently dressed man who has walked into this bar since I've sat down." She squeezed his hand with hers and reached out to clasp his shoulder with her other. "And you've arrived slightly earlier than I suggested. I anticipated both, and you don't disappoint."

"At your service, Madam. Just let me get a cold one from the bar. Can I get you another one?" He was shuddering from her touch and needed a drink.

"A glass of their pinot noir would be perfect, thank you, Mr. Blue."

He walked up to the bartender, feeling her eyes burning into his back. He felt he was being tested, and he so desperately wanted to pass. He sensed that he had to let her take the lead for the evening, while he could concentrate on not coming off as a bumbling fool.

He stood at the bar, waiting for the drinks, and took the opportunity to watch her as she gazed into a small gold pocket mirror to apply a new coat of Ferrari-racing-car-red lipstick. She was so freaking stunning he was breathless. She had icy blue eyes framed by arched eyebrows that made her look haughty and playful at the same time. Her blond hair grazed the top of her shoulders, the perfect length to run his fingers through, and had that slightly tousled look that probably took hours to achieve, but made her look like she had just rolled out of bed. And he hoped with every fibre of his body that she would soon be ready to roll back in.

He returned with the drinks, setting her wine glass down gently in front of her, on a crisp new scalloped paper coaster. He took a short swig from his beer bottle and set it down as well.

She slipped the mirror and lipstick back into a small black clutch purse that lay on the table, and looked up at him, running her tongue across her freshly painted lips. He sat down across from her and tried not to fidget.

"Mr. Blue." She took a deep breath and leaned forward a few inches. "Are you going to tell me your real name?" She smiled, put her elbows on the table, and cradled her chin in the palms of her hands.

"John…John Graves." He felt like he was at a job interview. He started picking at the bottom of his beer label.

"John Graves. Good strong name." She paused and took a sip of wine. "I like it. Suits you." She twirled the wine in her glass. "Do you have *any* interest at all in who *I* am?"

"Oh, God. Of course I do!" He felt hot splotches on his face and knew he was turning red. He could also feel little dots of sweat along his hairline. "I've got so many questions I don't know where to begin."

"I'm Lady MacBet on the Buckingham site."

"You're MacBet? I don't get it. I've posted on the forum page a lot, and I got the feeling from a few things you wrote, that I would be your last pick for a date."

"Oh, we don't mean half the things we say on-line, do we?" She removed a tissue from her purse and rubbed a small smudge from the stem of her wine glass.

"What's your real name?"

"I think I'd rather we keep using our on-line names tonight. It adds to the fun and games. Don't you agree, Mr. Blue?"

He nodded and took a gulp of beer from the bottle. He went back to work on the label, peeling off ragged damp strips. "Did you win a tournament entry from Buckingham?"

"No, I came here on my own steam, just soaking up the atmosphere, and hoping to meet some of the on-line players I've got to know over the last few years—like you." The bartender walked towards their table and she waved him off. "I felt so bad for you last year, when you posted about having to leave your wife. Then, when I heard your name being called at the poker table today, I couldn't resist going over and inviting you here. I'm sorry I whispered and ran, but they don't really like people hanging around the tables during the tournament. So I took the chance you would turn up." The corners of her lips turned down in a pout and she leaned over the table to run her satiny finger down his arm. "You don't think I'm too forward, do you?"

"Shit, no! Excuse my French. Christ. I had a bad year. No denying that. My wife didn't understand the passion I have for poker at all. I tried to explain to her that the only reason I'm losing is because I'm playing at low stakes, and the players there are crap. So I had to start playing with a bigger bankroll. Unfortunately, I've discovered plenty of dumbasses at higher stakes too. But soon I'm gonna start winning, there's no doubt in my mind. I finally had to leave the bitch."

He noticed her eyebrows slide up even higher and wished he could take that last sentence back. He had to watch his language with this one. She was in a different league from most of the women he met.

"You see, Mr. Blue? That's exactly why I thought meeting you would be a good idea! Sounds like you could use some cheering up, my dear man. I'm staying at the motel right next door. Why don't we go for a cool swim and a few more drinks?" She reached under the table and pulled out a big black straw bag.

Graves breathed a sigh of relief that he hadn't blown it. He drained his beer and smacked it hard on the table. "Lead the way, Lady M."

As they got up he heard a clink when the bag hit the leg of her chair. He suspected she had thought ahead and picked up some booze.

He followed behind her for a few seconds, enjoying the view immensely. When he caught up to her, she handed him the bag to carry for her. Peeking in, he saw a bottle of wine, as well as some cans of beer, and two plastic glasses. They were all safely snuggled into a nest made by a big bath towel. He shivered. This time it wasn't because of the air conditioning.

9

It was a short walk through the parking lot to the Roulette Motor Hotel. To say he was surprised at her lodgings would be an understatement. He couldn't believe this sophisticated woman would even know this place existed, much less book a room here. He speculated that maybe she got some weird kick out of roughing it. It was a one-story motel with the office down at one end, and eight doors spaced evenly along the full length. Each unit had a window and some had white plastic lawn chairs beside their doors. The entire stucco building was painted pumpkin-orange, and peeling like a bad sunburn.

There was no sign of life; no flicker of TV light slicing through the broken venetian blinds, no cars parked in front of doors, no glow seeping from the office. He followed her around to the back, expecting it to be barren land, but there was a swimming pool and hot tub.

The pool area was surrounded by a six-foot chain-link fence. When they arrived at the closed gate, he noticed a broken padlock dangling from one of the fence loops. Green plastic woven through the links provided complete privacy for the swimmers, not to mention protecting the swimmers from the horrendous view of the dilapidated motel. There were no pool lights on and his eyes were having difficulty adjusting to the darkness. Pale moonlight was the only illumination.

He followed her to one end of the pool, where she placed her purse and bag on a white plastic table that had a torn umbrella protruding from a centre hole. She removed a can of beer and a small glass vial of clear liquid from her bag. She opened the can.

"I have a treat for you, Mr. Blue. An aphrodisiac."

"I sure as hell don't need one, Lady." He reached for the can of beer, but she pulled it away.

She sighed, loud enough for him to hear, opened and emptied the vial into his beer and handed it to him. "Tonight will be unforgettable if you do as you're told. I took mine at the bar. It turns me into an animal, Mr. Blue. Don't you think you'd like that?" Her other hand dropped to the waistband of his shorts and twirled the top button. "Sit down here and drink up."

He sat on the rickety lawn chair, took the can from her and could barely get it down quick enough. She took the empty can and put it in her bag. He watched her as she poured a glass of red wine and drank it slowly. She took his hand and brought him to the cement steps of the pool that led down into the water.

"Out of those clothes and into the water," she said.

He wrinkled his nose and looked at her like she was crazy. "It stinks like a New York subway around here."

"Oh, Mr. Blue! That's from the demolished building next door." She faced him and stood inches away from his body. Now he could smell coconut and vanilla. She put her hands on the waistband of his shorts and one fingertip glided up and down his fly and rested on the top button of his shorts. "Don't be a spoil-sport." She pulled his fly down. "You'll disappoint me. Get in the pool now."

She didn't have to tell him again. He tossed his clothes to the ground while she attached a small inflated pillow, with suction cups, to the top dry step. He descended the slimy steps into the tepid water.

"You lie in there and relax while I get myself ready." She reached over to her purse and pulled out another small glass vial. The liquid in it was yellow.

"I have another treat for you Mr. Blue. Jasmine oil to put in the water. The scent is very exotic." She folded a towel up and knelt on it, at the side of the pool, beside his head. "I want to feel like we're in a tropical garden instead of a motel parking lot." She emptied the vial into the pool. "You don't mind, do you?"

"I suppose it's too late if I do," he responded petulantly.

She leaned over and he got a rewarding view of her breasts, which were spilling out of the top of her blouse. He noticed her jaw tense as she glared at him. She stood and walked back to the table.

He lay there in the water silently congratulating Lady MacBet on her resourcefulness in finding such a desolate location within walking distance of Fremont Street. He moved his head to see if she was stripping but it was too dark to see clearly. He could see the outline of her body near the table. He could no longer smell the rotten stench of the pool. Then he realized he couldn't smell the jasmine oil any longer either.

He closed his eyes and revelled in the fantasies running through his mind. An incredible woman was about to slip out of her clothes and slide into this oily water with him. The lukewarm sliminess of the water didn't bother him any longer. She certainly had every little detail of this planned out. He couldn't remember where Lady MacBet was from, and he hoped it wasn't far from here. This was a relationship he was keen to pursue.

He opened his eyes, and saw her fussing with the clothes he had hastily dropped on the ground. Her movements were agonizingly sluggish.

"How are you feeling Mr. Blue? Do you want me to come over there yet?" Her voice was slightly muffled. He opened his mouth to suggest moving the party out of the pool, but the words couldn't make the trip from brain to mouth. All he could muster was a slow head nod. His head felt like it weighed a hundred pounds, and his vision was beginning to blur. He thought that the heat of the desert air was getting to him and it might be time to get out of the pool and take her to her room.

She walked over and knelt down near his head. His wallet was in her hand. She placed her satin hand on his cheek, and stroked it so gently he couldn't feel anything. "I'm surprised at you, Mr. Blue! You wrote on the forum about your wife and children. How you couldn't support them anymore." She opened his billfold. "Maybe we should send all this money to them." She removed the wad of bills and smacked them against his cheek. "What do you think? Yes? No? You're not answering me, Mr. Blue. That's not very polite." Her face loomed over his. He tried to speak but his lips opened only a fraction.

"You'll be fine in a few minutes, Mr. Blue. This won't last long. Slither down into the water for me like the snake you are." She smiled. He couldn't believe what he was hearing.

She whispered in his ear. "On second thought, Mr. Blue, I'd much prefer to help you. We'll share the moment, shall we?"

Her gloved hand moved from fondling his cheek to the top of his head and pressed downwards. He tried to struggle, but his limbs weren't reacting. He tried to scream, but nothing came out of his mouth. There was nothing he could do but glide down the steps.

His lips were apart and he couldn't close them. The greasy water rushed into his mouth and down his throat. She continued pressing on his forehead and his head submerged; his eyes stung, his throat constricted, and his lungs began to fill with water. He looked up through the oily water and saw her beautiful face smiling down at him, as he had fantasized her looking down at him in bed. He struggled to lift his head that precious inch to air as his mind began shutting down. Just before he blacked out he saw her smiling down at him, licking her blood red lips with pleasure.

10

Joe arrived home shortly after 8:00 a.m. He had met the mortician at the airport and signed all the documents in the Canadian customs office there. He hadn't slept well on the red-eye flight, and fell right into bed.

He woke up surprisingly refreshed at noon, had a shower, and walked up the hill to his office to tackle mail and phone messages. Joe reached the door as the phone started ringing. He picked up on the fourth ring, as the answering machine was clicking in. Before he had a chance to speak, he heard "Joe, you there? It's Becky Newcross." Her voice was strained.

"I'm right here. What's up?"

"We were called out to a crime scene this morning, at an abandoned motel off the strip. A resident of an apartment building across the street looked out his window and spotted a floater. Naked in the pool. We've barely begun the investigation, but get this. He had a tournament card in his wallet, for the Poker Palace tournament. The clincher? He was being sponsored by Buckingham. He won his entry ticket on-line."

"But what about Harper? That changes things, doesn't it?" He sat down at his desk, swung around in his chair and put his feet up on the window sill.

"Sure as crap might. We don't believe in coincidences like that. Vegas Metro has been in contact with Montréal, in order to coordinate the investigation. You have one of the bodies now. Your cops will deal with Harper's sister, and bring her up to speed. We're trying one of these new cross border initiatives. Get this. Our boys call it a cop-to-cop bridge. Anyhow, it's basically a joint investigative operation that falls under the MLAT treaty between our countries."

"What's MLAT when it's at home?"

"Stands for Mutual Legal Assistance Treaty. Both countries have an interest, so we get to cooperate and collaborate on the case."

"Sounds progressive and perhaps disastrous both at the same time."

"Yeah well, open mind and all that. I'm being sent to Montréal to liaise with the Montréal police, and Montréal is shipping one of their finest down here. Reminds me of when I went on a student exchange program in college."

"Good of you to call and let me know what's happening."

"Well, to be honest, I mostly wanted to give you a heads up that it's a whole new ballgame, and you can't play anymore. You're on the bench now."

"Well, to be honest right back, my job was done anyhow. When do you get here?"

"It looks like I'll be flying out tomorrow morning. Look, Joe, I really can't talk more, I have so much to get done before I leave."

"Any chance you can call me when you get here? Maybe get together?" Joe picked up a pen from his desk and starting twirling it like a baton.

"I might do that. Gotta run now."

"One question. How did you get my number?"

"I'd hardly be much of a detective if I couldn't find someone's phone number for Chrissake!"

"In that case, I won't…" Joe realized he was talking to a dead phone.

11

Joe detoured for breakfast to a snack bar on Saint Marc Street, a few blocks west of his office. By the time he got into work, it was close to nine o'clock, and the red light was flashing on his answering machine. He pressed the play button and heard Becky's excited voice, "Joe, I'm flying out to Montréal later this morning. If you're around later maybe we can grab a bite to eat for supper. I've booked a room at the Nelson Hotel near the morgue. Call you later. Bye for now." He smiled, thinking that there weren't a lot of people who would choose their hotel based on proximity to the city morgue.

He figured that the late morning flight from Vegas would bring her into Montréal by early evening. Young Kelly Harper's despair tugged at his heartstrings so much that he had immediately been drawn into the drama, but he couldn't deny that the thought of spending more time with the lovely Detective Newcross was now a drawing factor.

Joe spent the rest of the morning working on his month-end accounting, entering bill and cheque amounts into some magic program that lived in his monitor, and got accessed every three months by a live accountant who would then phone him to give him a list of all the entry errors he had made. Then she would come over to the office and spend another morning going over the ins and outs of the program. He'd confirm that he understood everything, and then three months later, they'd do it all over again. It was a bit of fun, and he was convinced that they both looked forward to their quarterly date.

It was July 1st, Canada Day, and a parade would be marching through downtown Montréal around one o'clock. Joe wanted to avoid the hordes, so at noon he activated call-transfer on his office phone, on the off chance that Becky wasn't as shit hot a detective as she evidently thought she was, and locked up the office.

His condo was a fifteen-minute walk south of his office, in what was becoming a residential sector of downtown. It was an old neighbourhood, called Griffintown, and was being rapidly revitalized by young up-and-coming professionals. Over the last few years nearly all the old factories, warehouses, and quaint row houses had been demolished or, in some cases, gutted and renovated, to become trendy open-plan lofts.

The area was growing at a startling speed. Cranes sliced the skies and, from morning to late-afternoon, there was a continuous thumping of hydraulic hammers breaking rock coupled with the incessant pounding of pile drivers. Although the loss of architectural history disturbed Joe, he was coming to love all the little family-run restaurants, bistros, and indie coffee houses that were appearing.

The main street was Notre-Dame, where he had a bought a condo a few years ago after his divorce. He stopped halfway to get a Chinese takeaway for lunch and continued on, stopping at a small corner shop. In Montréal they were called dépanneurs but he had grown up calling them corner shops and couldn't break the habit.

He picked up wine and beer, in the hopes that he'd be entertaining Becky later in the evening.

Shortly after eight o'clock his phone rang.

"Hi, it's me. I'm just about to go through airport border patrol. Thought I'd see if you felt like grabbing a meal before I go and check in to my hotel." Becky's voice was hurried and he could hear the background babble of flight announcements.

"Great idea. I could easily fetch you at the airport and then we come back here to order in some food. It would be a lot quieter. Tonight is pretty crazy downtown with Canada Day festivities. It's like your July 4th."

"Don't bother, I'll get a cab. You get beer and pizza into the house. Oh, gotta go, my turn for the inquisition," she said, hanging up.

He was about to hit re-dial to give her his address, but didn't want to give her the satisfaction of telling him she already had it, which she no doubt did. So he looked through his kitchen drawer for the pizza menu. He called up the local pizzeria, ordering one all-dressed pizza and one posh mushroom-basil pizza. He liked them both, so wouldn't mind having left-overs in the fridge. Both the pizzas and Becky should arrive at nearly the same time.

Feeling like a jittery teenager, he went into the guest bathroom to to make sure the place was clean enough for company. He threw some cold water on his face, dried the sink with a rag from the cupboard below and rumpled his graying brown hair with his fingers. He folded the hand towel neatly over the ceramic bar next to the sink.

His doorbell rang, the first stanza from *Flower of Scotland*, and after verifying it was the pizza, he buzzed the delivery boy up. Joe stood in his doorway waiting for the elevator to climb to the fourteenth floor.

"Healthy appetite tonight, Mr. C?"

"You head of the neighbourhood weight watcher gang now?" he said, handing him the exact amount of the pizza order. He was pleased to see a splotchy blush creep up the boy's neck.

"Sorry, sir. Uncalled for."

Nodding, Joe reached back into his pocket to retrieve the five dollar tip he had pocketed. "Close call there, son."

"Thanks, Mr. C. Much appreciated, as usual. Have yourself a fine evening."

Joe closed the door and brought the pizza into the kitchen. He removed them from their boxes, so they wouldn't develop the dreaded cardboard flavour, and set them on the cutting board. He brought out a pizza cutter, two plates, two beer glasses, and two wine glasses.

The kitchen counter island faced the living room and was ideal for a little buffet that they could easily access from the sofa. He grabbed a jar of mixed olives from the fridge, drained them, and placed them into a fancy olive bowl someone had given him years ago. He had never used it till now. It had a built in wee bowl in the centre of the larger bowl, so that an olive eater would have somewhere convenient to dump the pits.

He opened the cheese drawer in the fridge, and found a good selection: a big chunk of Jarlsberg, some smoked Gouda, a half wheel of Camembert, and an unopened six-year-old cheddar. He arranged them on a Lazy Susan cutting board with some cheese knives and a selection of water crackers, and went back to search the fridge for more things to add to the buffet, but unless she wanted to munch on some jalapenos, or put mustard and mayo on her pizza, he was out of options.

The doorbell rang again, and he went to the intercom. They exchanged greetings and he buzzed her in. He went to the elevator to meet her, in case she needed help with luggage and reached it just as the stainless steel doors were sliding apart. She stepped off, wheeling a carry-all with one hand, and holding a laptop case in the other.

"Good to see you again, Joe."

"An unexpected pleasure. Come on in."

She smiled, handed Joe her carry-all, and followed him down the carpeted hallway. They arrived at his open door, and he stepped aside to let her in first. She walked down the five-foot-long hallway which opened up to the kitchen, dining area, and living room. From the fourteenth floor of the high-rise, with floor to ceiling windows on two adjacent sides, the views were impressive: the St. Lawrence River from one window, and the downtown skyline from the other. Placing her laptop on the dining room table, she stood still for a few seconds before turning to face him.

"This wasn't what I expected at all. No offence, but I envisioned more of a mish mash of a bachelor pad. Your home is stunning. But still cozy." She grinned. "Plus, I see food." She put the palms of her hands together in a prayer. "Please tell me there's cold beer to go with that."

"Take your pick, ma'am." He opened the fridge door and pointed at the top shelf full of beer and wine.

She grabbed a Corona and handed it to him to uncap, while she helped herself to one of the pilsner-shaped glasses which he had set out on the counter. She wandered around the room, like a prospective buyer at an open house. Her first stop was at his bookshelf, where she perused a shelf of titles, running a finger along the spines. She picked up a few framed photographs that were scattered on the shelves; one of Joe as a child with his parents in front of the family Christmas tree, his high-school graduation, and the one she held now, a photo of him and his ex-wife on their honeymoon outside the Guinness factory in Dublin.

"This is your wife?"

"It is…was…yes…Anna. She lives nearby, with her husband. They're both interior decorators."

"She's very pretty, and kind looking, and good taste in beer from the looks of it."

"And in men," he quickly replied.

She laughed loudly, although he didn't think it was that funny. She moved to the east window and stared down at the river. Cargo ships were being steered in and out of the docks. All shapes and sizes of pleasure-craft and tour boats were moving around the waters like a choreographed dance.

Becky moved her laptop from the dining room table to a coffee table, and removed it from its protective case. She returned to the kitchen island to join Joe, where he had begun slicing the pizza. They both filled their plates with a slice from each pizza and a handful of olives. Becky ignored the cheese platter, so Joe decided to give it a miss as well. They carried their plates and beers to the living room and began to eat.

"Joe, do you mind if I check my emails to see what's been going on with the investigation back in Vegas?"

"Of course not. The Wi-Fi is *Cameron* and the password is pokerscot—all lowercase."

Her fingers raced across the keyboard, logging on. "You play poker?" She shot him a quick glance and continued typing.

"Your detection abilities are beginning to astound me."

"Do you play online, or just live?" Her fingers kept tapping as she talked.

"Both really, although I don't get much opportunity for live poker. Do you play?"

"No, I don't gamble at all. I see what it does to people every day; the sadness, the despair, the depths that people sink to. Tragic." She hunched over the keyboard, shaking her head, and typed like a secretary on amphetamines. "Have you been on the Buckingham site, where Harper played?"

"Not yet, but I thought I'd check out the Forum that the organizers talked about." Joe got up from the sofa with his empty plate and walked to the kitchen. He took two more beers from the fridge. He was collecting crumbs around the countertop with a damp cloth when Becky shouted over.

"Holy Shit. They've been busy back home, Joe. Come take a look at this." He came back and sat closely beside her on the sofa so that he could see her laptop screen. She was on the LVPD website and had the preliminary forensics toxicology report on the screen for the guy found in the motel pool the previous morning.

"There are definite traces of Ketamine in his system, same as Harper. We won't know quantities until the final tox report comes out."

"I don't know much about Ketamine except for the fact it's used in date-rape. It's called Special K, right?" Joe asked.

"Yeah. It basically knocks a person out. It's not very popular in Vegas, although we've come across it. It's the fact that both were Buckingham players that rankles me."

"And both dead in the water, so to speak," Joe said. Becky groaned appreciatively. "What more do you have on him?"

She bent over the keyboard and pressed a few more keys. "John Graves. Caucasian. 35 years old. Originally from New York City. Moved out to Vegas a few years ago with his wife and two small children. They've since separated. She's still living in a Vegas suburb. My partner and the Montréal cop will be interviewing her today or tomorrow."

"So what are your plans for tomorrow?"

"I'm meeting a Detective Andrew Miller at the morgue tomorrow morning. We'll talk to the pathologist there who's going to review our reports and I presume he'll perform an autopsy of his own on Harper. Then we'll set up an action plan".

"Hey, I know Miller. I worked with him on the force for a few years and we became good mates. He's a real nice guy and a super detective. We have a drink now and again at the same pub near his station. Warn him that this case has caught my interest, so he can throw me a bone now and then to keep me happy." As Joe was talking, Becky closed down her laptop, and polished off her beer. She got up to put her plate on the counter and Joe realized the evening was ending.

"Will do, Joe. I'd better get going and check in to the hotel. I need a good night's sleep. Really appreciated the food though. Can you call me a taxi?"

"On the promise that if you have time tomorrow, you let me take you to dinner. Deal?"

"If there's time to eat tomorrow, then yes, that would be great," she agreed.

He walked her outside to the taxi rank at the corner. For some inexplicable reason, it took exactly 90 seconds to walk to the first taxi but five minutes for the taxi to drive over to the front door if they were phoned. One of those unexplained mysteries of life. Joe waved to the back of her head as she rode off, returned home, finished off one of the pizzas with a beer, tucked all the leftovers back into the fridge, and went to bed, hoping to dream about Becky.

12

Joe woke the following morning feeling more tired than usual, possibly still a bit jet-lagged. He decided it would do his head good to walk up the hill to work. It was only 8:00 a.m., but the temperature was already in the high 20's and would, no doubt, break into the 30's again today. The heat was made slightly tolerable by a breeze coming in off the St. Lawrence River, so after his shower he strolled up the hill, stopping only to buy a large coffee and a Danish at a snack bar near work.

He arrived at his office at close to 9:00 a.m., and wolfed down the pastry. He regretted not buying a second one, or bringing along a slice of leftover cold pizza from home. He sat quietly behind his desk, feet firmly balanced on the sill of the bay window.

For some reason this case was really niggling away at him and it made him miss police work. Two dead bodies now: both poker players, both drugged, both drowned. He was already hatching a plan so that he could not only find out what was happening, but could spend more time in the company of Becky. He sent a text off to Andrew.

U and new sidekick wanna meet 4 lunch 2day?

A few minutes later the ping of his phone announced an incoming message.

Donegal Pub. 1pm.

Andrew and Joe often met at the Donegal for a few drinks and lunch and frequently would bounce ideas off each other about ongoing cases. They had been friends for years. Andrew was a newlywed after having drifted from woman to woman and never settling on one to stay with for more than a few months. His wife, Lauren, was a clothing designer and owned a boutique in the trendy Plateau area of Montréal. Since his marriage, he and Joe didn't get together as regularly in the evening, but kept up their lunch dates.

Joe was firmly attached to his favourite bar stool well before one o'clock. The Donegal was all mahogany, brass and mirrors. There were a few other people in the pub, eating and talking quietly. There was a strong scent of lamb in the air and Joe suspected there was an Irish stew on the stovetop despite the summer heat. It was a popular lunch spot with the business folk in the area. The owner, Nicola, came away from chatting to one of the customers, and stood at the taps, which happened to be directly in front of Joe—hence, his favourite bar stool.

"Good to see you, Joe. You here for lunch, or just a pint?" Without waiting for his answer, she began to pour a Guinness.

"I'm here for both, Nicola. I'm meeting Andy and another cop for lunch."

She handed him the glass, expertly poured as usual, and excused herself to go in the kitchen to give a lunch order to her daughters, who served as cheap labour. Nicola was a lovely woman from Malin Head, a sleepy town on the Northwest coast of Ireland.

She had come to Montréal as a student in the 1970's, working part-time in various university ghetto bars and coffee houses, while she worked towards her Commerce degree. She eventually became manager of this pub. After her parents passed away back in Ireland she took her inheritance money, finished her degree, and bought the pub, changing its' name to the Donegal, in honour of the county where she was born. She put down roots, married one of the "regulars", and now had two girls attending the same university that she had gone to all those years ago.

The pub had become a popular second home for the Brits who immigrated here to fill the many engineering positions available in Montréal in the 70's and 80's. It had established itself as a good solid neighbourhood pub. During the week the patrons were mostly locals who either lived or worked in the area. They would pop in for drinks, catch up on the local gossip, banter amicably over an English or Scottish football game on satellite during the season, or the occasional hockey game. Students would turn up on the weekends, as it was close to one of the university campuses. And there were still a few of the ex-pats who lived in Montréal who would make the trek to the pub for old times' sake. Sunday mornings brought a group of Coronation Street fanatics, and Nicola would serve a traditional fry-up breakfast while the large screen TV would dish up the latest disaster from the old Manchester Street.

All in all, it was a quiet and pleasant pub, and Nicola's daughters were well-trained to cook up Irish delicacies. It wasn't an immense menu, but it varied from day to day, and you could count on getting a fine meal at a fair price. As it was summer break from school now, they would be the cooks for lunch and for dinner. During the school year Nicola had to hire extra staff.

Andrew and Becky walked in, and Joe moved from the bar over to a table so that they could eat and chat comfortably. He already had his Guinness in hand, so the two detectives stopped at the bar and got themselves a couple half pints of draught beer. Becky was dressed casually in pale blue jeans and a plain sleeveless white blouse. Andy was in khaki trousers that looked custom made. He wore a loose-fitting tan shirt and loafers of the same shade. He had sunglasses perched on his head. They were standard police-issue. Nothing else about him looked law-enforcement. His jet-black hair was thick, wavy, and touched the top of his collar. He was six feet tall and didn't have an extra ounce of fat on him. His blue eyes were mesmerizing—very Paul Newman. They joined him at his table, looking comfortable with each other, as if they'd worked together for years.

Joe looked at Becky. She wore a slender gold chain around her neck and no other jewellery. Her blond hair looked a little kinked from Montréal's high humidity. "So, how did you get through an entire morning working with this character?" Joe asked her.

"We actually spent a delightful few hours in the morgue, reviewing the results with the pathologist. Then we went to the station for a conference call with our partners." She picked up a laminated menu that was jammed between the napkin holder and the condiment bottles.

"Andy, did Becky bring you up to speed with how I initially got involved with the Harper case?"

"That she did. Must have made a novel change for you, being hired for something other than taking photos of cheating spouses and tracking down lost cats." His expression was deadpan.

Nicola dropped two more menus on their table, "Anyone need a top-up?"

They all decided to switch to water in honour of this being a work day, and buried their noses in their menus. The specials-of-the-day list was short and sweet, and they were ready to order by the time Nicola returned with a pitcher of water and glasses filled with ice.

"The girls have made my favourite Beef Barley soup. I'll have that with a plate of Bangers and Mash please. And tell them not to be stingy with the gravy," Joe said.

"You got it, love. What about you, Andrew?"

"Too hot for soup. I'll just have the Shepherd's Pie. Thanks, Nic."

"Tough decision here, it all sounds great." Becky diplomatically remarked. "But I'll try the same as my partner Andrew here."

Joe took the last swig of his Guinness and looked at Andrew. "You're in luck, Andy. As it turns out, I'd be pleased to lend you my criminal-catching expertise on this case. I have, as you know, an invaluable knowledge of on-line poker playing."

"Wouldn't want to keep you from your own work, Joseph." Andy had a tendency to use Joe's full name when they were in involved in light-hearted razzing.

"Once again, mate, luck is on your side. I'm in between Lotharios and kittens at the moment."

Becky was watching them like she was a spectator at a volleyball game. "Look, we were supposed to conduct two interviews today. One with Harper's boss and another with the shrink whose name was on his prescription bottle. Why don't we split up? Andy, you take the boss, and Joe can lead me to the Doc's office."

Joe jumped in, ecstatic at the thought of spending the afternoon with Becky, as well as keeping his toes in the water of the Harper case. He looked at Andy. "Great idea. Would move things along quicker for you."

"Fair enough. As long as you keep your mouth shut during the interview with the Doctor. Leave it totally in Rebecca's control. I'm not kidding, Joe. If you get some brilliant insight, write a note to her and let her handle it. I don't want you muddling this case up."

"As if. But I agree to your nonsensical terms. What's your plan with the sister, Andy? I've met her and she's a sweet kid."

"We're hoping she can give us a bit of background on him, a list of his friends, and we need to have a poke around his room. Then there's the ex-wife to look into. Rebecca and I will get all that done tomorrow. Forensics is going to Harper's apartment today to pick up his computer. They'll check out what he's been up to, particularly on the Buckingham site. Mind you, there's still the possibility that the Harper kid is a suicide, and that the murder of the other Buckingham player is just a coincidence. Don't forget, there was a suicide note, and no sign of a struggle in the hotel room."

Their meals arrived and they dug into them like frenzied animals who didn't know when they'd have time to go out for a hunt again.

"So what's the strategy in interviewing Harper's shrink?" Joe asked Andy in between bites.

"We just want to get some objective insight into his character and mental stability. She had him on Remeron, which is a common enough prescription drug for depression, but we'd like to know more about that. This shrink, Doctor Kathleen Wentworth, runs her practice out of her home in Westmount. Based on the address, on Grosvenor, it must be one of those grand old greystones halfway up the mountain. Now that you mention it, it'll be good for you to tag along. That way you could possibly get a much needed appointment for yourself, Joseph."

"The Comedy Festival starts soon, Andy. You should get yourself a gig."

Ignoring Joe completely, Andy focused on Becky. "Rebecca, let's meet back at the Station when we're done. We can get on the phone with Vegas then and see what they accomplished today, and devise a plan of attack for tomorrow."

Joe sat back, while they planned their meet-up, taking a small pleasure in the fact that Andy was calling her Rebecca. It seemed much more formal. Normally women fell all over the detective, but Becky didn't seem fazed by his Hollywood good looks at all.

"Actually Joe, now that you mention wanting to help, I could use a crash course in understanding the domain of on-line poker. Never got into it myself, so it might be helpful when Forensics starts to tell me what's on the computer. And Rebecca mentioned that she doesn't indulge in the sport either, although she knows a lot more about the gambling world than I do."

"Sure, no problem. It's fairly straightforward, and you don't really have to know much about poker to understand the logistics of how the site is run. I'll use the Buckingham Poker site as an example. First you download their software, which will install a virtual casino on to your computer. Then you set up an account like you would with any website, like eBay or Amazon."

"Do you have to deposit money?" Andy asked.

"Not necessarily. There are poker tables where you can play against people with play money that the site provides you with. But let's say you decide that you want to play for real money. Your account information will include your personal details: name, address, age, phone number, all the usual details when you join a club of any kind. The one difference here is that you never use your own name when playing. You have to choose a "player name," which is basically a fictitious nickname. For instance, Ryan Harper was TexasHarp. You choose your preferred method of funding your account with money. Depending where in the world you live, you might be able to deposit money simply by using your debit or credit card. There are many different methods of uploading funds nowadays. More and more electronic money service companies are popping up to fill the void as the mainstream methods stop allowing the uploading of funds for gambling purposes. Anyhow, as soon as you have money in your account, however you got it there, you're good to go. Then you can browse the poker site and sit at a table to play anything from pennies to thousands of dollars. You can just watch games being played as well. A lot of big poker names are hired by different sites to play and attract customers who want to play against the "greats". There are even film stars and sports personalities who get contracts to play on the poker sites to attract people. One enticement is that when you sit and play at a table with these people, you can talk to them via the chat box on the screen."

"How do these poker sites make their money if people just compete against other people?" Andrew asked.

"A multitude of ways. It's all very transparent. In a tournament, the site will take a specific amount from each participating player up front. For instance, if you're playing a tournament that you buy into for $110, maybe $100 is going into the prize pool, and $10 to the house. Another way they make money is if you sit down to play with a portion of your money against other players in a cash game. The site takes a percentage of each pot that's played. Another way is by providing side games, like Blackjack or Roulette or Slot machines, where you're playing solely against the House. The odds are always in the House's favour, so they can make a lot of money providing these games. Yet another way for them to make money is by investing the money that the player has deposited with them. Many players keep thousands, even hundreds of thousands of dollars on the sites. There are regulations as to the extent of risk a site can take with these funds, but even low-risk investments can be a huge revenue source considering they don't pay the players any interest on the funds they've deposited with them. Am I boring the tits off the two of you yet?"

Becky responded immediately, looking down at her chest and back up again, "I've still got some left, but your pal is looking a bit flat." Both men had a good laugh before Joe continued his explanation.

"Not much more to tell you really, except perhaps the most important part for this case, and that's the social angle of playing online. All the sites have little chat boxes on the screen, so you can talk to other players. You get a diverse cross-section of chatters. A lot of people just use the chat box for typical greetings and remarks; *good luck*, *good game*, that sort of thing. But if you play regularly for the same stakes, you tend to play with the same people over and over again, and friendships really do develop. Sometimes to the point where people will give out their email addresses and real names, and even plan a live meet-up at a local casino to play a game. Some people become true friends with like-minded people. I've even known marriages to come about. But I've also known players to meet up in a bar and get the shit kicked out of them by some of the "friends" they agreed to meet. More and more sites are increasing the social aspect of the game by creating interactive websites and Facebook groups, where folk can message each other and chat outside of the game. Buckingham is one of the more socially oriented sites. Making online friends has the potential to be fun, but there are a lot of whackos in cyberspace. You really have to be wary of that."

"So we have to find out who these two guys socially interacted with on Buckingham, whether in the chat box, the website, or even a Facebook group?" Andy asked.

"That's about the size of it, mate. Good place to start, for sure."

They had all finished eating. Andrew made a quick phone call to Harper's boss to move the time of their meeting forward. They each paid their own tab to Nicola, and walked Andrew back to his car at the station around the corner. Joe and Becky decided to walk to Wentworth's office. The interview was set for 3:00 p.m., so they had 45 minutes to get there which would be just about the right amount of time to stroll along Saint-Catherine Street, and then cut through Westmount Park to get to Grosvenor Avenue. They chatted idly along the way, mostly about Montréal's history. Becky reinforced the fact that this was her interview and Joe was to keep his comments and questions to himself.

13

Joe and Rebecca arrived at the home office of Dr. Wentworth a few minutes before their scheduled appointment. The outside of the home was breathtaking. Set back twenty feet from the sidewalk, a granite pathway weaved its way to five stone steps and a large wooden wrap-around balcony. The front yard was lush with plants, flowers, and an intricate rock garden.

A wrought iron sculpture of a twelve-foot tree stood in the centre of one half of the yard; majestic in its simplicity, dozens of leafless branches jutting out sporadically. It appeared to be constructed from sheets of copper which had partly oxidised and were turning green in patches, which made it fit the surroundings as if it had grown there. Parts of the trunk and some branches were shiny as if they had just been polished. It made a striking contrast to the century-old maple tree on the other side of the walkway.

Grosvenor Avenue was one of the main roads that meandered up Westmount Mountain. Most of the homes on this street were elegant, and this one was no exception. A classic turn of the century home. At the top of five steps was a main front door opening onto the front porch. To the right of the imposing door was a small copper plaque, announcing the offices of Dr. K. Wentworth, with an etched finger pointing to the right side of the house. Walking around to that side, they found another smaller door, and another plaque confirming that they had reached their desired destination. Although it was part of the main building, it had probably been the servants' entrance when the house was built.

They entered the side door into an elegant, but sparsely furnished, reception area. It felt like a miniature living room. There were three doors in the room; one of them was closet-sized, another was a sliding pocket door leading towards the home; the third was average size and presumably would lead into the doctor's office. A blue velvet loveseat, flanked by two side tables, sat across from two yellow and blue pin-striped club chairs. Between them was a coffee table with a beautiful bouquet of white freesias and a few artsy coffee table books. There were plenty of healthy looking plants, all in terra cotta planters. The floor was a dark hardwood, but an embroidered silk oriental carpet covered almost the entire space.

The walls and ceiling were painted a robin's-egg blue, and all the plaster trim was a soft white enamel. The only lighting was the soft glow of three table lamps. Blue velvet drapes, which matched the loveseat, were closed across the one window in the room. The entire effect was extremely peaceful and non-medical. They were just about to test the chairs when the door opened, and a woman stood there. She shook Becky's hand first, and then Joe's, introducing herself as Dr. Wentworth, adding that she would prefer to be called Kathleen.

Becky introduced herself as Detective Newcross, and produced her badge. Joe added that he was Detective Cameron. She invited them into her office, which had many similarities to the outer waiting room, but triple in size. There was a navy blue velvet loveseat, and two high-backed wing chairs which were both a pale blue tweed. There was the addition of a huge wooden oak desk, which was undoubtedly a priceless antique, a modern ergonomic chair behind the desk, and a bank of vintage tiger oak wooden filing cabinets along one wall. There were two smaller oriental carpets, one under her desk and chair, and the other anchoring the loveseat, chairs, and coffee table.

Again, there was an array of potted plants, and two matching vases of white freesias; one on her desk, the other on the coffee table. There was a tall bookcase in between two of the windows which held an assortment of medical text books interspersed with candlesticks. All different shapes and sizes and materials, and many of the larger heavier ones were being used as bookends.

The doctor sat on the loveseat, so Joe and Becky each took a chair across from her. On the coffee table between them was a glass pitcher of ice water on a tray. Slices of lemon floated on top of the water and the delicate citrus aroma mingled with the gentle scent of the flowers, hanging in the air like an invisible cloud. They both accepted her offer of a glass, which she poured for the three of them. She stepped over to her desk and returned with a plate of shortbread cookies.

"I buy these at a small patisserie near here. Try one, please," she said.

Becky declined with a small halting motion of her hand, but Joe took one, and savoured each bite of the buttery crumbliness.

Dr. Wentworth was a good-looking woman. Her skin was nearly translucent, she had high cheekbones, and she wore very little make-up. She didn't need any. She was dressed very conservatively, without looking too solemn, in a black linen skirt and pale blue cap-sleeved blouse. She had a string of pearls on her neck and, as she poured, Joe glanced at her hands and noticed she had no wedding ring, just a simple pearl ring on her right index finger. Her hair was auburn, quite short and dead straight, both sides tucked behind her pearl-studded ears. Her bangs reached the top ridge of her eyebrows. Her eyes were a mesmerizing pale green, like the inside of an avocado, very kind-looking and they held an irresistible twinkle. Joe thought she must be in her mid-thirties.

"I've been looking through Ryan's file while I was waiting for you to arrive. I don't know if there's anything in it that can be of any help to you, but ask away. I was very fond of the boy. When his sister first called me, and told me that the police were calling it a suicide, I found the idea outlandish. He was making great progress with me."

Becky took the lead, asking the first question. "But he was taking Remeron, prescribed by you, is that right?"

"Correct. He's been taking Remeron for nearly a year, along with regular therapy sessions. He suffers ... sorry ... suffered, from depression and mood swings, when he was initially referred to me. That was two years ago. We tried a variety of different medications at the beginning, and finally settled on Remeron. He's been doing so well lately that I was planning to stop his medication soon, and continue solely with therapy."

"When did you last see him?"

"That would be a little over a week ago, just before he left on his trip."

"Can you tell us his state of mind at the time?"

"Well, that's the thing. We sat here and he told me about the Vegas trip he had won, and asked me what I thought. I have to admit, I wasn't thrilled with the idea of him going, but he was so happy, and he felt that this would be some sort of test for himself. And if he passed he would be able to move on with his life. So I told him I had faith in his strength, but that I would be a simple phone call away if he needed to talk. He booked an appointment with me before he left, which would have been tomorrow. He was looking forward to telling me about how he made out down there, regarding, as he put it, "flipping out if I lose" and, I must admit, from a clinical standpoint, I was looking forward to hearing about his escapade and what effect the trip had on him."

"What do you know about Ketamine, Dr. Wentworth?"

"Please, call me Kathleen. Ketamine is an anesthetic drug used primarily by veterinarians. Unfortunately, it's also gained popularity as the primary date-rape drug. Some people also use it intentionally, in low doses, as a recreational drug. Do you mind telling me what this has to do with Ryan?"

"An amount was found in his bloodstream. We're still waiting for the final tox report for the quantity. Are you aware if Ryan ever took the drug?"

"Certainly not to my knowledge. And it would have been disastrous combined with either Remeron or alcohol."

"Based solely on the empty prescription bottle, the filling-date, the recommended dosage and the presumption that he took the balance of the pills that night, we estimate that he swallowed 300 mg of Remeron, alongside a still-unknown quantity of Ketamine. He also had at least a few beers."

Dr. Wentworth's eyes were welling up and threatening to overflow. She stood up abruptly, excusing herself. She walked to the other side of her office, entered a small door, and closed it behind her. They heard a tap running and a toilet flushing, and when she returned, the bottom rims of her eyes were slightly red. She looked sheepish.

"I apologize. This is all quite a shock. Although we aren't supposed to have favourite patients, I'm only human, and Ryan indeed was one of my favourites. And I find this all very difficult to comprehend. He wasn't a *stupid* boy. He would know not to mix drugs and alcohol like that, I'm sure of it."

"Based on the amounts of Remeron I mentioned, what would the effect have been with that combination of drugs?"

"Without knowing exact amounts of the Ketamine and alcohol intake, I can't tell you positively what the effect would have been. But I can tell you that there are a variety of potential side effects. You have to understand, Ketamine is a dissociative anesthesia. So someone could experience hallucinations, respiratory depression, confusion, aggressive behaviour, vertigo, analgesia, and in extreme cases, coma, and death."

"Can you tell us how long it takes to feel the effects of the drug?"

The doctor stood up again, walked over to the bookcase, and took down a huge tome. She stood there and flipped through the pages. She paused nearly half way through the book and her lips moved slightly as she read silently for a minute. She replaced the book and turned back towards them. She glanced at Joe but then directed her answer to Becky.

"When taken orally the effects take ten to twenty minutes to be realized. When taken intravenously the effects are instantaneous."

"If you slipped it into someone's drink, would they taste it?"

"Probably not, but they might see it, because it would cloud a clear liquid."

"Kathleen, can you give us any more insight into Ryan's personality or state of mind? Anything at all?"

"Up until a year ago, he suffered from severe depression and mood swings. But, as I said before, I've seen a marked improvement in him, and I believe he would have been off Remeron over the next few months. I've never seen any indication that he was abusing any drugs whatsoever. Even his alcohol intake has decreased over the last half year."

"We still haven't confirmed whether Ryan's death was suicide or criminal wrongdoing. You've had therapy sessions with him over the last year. Do you know of anyone who he may have confronted recently? Any enemies he may have had?"

She stared at the window and concentrated on it as if she was watching a movie. She spoke woodenly as if she was transcribing notes into a voice recorder. "Ryan had a problem with controlling his anger, but I find it difficult to believe that he would get anyone angry enough at him to want to kill him. To the best of my knowledge, the only person he has ever physically assaulted has been his wife, and that was quite some time ago. It's a matter of record. You can look up the police file. He has no contact with her now whatsoever." She looked back at Joe, and then at Becky.

Becky stood up, and reached her hand out to Kathleen. "That's all the questions I have for you, Kathleen. Thank you for taking the time to meet with us at such short notice."

"I'm so sorry, I don't feel like I've been much help." She reached over to her desk and slipped two business cards out of a small silver tray. "Please call me if you have any other questions. And would you please tell Ryan's sister that if she wants to get in touch with me to talk, I'm available. I've never met the girl, but Ryan spoke so sweetly of her. She was very important to him. She must be in great pain." She handed Becky a business card.

"That's very kind. I'll let her know."

Joe shook her hand and accepted a card. As the three of them walked towards the front door, Joe spoke up for the first time since the initial introductions, "Thank you so much for your help,

Kathleen. You've really given us a lot of worthwhile information about Ryan as well as the drugs. We appreciate it. We really do."

"Please call me if there's anything you think I can help with. And I'd be very grateful if you'd keep me informed, whenever you can, about the case."

"I'd be pleased to," Joe answered, "and here's my card as well." They walked out the door, around to the front of the house, and down the steps.

"Joe, that was stupid. Giving her your card?"

"It was just habit. Didn't mean anything by it."

"You're not even *on* the case. How do you expect to keep her informed? You're so bloody transparent."

"Easy on. I apologize. I felt like I was back in the thick of it for a few minutes. It felt good." Becky was silent for the few minutes it took to reach the corner of Saint-Catherine. He didn't know what to say. He knew she was right. It *was* stupid to have handed his card over. He was a P.I.—not a cop. A taxi was stopped at the light and Joe hailed it. He held the rear door open for Becky and followed her in. He gave the driver his office address and turned to Becky.

"Do you want me to drop you at the station?"

"Please. Andrew may not be back yet but I can write this interview up while I wait."

She checked her phone and replied to text messages during the ten minute drive to the station. As the taxi pulled up to the station, they saw Andrew entering the front door.

"Text me later if you want to go to the Donegal or for a bite to eat? I'll buy you an apology pint," Joe said.

"It'll take more than one." Becky stepped out of the car, closed the door, and followed Andrew into the station.

14

Detective Hank Mason arrived in Vegas from Montréal and, like Joe Cameron before him, checked into the Poker Palace hotel so that he'd be near the Vegas Metro police station. After a night's sleep, he dressed in a golf shirt and cotton trousers and set off for the station to meet his temporary partner.

Mason had been on the force for nearly 30 years, and was planning to retire soon. He had a reputation for being an old-school cop and was proud of it. He was a stocky man and totally bald. All his features were roundish. When he was younger, his school friends said he had a beach ball head. His nose was squashed onto his face, like a bulldog's, from countless schoolyard battles. He knew his squad called him Humpty—mostly behind his back. But everyone on the force had a nickname and it didn't bother him any longer, so more and more of his team were calling him Hump instead of Hank. The only sharpness about him was the piercing glare in his eyes. He had an intimidating look and he got quicker results in an interrogation room than most others because of it.

He had started on the force in Baie Sainte-Anne, New Brunswick, the same town he was born in. He transferred to Montréal after a few years because he craved more crimes to solve.

The Acadian French that he'd grown up with was a totally different dialect, but he got the hang of Québécois French and had grown to love Montréal. Recently though, he was becoming disillusioned with the modern world—he could barely figure out how to operate his television—and had been mulling over fond memories of his small-town childhood. He was putting feelers out about buying a little place near the ocean on the east coast. Just him and his fishing rod.

He'd give technology one final shot and join that Facebook thing. Try and get back in touch with long lost cousins and high school friends. He had few friends in Montréal, although he got along with all his colleagues. They invited him for drinks after shifts and family BBQs in the summer but he expected they felt sorry for him because he had no family here. He'd never married. Hadn't even dated in the last few years.

He walked through downtown Las Vegas until he reached a residential area. He continued along a few blocks of dilapidated, sometimes abandoned, houses. The yards were dirt and stone. Shopping carts, old car seats, and bicycles were the only lawn ornaments.

It took him ten minutes to reach Metro, by which time he was dripping with the heat. 9:00 a.m. and the temperature had hit 102°F. The police headquarters was a modern red-brick three-story building. He entered the station and stopped at the desk, which was left of the door on a raised podium and framed by bullet-proof glass. He asked for Detective Arthur Thibodeaux of Homicide.

While he waited, he inspected his surroundings. It was more contemporary than his station. The floor looked like marble, and there were small windows, each covered with a fine mesh grate. Under the windows, running the full length of the outer wall, were black moulded plastic benches, on which a few silent people were seated. Along the back wall were two elevators and a number of doors leading into the centre of the building. The room felt spacious and non-threatening. More like a dotcom office. The walls were painted cappuccino brown and displayed dozens of framed black and white photographs of Las Vegas from days past.

"Look at you—dressed like that! You must be as hot as two bunnies screwin' in a wool sack!" He turned to see a young man walking towards him with outstretched hand. "Art Thibodeaux." Art's accent reminded Hank slightly of the Acadians of his youth but even more so the characters he'd watched the year before on the Tremé TV series set in New Orleans.

"Hank Mason. Good to meet ya." He shook Thibodeaux's hand, and felt the grip of someone who worked out regularly.

Thibodeaux was dressed in tan shorts and a loose canary-yellow t-shirt. They couldn't have made a more incongruous pair. Tall and slender, surfer blond hair long enough to be tied in a little pony tail. Mirrored sunglasses straddled his head. His eyes, the colour of pewter, were bordered by crisscrossing crow's feet.

"Seein' as how you're my new partner, call me Gumbo. Everybody does. You know these guys on the wall here?" He didn't give Mason an opportunity to respond. "This photo here is the illustrious Bugsy Siegel. He's the New York gangster who was the force behind building the Flamingo Casino. Before that, we just had gambling saloons downtown. He got the bright idea to build a fancy resort in the middle of this cowboy town and bring in Hollywood rich kids. Separate them from their money amidst the glamour of gambling, booze, and bombshell women." He shook his head. "Rest is history. He never got to see his dream. Murdered by his colleagues within a year."

"Who's this kid?" Hank pointed to a photo of a young guy with mop-top hair, wearing John Lennon glasses and a toothy Mick Jaggeresque-grin.

"Sad case—Stu Ungar. He won and lost millions playing poker. Died at 45 in a cheap motel room on the Strip. Heart failure brought on by years of drug abuse. Life is short, but it's long enough to ruin a man." He shook his head again and started to walk away. "We'll have a coffee and I'll bring you up to bumper car speed with what's been goin' down 'round here. Interesting project, this cross-border shit. First time we've been involved with it. You?"

"Never even heard of it and I've probably been on the force longer than you've been alive. Makes sense in theory, but I'm curious to see if we all survive the warm and cuddly sharing bits."

Thibodeaux laughed. "I promise the fondling won't be more than a mild caress." He proved his point with a friendly pat on the back while guiding Hank through the nearest door. He handed him a visitor's badge—already filled in with his name and rank—to pin on his shirt.

They walked through a work-station area of men and women glued to their computer screens, tapping on keyboards like concert pianists, and entered a fishbowl conference room. An oval teak conference table took centre stage, surrounded by eight leather-backed padded chairs. A welcome smell of freshly-brewed coffee wafted over from a machine on a large credenza under the window. The window also had a mesh barrier, and small slat venetian blinds, which were partly closed, shredding the harsh sunlight in the room. Beside the coffee was a tray set up with milk, sugar, real cups and cutlery, as well as a half-full box of croissants.

On the wall at one end of the room hung a large monitor, and on the other end of the table was a touch panel showing the last video conference caller's address as well as a list of other police station addresses throughout Vegas and major cities around the country.

"We can sit in here without being disturbed while I fill you in on the case. Later today we'll hopefully have more information than we do now. Coffee?" Gumbo asked and poured two cups out without waiting for an answer.

They both fixed their coffee, grabbed a croissant, and sat beside each other at the conference table. Gumbo pushed a few buttons on the central panel to light up the wall screen.

"Christ, Gumbo. What the hell did we do before all this technical crap?"

"Well, for one thing, we didn't collaborate. We've moved along since the telegraph machine," he laughed in reply.

"Sometimes it feels like I spend more time trying to figure out the latest program on my computer, and filling out forms, than I do working a case."

"There'll be enough of working the case the old way, don't worry about that. We'll be as busy as kittens burying turds on a granite floor. I'll handle the tech stuff." He continued to press buttons and turn dials.

"Pinball machines are about as high-tech as I wanna get."

Gumbo pressed another button on the panel. A photograph of a naked male body—floating face up in a kidney shaped pool—filled the screen. Beer cans and plastic bottles were floating in the slug-coloured cocktail of a pool.

"This is our vic, Graves, at the Roulette Motor Hotel. 37 years old. He lived in Vegas. Moved out here a few years ago, from New York City, with his wife. They split up soon after. His online player name with Buckingham Poker was MrBlue."

The screen changed to a photo of the same body—removed from the swampy pool—and now lying prone on the flaking blue cement.

"I thought Americans couldn't gamble on-line anymore," Hank said.

"You're right about that, but there are ways around it. An American can set up his computer to virtually bounce off a server in a country where it's legal, like Canada or the United Kingdom, and then register with a street address and an IP address from that country. Then he's off and running. Millions of people are doing it worldwide."

"You think the two guys knew each other? Harper and Graves?" Hank asked.

"No indication of it yet, but we have our IT forensic boys looking through Graves' computer. Particularly his email and his participation on the poker site. It's my understanding that your boys back in Montréal are doing the same thing with Harper's computer. We have Buckingham Poker running a data check on their gaming histories to see if they ever played the same table at the same time. Granted, it's bound to have happened at some point because it's a small website. We'll see if they chatted beyond the usual "good hand" or "wtf"." Hank got up and went over to the coffee machine. He poured another full cup and asked Gumbo if he wanted more.

"No, merci."

"Was it definitely a death by drowning?"

Gumbo nodded and pressed a button, bringing up a photo taken from a distance of about eight feet from the body. "Poor bastard was like a submarine with a screen door." A pile of clothing was folded neatly on top of the damaged poolside table. "He also had quantities of Ketamine in his bloodstream, according to the toxicologist. No sign of a struggle. Based on his nakedness, we're running on the assumption that he entered the water willingly and was with someone who he planned to have some fun with. He must have been pretty blotto or horny or both not to notice the state of that pool. Whether that other person was a man or a woman, we'll have to investigate this guy's background more thoroughly, even though he was once married. Doesn't mean nothing anymore."

"Anything else so far?" asked Hank.

"We have uniforms doing door-to-door near the motel. The body was spotted from an apartment building across the street, so maybe somebody else saw something. We've begun a more thorough investigation of the Paradise hotel staff, and people who were staying on the same floor as Harper. A lot of them have checked out so we're phoning them. The casinos are providing us with DVDs from their CCTV for the dates and times we provided and we'll go through the footage. We'll look at both the vics; when they played in the casino, when they left, who they interacted with. If there's any common denominator, we'll damn well find it."

"What have you lined up for today then?" So far, Hank was impressed with the procedure his new partner was following. He wouldn't have done anything different.

"I figured I could walk around the station and pick up all the reports from the different departments and the footage from the casino. You can get hold of the NYPD to see if they've got a file on Graves. I emailed a request to them earlier. When I get back, we can go interview the ex-wife together. After that we can connect with our partners up in Montréal, and see what they've got."

"Solid plan. Set me up somewhere and I'll get on it," said Hank.

They walked down the hall to a large room where there were half a dozen guys seated at computer screens. Gumbo stopped and made introductions at one of the desks. "Hank, this is Bob. You need anything when I'm not around—you ask him." Bob nodded without looking away from the monitor and Gumbo dropped Hank off in a dusty abandoned cubbyhole of a room; a desk, a chair, a phone and file folder on the desk. Nothing else.

"Here's the number for our NYPD contact, Lieutenant Gómez. I shouldn't be more than ten minutes. I've programmed *1 on the phone to reach my mobile." Gumbo smiled and closed the door behind him. Hank sat down at the desk and opened the drawers one by one. He found a pad of paper and a few pens and pencils in one of them. He phoned Gómez, who picked up immediately. Hank explained who he was and why he was calling.

"Right. I guess it was your partner who emailed us earlier asking if we could dig up anything on your guy. I had one of the uniforms look him up. The file's here somewhere. Hang on." Hank sat back, listening to a background of paper swishing, interspersed with swearing and phones ringing in the background. The receiver was picked up again. "Got it. Not much on him really. Born here in New York, in the Village, in 1979. 2004, he married a Stephanie Corrigan. He had a DUI in 2005—licence suspension and fine only. We also had five domestic dispute call-outs between 2006 and 2012; four times from neighbours, once from the wife. She was pregnant at the last call-out, towards the end of 2012, but dropped the charges. Seems they moved to Vegas in early 2013. That's all we have on him. Anything else I can do for you guys?"

"Not for now. We just wanted to know what he got up to before here. Could you email a copy of that to Thibodeaux, Lieutenant?"

"No problemo. Good luck with your case," he said, and hung up before Hank could say goodbye.

15

By the time Gumbo returned, Hank had reviewed all the files and photographs from both the Harper case and the Graves murder. There were many similarities between the two deaths. Hank didn't believe in coincidences but still couldn't find a connection.

"You ready to go have a chat with Graves' ex-wife?" Gumbo asked as he stood in the doorway.

"You bet. Any news from the door-to-door?"

"No one around the motel saw anything. No one heard anything. About what we'd expect from that part of town. It's sketchy—a lot of people living on the fringe—they tend to keep to themselves."

"What about the casino where the tournament was held?"

"They talked to staff at the Poker room, bar, and hotel. Again, everyone was deaf and blind. Maybe the Casino CCTV will give us a lead. This city has more cameras than Hollywood but the Paradise is a 50-year-old dump that only has cameras on the casino floor. My men will log any footage that shows the vics and we can view it when we get back."

They took an elevator down to the parking garage, and made their way to an unmarked apple-red vintage Ford Mustang with plenty of chrome and a pristine white interior. They got in to the car and shot through the underground parking. Thanks to an unseen

98

electronic eye, the garage doors slid open, and they were heading north.

"You get anything from NYPD?" Gumbo asked.

Hank repeated what Gómez had told him. "I see from the case file there's been no incidents here in Vegas—at least nothing that was ever called in."

"Nada. Rien. Nothing. They separated about a year ago. She kept the house in the suburbs with the two kids. He moved to a flop house not far from here. Just behind the bail bond area along the Strip. Took all of five minutes the other day to go through his worldly possessions. Nothing of value but the computer. Forensics is going through that now." He reached over and turned on the GPS. They took the on-ramp to Highway 15 heading north. "It's not too far. She lives near Nellis Air Force Base."

Ten minutes later, they were on a four-lane road lined on both sides with tract homes, fast-food restaurants, cheap bars, cheaper motels, and used-car lots breaking up the boredom of desert landscape. The air conditioning had finally chilled the car as Gumbo slowed down and turned left onto a smaller suburban road.

There were two small gangs of teenagers—one on each side of the street—like border control. For as far as the eye could see down the block, identical housing units were constructed on the dusty ground like giant Legos, four homes per unit. Pale yellowish-tan adobe, bars on all the windows and front doors, and front yards of dry sand. The neighbourhood swarmed with kids: skipping, hopscotching, running wild. They dodged a maze of children chasing a soccer ball along the street and shouting at each other in several different languages.

Gumbo parked in front of one of the apartment units as the GPS announced their arrival. As they stepped out from the cool interior of the car they caught the stench of rotting food drifting over from large industrial size refuse containers that stood between each building. Many were overflowing onto the play area—like toy boxes for rodents. The homes resembled mini-motels. Wrought iron staircases spiralled to the second floor apartments. Satellite dishes of various sizes clung to a multitude of window bars.

Two children were imprisoned in a play-pen, shaded by the overhanging balcony above. They looked to be the right age to be the Graves kids: the youngest girl just over a year, and the older sister closer to three. They approached the front door along a shattered flagstone walkway. The inner wooden door was open, but the metal door with the security bars was locked. Gumbo gave a yell. "Mrs. Graves! It's Detective Thibodeaux, Vegas Metro!"

They stood at the doorstep, watching the older of the two kids hitting the other one over the head with a plastic truck amidst squeals of delight. Both were dressed in stained and torn white T-shirts. A grimy diaper was hanging dangerously loose off the youngest girl, and the older one was wearing striped shorts that she probably wouldn't grow into for another year.

A woman walked along the hallway towards them, loosely tying the sash of a silk kimono around her waist. She was 35 years old but her pixie face looked dog-tired and caked with a few days worth of makeup. Her hair was muddy-brown and hung limply to her shoulders. The skin on her arms dangled too loosely from her bones, not doing her tattoos any favours. The only jewellery she wore was in her ears, but she couldn't have accommodated one more stud or loop without growing a third lobe. She lit a cigarette as she approached them.

"The fuck you want? Cops were here yesterday to give me the good news." She greeted them with the gravelly voice of a hard-core smoker.

Hank reached down to retrieve a toy truck that had flown across the yard and hit his shin. He took a few steps over to the play-pen, dropping it in, and gave one of the kids a friendly head tousle.

"Wouldn't do that if I were you. They're crawling with cooties." She laughed until a bout of coughing took over. Hank scrubbed his palm against his thigh, hoping to kill any of the little buggers if they'd hopped on, staring at her with blatant distaste.

"Can we come in and talk, Mrs. Graves?" Gumbo asked.

"I don't use the bastard's name anymore, so you can quit with the Mrs. Graves shit. Haven't used it since he walked out and I'm not about to start now," she said, making no move to open the security gate.

"Stephanie, then? Can we come in and talk?" he asked again, trying not to lose patience.

"We'll stay out here. Lotta wierdos around here. Can't leave the kids on their own," as if she'd been reading them a story when they'd driven up. "Whadya want?"

"When did you and your ex part ways?" Gumbo began.

"Not soon enough, that's for sure. A year ago. Something like that."

"What were the circumstances?" he continued.

"Circumstances? He becomes some hotshot poker player. Or so he thinks. Wins some big tournament downtown and informs me he's had it with this shit and moves out. I don't think he even knew the little one's name. Didn't gimme a dime when he left. What the hell. We're better off without the asshole living here."

"Why didn't you move back east?" Hank asked.

Stephanie looked at him like he was intellectually challenged. "Simple. Bigger welfare check here. Cheaper to live, too."

"When was the last time you saw him?" asked Gumbo.

"The last time he needed money, I guess. Maybe two or three weeks ago. I dunno. Time flies when you're having fun. He turns up once in a while when he's drunk and broke. Normally just after my welfare check has arrived."

"And you gave him money?" Hank asked. He couldn't keep the disbelief from his voice.

"It's that or he gives me somethin' that I can happily do without. Why? You were thinking maybe he drops by for tea and cake to give me some of his track winnings?" She spluttered through her phlegmy chuckle.

Gumbo put his hands up in the air like he was being held at gunpoint. "Stephanie. This is serious. Your husband was murdered. He's their father," pointing at the two in the play-pen. Hank could hear the strain in his voice and chimed in.

"Was he on any medication that you know of?"

Stephanie looked over at Hank, again like she'd have to explain something to a child. She took a pack of cigarettes out of her pocket and lit one off the stub of her butt. "Shoulda been, but I doubt if the slob could afford meds." She threw the butt on the ground and buried it into the dirt with the toe of her shoe.

"Did he ever phone you?" Gumbo asked.

"He don't have the number. Never will now, thank fuck."

"Can you tell us where you were the night of his death?"

"Where the hell do you think I was?" She looked pointedly over at her two children. "On stage with Penn & Teller?"

Gumbo and Hank were both silent and stared at Stephanie.

She tightened the robe and folded her arms across her chest. "I was here, of course, with these two nose-miners. Don't get me wrong, boys. I'd love to take the credit for it. When you find the guy who did it, gimme his address so I can add him to my Christmas card list."

"I suppose it's too much to ask if you knew if he had a girlfriend or close friends?" asked Hank.

The only response he got was an eruption of hacking laughter.

"Enemies?"

"I'm sure he had plenty. Get it through your thick skulls. We don't chitchat. He turns up here. I give him a few bucks to leave me be, and then I pray he wins enough to not come around here again for a very long time."

"Well, you must have prayed real hard last time, lady," Hank said, while she doubled over in a bronchial fit of happiness.

"Thanks for your time. Watch those kids now," Gumbo said.

They walked back to the car and got in. They both rolled the windows down, as a precaution so they'd hear the children running around the streets. As they were slowly driving away, they could hear a faint yell, over the hum of the Mustang, "Hey boys, did the fuckin' cocksucker leave me anything in his will?"

16

"What's your take on the grieving widow, Hank?"

"She sure as hell has motive, but lacks the deviousness. And the planning and execution? I don't see it."

"Agreed. She's a rough little number but I reckon Miss Steph is about as sharp as a basketball. I want to look into her though."

They got back to the station without further conversation. Gumbo turned the radio on to a country channel, humming along, and Hank sat back and enjoyed the view. They were surrounded by mountain peaks peppered with blackbrush and reminded Hank of the backdrops of western movies he'd loved as a child. Out of sight, but only a few miles away, was the madness of the Strip where hotels and resorts were impaling the cloudless pale blue sky.

Gumbo parked the car and they took the elevator up to the second floor. Hank followed Gumbo to a frosted glass door. I.T. Forensics was etched at eye level. Gumbo swiped a card in front of a digital reader to open the door.

"You wait here, Hank. I'll just pick up the reports from the team, and then we'll get in touch with Montréal to compare notes."

Gumbo wasn't gone more than a minute, returning with a half-inch thick yellow file folder and three DVDs in transparent cases. Hank took the DVDs from him, reading as they walked to the conference room. There was a white sticker on each case. "June 26th, 2015, 9:30 p.m. to 10:00 p.m., Poker Palace Casino, Poker Room, Camera 8." "10:00 p.m. to 11:00 p.m., Poker Bar, Camera 3." "June 29th, 2015, 9:00 p.m. to 11:30 p.m., Poker Room, Camera 4".

"I sent a text to my partner, Newcross, to initiate the computer link in Montréal when they're ready," said Gumbo. "In the meantime, we can watch the Casino DVDs and see if we spot anything. The quality of footage, from most CCTV cameras here, is as good as a Hollywood studio production. They can be a lot of help when we're trying to track someone. Unfortunately, the Poker Palace is small fry, and independent from the multi-billion dollar chains. They haven't upgraded their equipment in years. But still, better than nothing."

*

Rebecca Newcross walked with Andrew Miller to his car. The intense heat wave had moved on and made room for a temperate day. There was a sweet breeze carrying the scent of lilacs from the garden of the monastery further down the block. They were going to see Kelly Harper, the sister of Ryan Harper. She lived in Ville Saint-Laurent, a suburb of Montréal, but not a sleepy one. It would be a 15-minute drive north on the expressway to reach the apartment they had shared.

Rebecca thoroughly recounted her interview with Dr. Wentworth. Andrew knew a lot about Ketamine, as it had become a serious problem in Montréal recently.

"Special K started making an appearance in bars around town a few years ago. We devote as much time as we can to awareness campaigns. We give talks in high schools and colleges, warning kids to have a friend mind their drinks, to never leave a bar with a stranger, and to watch out for friends that appear drunker than normal, that sort of thing. The problem now is that kids have discovered that low dosages of the drug can result in a somewhat euphoric state. Unfortunately there's a fine line between euphoria and catatonia. And if someone also consumes alcohol, they can misjudge the recreational amount with disastrous consequences. You probably know all this."

"I don't know as much as you do, Andrew. The drug isn't as big a problem in Vegas. Don't get me wrong. It's there, but not as prevalent as other drugs. Thank God. We've got plenty of other distractions, I suppose."

Andrew turned off the highway, and drove along a tree-lined Boulevard, explaining that Decarie Boulevard was the heart of old Saint-Laurent and had grown from a village speckled with farms and riding stables to a melting-pot city of ethnic families and young couples first-homing. They turned onto a street of post-war red-brick apartments. The block was bookended by a car dealership at one end, and a grocery store at the other. They parked and entered one of the three-story buildings, ringing a doorbell above a mailbox labelled Harper. After climbing two flights of stairs, they arrived at door #22 as it was opening.

"Hi, you're the police?" A young woman stood there clutching a paperback romance novel in one hand and a wad of scrunched up Kleenex in the other. Her brown hair was tied back in a ponytail. Wearing a pair of cut-off jeans and a summery dark pink blouse, she was barefoot and her toenails were painted pale pink.

"That's right, I'm Detective Miller, and my partner is Detective Newcross." He held out his ID for Kelly to check. Newcross followed suit, opening her wallet to expose her badge. Kelly only glanced for a second at the IDs when a fluffy overweight tabby cat shot out of the apartment and between Miller's legs. Newcross sprinted down the hall and scooped the cat up before it reached the stairwell. She brought it back to the doorway and transferred it from her arms to Kelly's.

"We're very sorry for your loss, Ms. Harper," said Rebecca while Andrew nodded his agreement.

"Thanks. Come on in." Rebecca closed the door and Kelly let the cat down. They followed her down a long and narrow—like a bowling lane—hallway to the kitchen. "I just made a pot of coffee." Plates, cups, glasses and cutlery were piled in and beside the sink. The counter was littered with pizza delivery boxes, and Chinese food containers.

The detectives stood silently as she poured three cups of coffee and pulled a small carton of milk out of the fridge. A sugar bowl was on the counter beside the cups. There was a small spoon balanced across its rim, crusted over with yellow hardened sugar. They both decided to drink their coffee black and unsweetened and carried their cups through the kitchen to the living room. A table-top fan was positioned on an old white melamine table, under the open living room window, but it felt like it was circulating only warm air around the room. The ammonia smell of a too-full litter box mingled with the aroma of coffee and the lemony smell of freshly polished furniture.

The living room was surprisingly tidy considering the state of the kitchen. Kelly sat on a small footstool beside the coffee table, and the two detectives sat beside each other on the worn orange plaid sofa. The cat took up residence on a miniature chaise longue, covered with paw print upholstery, near the balcony door and settled in for a grooming session.

"We need to ask you a few questions about your brother, Kelly," said Rebecca.

"Do you have any news or anything?" She gripped her coffee mug with both hands. Her knees were thumping up and down as if she had an invisible baby on her lap.

"We've opened a full investigation into his death. It would assist us a great deal to learn more about him. You can help us with that."

"I'll help any way I can." She put her cup down on the coffee table and wrapped her arms around her knees.

"Are you aware of Ryan taking any drugs?" asked Andrew.

"He took some anti-depressants. Not all the time, but once in a while. They're like prescription though. I can't remember the name of them, but there's some in the medicine cabinet if you want to look at them."

She started to get up and Andrew said, "That's okay, Kelly. Are you talking about Remeron?"

"Yes, that's it," she said, wriggling back into her seat. "He smoked a bit of weed now and then, but nothing stronger than that."

Andrew leaned back on the sofa which cued Rebecca to resume asking the questions.

"What about his ex-wife, Valerie Mackay? Did Ryan keep in touch with her?"

"With Val? No, I don't think so—not since the divorce. They never had kids, and they weren't married for very long. Like, a year or so, I think. So there wasn't even alimony or anything. They just got divorced, no lawyers, nothing."

"What about you. Are you friends with her?"

"No. We never really got along from the start. She lives out on the South Shore somewhere. So it's not like I would run into her or anything. Does she know about Ryan?"

"Yes, she's been informed. Tell me about Ryan. What did he do for fun? Did he have friends he went out with? Anyone you think we should talk to?"

"I can't imagine who. He never really went out—except to work —and that's like just down the street, at the Hardware store on Decarie. He'd get home from work, make a sandwich, open up a beer, and go to his room, and play on his computer till bedtime. Sometimes, like on payday, he'd pick up pizza or something on his way home, for us to share. But even then, we hardly ever ate together. Most of the time he'd just take his plate, and go into his room. I'd only see him if he came out to get another beer."

"You two get along okay?"

"Oh my, gosh! Yes! He was my big brother!" Tears started rolling down her cheeks. "I didn't mean he was bad or anything." Her shoulders began to shake and the cat ran out of the room as if he'd witnessed this event before and didn't desire a repeat.

Rebecca got up from the sofa and knelt down beside her. She clasped Kelly's knees in her hands and gave them a gentle squeeze. "It's alright, Kelly. We know that you and your brother were close. You mind if we take a look round his room?"

Kelly blew her nose and shook her head at the same time. "Of course not. I haven't touched anything. The other cops told me not to. They took his computer away yesterday." She pointed at the closed door to the left of the kitchen.

Rebecca and Andrew left Kelly in the living room and opened the door to Ryan's room. The window was closed and the room was stuffy and warm. Mounds of dirty clothing decorated the floor and the place smelled like a high school gym locker. One that hadn't been cleaned out by last years' occupant and was inherited in September by some other poor kid.

A Canadian flag had been staple-gunned to the top frame of the lone window. The bottom of the makeshift curtain hung a few inches short of the sill, which was being used as a book shelf. There were three books on poker strategy and a Las Vegas guide. Balancing precariously on the other end of the sill was a stack of magazines which all proved to be well-thumbed Playboys. It was a small square room, and impossible to tell whether someone had actually painted it yellowish beige or if it was nicotine-stained.

They both reached into their pockets and put on latex gloves. Rebecca flicked through the pages of each book while Andrew tackled the magazines.

The desk was beside the window. The only objects on it were three empty beer bottles, an overflowing ashtray, and a wireless computer mouse. There was a dust-free rectangle where the laptop had been.

Andrew peered under the unmade double bed. He saw clumps of dust bunnies and a pair of dirty white socks. On top of the bedside cabinet was a lamp, a box of Kleenex, and an ashtray that held a few cigarette butts and a wad of pink gum. He opened the drawer and saw two empty plastic pill bottles, a pack of illegal cigarettes from the Mohawk Reserve, a handful of small change, and the most recent edition of Playboy. He held the cigarettes up to show Rebecca.

"This is a problem here in Montréal. People drive over to the Reserve and buy cheap smokes. They manufacture them now and don't have to pay government taxes."

"Aren't there any regulations in place?"

"Tough to manage. They have smoke shacks up and down the main routes that cut through their land. They're supposed to sell only to natives, but it's not easy to pass up such huge profits." He shook his head and threw them back in the drawer.

Rebecca had been searching a three-drawer bureau but she only found the usual assortment of underwear, socks, jeans, and T-shirts. She went to the closet and opened the door. There were a few wrinkled shirts, a pair of black dress trousers, two jackets, and a parka dangling from hangers. Shoes and runners littered the floor, some with socks bunched up in them.

Andrew lifted the suitcase that was on the floor onto the top of the bed. The handle still had the flight tag on it. He unzipped the case and removed everything; clothing, toiletries, empty pill bottle, a *This Week In Vegas* magazine, his tournament entry papers, passport, and wallet. His wallet contained a few hundred dollars, a Casino Players Card, driver's licence, and a Starbucks loyalty card. He tossed everything back into the case, zipped it, and placed it against the wall beside the desk.

"Shit, this room is gloomy," said Rebecca. "There's no hint of who this kid is: no photographs, no letters, nothing. Hopefully his computer will give us something."

"Yeah. It feels more like a cheap hotel room than a private bedroom."

"Yep. Only thing missing is Gideon's Bible." They stared at each other and sighed in unison. Andrew closed the bedroom door behind them and found Kelly, garbage bag in hand, tidying up the kitchen.

"We'll have a look in the bathroom now," Rebecca told her.

Kelly nodded and pointed at a door just to the right of the entry. They looked through the contents of the medicine cabinet and found a ten month old prescription bottle of Remeron which contained three pills.

"I expect this was long forgotten about. He had a recently filled out pill bottle with him in Vegas," said Rebecca. They put it into a plastic evidence bag so that Toxicology could verify the contents. The rest of the cabinet contained commonplace toiletries and Kelly's makeup.

After reassuring Kelly that they would update her on the case, they left for the South Shore, where they had arranged an interview with Harper's ex-wife, Valerie Mackay. From Saint-Laurent they had to drive the width of the island, and join the bumper to bumper traffic to cross one of the few bridges to get to the mainland.

Mackay lived in a suburb of Montréal called Chateauguay, near the Mohawk Reserve. They had agreed to meet her at four o'clock at her home, to accommodate her work schedule at a nearby restaurant.

They were a bit early for the appointment, but as they approached the small bungalow, a woman was hurrying up the walkway to the house. She had buds in her ears and a smartphone in her hand and didn't hear them turn into her driveway. When Miller and Newcross slammed the car doors, the woman dropped her house keys on the landing and swung around to face them.

17

"Valerie Mackay? I'm Detective Newcross. This is my partner, Detective Miller."

"Yes, that's me. You're earlier than I expected." She twisted her lips into a pout—more of a coquettish mannerism than a sullen grimace. She was thirty years old and looked much younger. Her jet-black hair was pulled up in a ponytail. She was a near-perfect hourglass shape—a little heavy on top—or the effect could have been attained with the aid of a push-up bra. Her clothes were of the chain store variety but the overall look was fashionably trendy. She wore a short purple skirt, with a pristine white scoop-neck tank top. Her shapely legs were bare and her pedicured mauve toenails poked out from straw sandals. A straw purse draped from one of her shoulders. She had an even tan all over but with that tinge of tangerine that comes from a bottle of cheap spray tan.

"Can never estimate how long it will take to cross the Mercier Bridge," Miller said non-apologetically. They walked up the pathway and joined Valerie at the front door. It was a 1950's style bungalow, a combination of pale grey brick and white vinyl siding. All the windows were on the small side compared to most of the neighbours who had upgraded to bow picture windows.

"Well, you might as well come in then." She turned the key in the lock and walked in, leaving the door open for them to follow. "And you might as well call me Val." They stepped into a living room that bore more resemblance to an Ikea showroom than a lived-in home. She sat on a chocolate brown wing chair. The morning Gazette and a lipstick-stained coffee mug were on the matching footstool. The parquet floor was partially hidden by a number of throw rugs. The detectives sat side by side on a beige loveseat. Newcross placed her notepad on the glass coffee table which was anchored on an imitation polar bear rug.

"We won't take up much of your time, Val. If you can just answer a few questions we have about your ex-husband, we'll leave you to the rest of your day," Andrew said.

"That's okay. I don't have much to do anyways. Ask whatever you like. I don't think I can help though. I'm really not in touch with Ryan anymore." She was beginning to look a lot more comfortable than she had outside, after being initially startled by their arrival. She leaned back in the chair and crossed her legs.

"When was the last time you saw him?" Miller asked.

"It's been a couple years since we got together. We divorced after just two years, without even any lawyers. It was a joint agreement and we just hired a facilitator."

"Have you had any contact with him at all since the divorce?" asked Newcross.

"He emailed me a few times to see how I was getting on. But it always felt like a pretext. He never came out and said it but I think it was really to see if I was getting along well enough to loan him money, which I wasn't." She spoke about him with more pity than irritation.

Since Miller had settled back into the sofa, Newcross assumed he was content to let her continue the interview. She picked up her notepad. "Can you give us names of any of his close friends?"

"Ryan was really a loner. Aside from his sister, I can't think of anyone he ever went out with or even talked to on the phone."

"Not even friends at work?"

"I don't remember Ryan ever holding down a job long enough to make friends. He was always searching for the perfect get-rich-quick scheme. He would start up a home business, like mowing people's lawns, thinking that within a month he'd have so many contracts that he'd have a fleet of mowers and could pay neighbourhood kids to work for him. Then he'd sit here watching the rain and getting drunk. Blaming the weather for his misfortune." She looked out the window as if she could see him mowing.

"He started buying cheap cigarettes from the natives on the reserve, and selling them in Montréal, roaming from bar to bar. He made a decent enough profit at that, but the money got miraculously turned into alcohol while he worked. He'd get home in the middle of the night, drunk and broke. Of course, that was the fault of the bartenders who insisted he patronize the bar or be thrown out for peddling illegal goods."

"Can you think of anyone at all that may have held a grudge against Ryan? Maybe someone he crossed during those times?"

"Not really. Nothing more than your average run of the mill bar fight for looking at someone the wrong way or trying to cheat at pool. That sort of thing. But I can't be any help with anything recent in his life. Honestly, I have no idea what he was up to these days."

"Did he gamble when the two of you were married?"

"He'd go to the race track once in a while. Or if we went to a bar and there was a pool table, he'd play against other guys for a buck or two. Later he got into poker, but not when we were together."

"How do you know he was playing poker lately?"

Valerie looked at Miller and back to Newcross. "He called me a few months ago. He was playing Poker at the Indian casino about a mile from here. It was late at night and he wanted to come and sleep here. I told him to piss off." She looked down at the polar bear and stroked its head softly. "He started to cry. I didn't feel bad at the time." She lifted her head and glanced at Andrew and then stared at Rebecca. "I do now."

"So was that the last time you spoke with him?"

"Yeah. There were a couple emails after that, but we never talked again."

"What was your marriage to Ryan like? Why did you get divorced?"

"We married young, we divorced young. We just drifted off in different directions. To be honest—he was a lazy bum. I know that's a horrible thing to say now, but it's true. He never wanted to work for anything. He didn't want children either. You'd think I would have asked about that before we got married. Shows how young and naïve I was. You two probably know more about him now than I ever did." She looked down at the newspaper on the footstool.

Valerie's voice was sincere. Newcross rose from the sofa and thanked her for her time. Miller followed suit.

"If you think of anything at all that may help us in our investigation, please call me anytime," Miller said, handing her his card. "And thanks for your time today. We appreciate it."

The three of them walked the short distance to the front door. The two detectives left her watching their departure from the front stoop.

"Andrew, did you notice the newspaper? On the footstool with the coffee mug?"

"I was sitting too far away from it. Why?"

"I expected it to be today's but it wasn't. It was the paper that came out last week about Ryan Harper's murder."

"You think that's suspicious or gloomy?"

"I'm not sure. It's just an observation. Although I always think everything is suspicious."

18

Andrew and Rebecca arrived back at the station to find a large yellow post-it dangling by one sticky corner from the middle of his computer monitor. *Call Vegas duo.* The time was inscribed to let them know the message had been written an hour earlier. They each grabbed a coffee and went into the vacant conference room.

"Rebecca, can you phone them to see if they're still waiting for us, while I fire up my laptop?" Andrew put his coffee down on the conference table, switched on the computer, and plugged it into the network.

She sat down next to him, in front of the phone, and looked around the room. "Where's all the teleconferencing equipment?"

"You're looking at it, although we tend to call it the laptop and phone. We have a system that hooks the conference room phone into the laptop, so we end up with the visual coming through the monitor, and the audio comes through the phone. My lieutenant checked that it's compatible with your teleconference system. No difference except we have to crowd in front of the laptop webcam if we both want to be seen."

"Hey, no complaints here, whatever gets the job done." She hoped she hadn't offended him. He seemed like an okay guy, and understood he was a good friend of Joe's. While he explained their system, she entered the number to the Teleconference Centre where their two partners would hopefully still be waiting. After three rings, she heard the soothing southern drawl of her partner's voice.

"Detective Thibodeaux here."

"Hey, Gumbo, how you doin'?" She pressed the button to put the audio on to the speakerphone, so that Andrew could hear the conversation.

"Becks, my girl, good to hear your voice. Ya'll ready for hookup? I'll log in to your system."

"Ready when you are," she said and waited while Gumbo worked his magic. A few seconds later the faces of her partner and Andrew's partner appeared on the laptop monitor. They were sitting across from each other with a whiteboard visible on the wall behind them. The names, dates, and details of the two cases were written on the board.

"You two look as cozy as shrimps in a po'boy," said Gumbo, as Andrew and Rebecca huddled in front of the eye of the webcam.

"Po'boy?" Andrew looked at Rebecca quizzically.

Rebecca grinned at him while Andrew and Hank looked like they were at a foreign film without subtitles. "It's a sandwich. Shrimps crammed together in a roll."

Introductions were made all around, and Andrew spoke up. "Why don't Becky and I begin with what we've been looking at up here? Jump in anytime with questions or comments though. I'll begin with Ryan Harper's background. Twenty-five years old and lived all his life here in Montréal. Married at the age of twenty. Divorced two years later."

"Wife's name?" asked Gumbo.

"Valerie Mackay. She's the same age as Harper. Lives here. Has a few priors for shoplifting as a teenager but nothing serious. They never had kids and don't seem to be in touch anymore." Andrew continued as Gumbo was adding her name to the whiteboard. "Harper has lived with his younger sister, Kelly Harper, since the divorce. He was busted once for drug possession, cocaine, two years ago, as well as assault."

"Did he spend any time in the prison system up there?" Hank asked, as Gumbo continued writing details on the board.

"The drugs were discovered on him when he was picked up during a raid on an illegal poker game being held in the back room of a bar. A fight had broken out over the game. Harper hit some other guy over the head with a bottle. Bar owner called us. Assault charges were laid, but later dropped. He was released into the sister's custody on the condition that he get professional help for his addiction to drugs and gambling as well as mandatory therapy for anger management." Rebecca motioned to him that she wanted to speak.

"I went to see Harper's doctor yesterday," she said. "She seemed to think that he was doing really well. She had him on Remeron for depression, but he was in the process of weaning off it. She saw no indication of him using any other drugs. She was disappointed that he was still gambling, but, at the same time, she said he was getting his life under control."

"So she doesn't buy the suicide theory?" Hank asked.

"Not at all. She met with him a matter of days before he left for Vegas. She saw absolutely no reason to suspect that he had any suicidal tendencies. She also felt that Harper would not willingly take Ketamine. He understood the dangers of drug interaction with taking Remeron."

"Okay. Let's assume, at least for now, that we're dealing with two murders. Let's also assume that it's the same perp," said Gumbo. "We visited Grave's ex-wife today, Stephanie Corrigan.

No love lost between them but we didn't get a guilty vibe off her. He sounds slicker than gator snot on a radiator. He's a deadbeat Dad and has a few priors for domestic abuse. Forensics are going through his computer. We've just begun to go through casino tapes. So far there's nothing jumping out at us."

"Have you been able to find both Harper and Graves on the night of their deaths?" asked Becky.

"We haven't reviewed Graves' footage yet. So far we've got Harper playing in the tournament. He got into a bit of an upset with another player when he got knocked out of the poker tournament. The camera has him being led away to the bar by one of the tournament organizers and a couple security bruisers as backup. It played out exactly how the Buckingham organizer told us. They drank some beer, talked, and then Harper walked towards the elevators, presumably to go up to his room. There are no cameras in the elevator or the hotel hallways. The casino floor and bars were busier than a two-dollar whore house on nickel-Tuesday, between the time that Harper left the bar and the estimated time of death."

"What about Graves? Anything on him?" Andrew asked.

Hank stood up in the Vegas conference room, and moved back a few steps to the whiteboard. He pointed at the photo of Graves lying naked on the pool cement. "The only difference between these two deaths is that his wallet was emptied of cash, assuming he had some, and tossed to the ground. And, of course, he drowned in an outdoor pool instead of a bathtub. His clothing was folded neatly on top of one of the plastic tables."

"So no signs of struggle with either of them?" Andrew asked.

"Not even a broken finger-nail between them," said Gumbo. "Both were willing to get naked and in the water. So, given their history of heterosexual activities, we're working on the assumption that the perp is a woman. He has a drink or two laced with Ketamine, gets ready for a bit of fun, and wham, bam, he doesn't get what it says on the tin."

"Who else have you interviewed down there?" asked Andrew.

"Between us and the uniforms, we've got statements from all the Buckingham Poker folk who are here from London, as well as everyone that was at both poker tables during the game," said Gumbo. "We've also interviewed the eight people who won tournament tickets through the Buckingham site. Along with the camera footage in the poker room and the rest of the casino, all the statements check out."

The telephone began ringing in the Vegas conference room. Gumbo picked it up on the second ring, with an apologetic smile to the camera. The three onlookers listened in on the one-sided conversation, which consisted of a series of grunts, nods, and hmmms. He put the receiver down and walked back to the whiteboard, picking up a marker from the narrow ledge of the board. As he wrote a file number beside Stephanie Corrigan's name, he explained to them. "Lieutenant Foxton just ran a check on the widow. She's on welfare, like she told us, but tops it up with some extra cash. She's been picked up a few times on Charleston."

Rebecca explained to the other two that Charleston Street was a common hooker hangout at the north end of Vegas.

"I thought prostitution was legal down there," Andrew said to Rebecca.

"It's legal in some districts of Nevada, but not within the city limits of Vegas. We have perfectly wonderful brothels, not far from town, which are safe and healthy, and you'll get treated well. They even take credit cards now. Most of them have an auto parts shop or gas station attached, so they can write up a receipt that would never raise suspicions back home, if that's an issue. But unfortunately there are still some sad bastards who think that picking up a thirty-dollar hooker on a street corner could be a thrilling experience. They have ten minutes of romance in the back of their car, or behind one of the strip malls." Turning back to the monitor, Rebecca asked Gumbo, "Are you guys gonna call her in for more questioning then?"

"We'll go out tomorrow and have a word with her. We'll let you know if we get anything more. I still don't think she's good for the murder, but I don't cotton to her hiding her profession from us."

"What did Graves do for a living? Anything aside from playing poker?" asked Andrew.

Hank sat back down at the conference table and Gumbo answered. "Picked up some odd jobs here and there. Construction, mostly. Then he'd gamble the money away. He lived pretty rough. He's been picked up a couple times in Vegas for bar fights, but never served time. According to his neighbours, no one ever came and went from his dump except him. There's no evidence of him having any friends. The Buckingham boys were able to get us a print out of all the posts he's made on their website over the last few years. That boy could get madder than a horse sittin' on a cactus at people on the website, but none of those people were here for the tournament. Graves isn't well liked in Buckingham's chatroom, that's for sure."

"Similar story with the Harper kid," Andrew added. "His only friend was his sister from the sounds of it. But he was holding down a job and appeared to be turning his life around. Such as it was. We're gonna look closer into the ex-wife here as well."

"We're missing something. There has to be some sort of personal link between them," Hank interjected.

Rebecca held up her hand and spoke barely above a whisper, "What if only one of them was the target, and the other was just to throw us off?"

"I think you're reaching there, Becks," said Gumbo. "Which of them would be the target? And who would have the knowledge to be able to target another Buckingham player, as well as the ability to procure Ketamine?"

"Let's run with it for a minute," said Andrew. "Let's say the real target was Graves. He lived in Vegas, so the odds are better that he would have enemies there. If someone wanted him dead, and that someone lived in Vegas, he or she would know how to score Ketamine and would also know their way around a poker room. At least well enough to pick someone to kill as a red herring."

Becky nodded. "You just have to walk over to the Buckingham information table to see a posted list of what players are in the room. They even write their table and seat number, as well as their online name and real name. If it's a woman, then the ex-wife, Stephanie, could be of serious interest. Although this could also be a hired kill if Graves had got himself involved in anything stupid."

"We'll look closer at her. We should find out where he was playing poker on a regular basis. See if he has any debts or crazed girlfriends," said Gumbo. Hank stood up and started pulling all his papers and photos together into a neat pile.

"Gumbo, I don't really see the point of me spending more time up here in Montréal. Check with the Captain, will you? Maybe I can fly home tomorrow night."

"Sure thing, Becks. I'll call you tomorrow."

They all said their goodbyes and shut down their computers. Andrew looked over at Becky, and gave her an approving nod. "I really think your idea has some merit, but I'm gonna keep looking into Harper."

"Understood. But I really think Vegas is where we'll find the answers. That's where both the bodies were. It's logical, whatever the motive was. I just wish I was there."

"Settle for the pub instead? We could call Joe to meet up with us."

"Sounds like a plan. Give me ten minutes to freshen up, and I'll meet you downstairs at the station door." She turned in the direction of the women's locker room.

"Somehow I don't think Joe will be too thrilled to hear that you might leave soon," Andrew said to her back.

Becky stopped in her tracks and turned around, debating whether to ask the question that she badly wanted to ask. He was intent on unhooking equipment and shutting down his laptop. She kept her mouth shut and left for the locker room. She showered and changed and as she walked through the squad-room to go outside she saw Andrew in the Captain's office. She was about to walk across to join them when he turned and went back to his desk. She met up with him there as he was locking his desk drawer.

"I was just updating the Captain. We can write it all up tomorrow. Let's head out and we can call Joe from the Donegal."

Becky took a deep breath and blurted out her question. "Andrew, what's Joe's story? Why did he leave the force?"

"You should ask *him* that. Not me."

"I could probably dig his file up and find the answer."

"No, you couldn't." He put his keys in his pocket, turned and walked away.

19

I love waking up every morning now. I love being awake early when there's no need to be. No work today—just play time—or at least thinking about play time. Makes me shiver. In a good way. Today I'll just make plans. Always worth planning it well. I get to enjoy it twice that way.

Oh my! Could I be any happier than this? But I must concentrate. Can't let anything get the better of me. Or anybody. They all trust me. Maybe they even like me. Or love me. God knows they should. Everything I'm doing is what should be done. No matter how you look at it. I'm as normal as anyone else. No I'm not —I'm better.

If this is the feeling I can expect each time, I never want to stop. No need to stop really. What I need is to find more. God, this is amazing. The tingling. I really should get up now. I'll treat myself to Eggs Benedict today. Oh, I can't wait. But I so love having this time to think quietly about all my people. I actually feel quite aroused. Oh dear. I think I'll just save that feeling for later and see what can be done about it. It'll be all that much sweeter.   I'll just get up and go out to eat. It's hot out. I can wear a little sundress. Oh, and my new shoes. I love those sandals. I'll see and talk to people like I always do. Until I find the right one. Then I can be me.

20

It was nearly five o'clock and Joe was still at his office. Business was slow lately. In fact, it was closer to non-existent. Normally he'd get a call or two a week from someone wanting a quote for his services. Exposing and photographing cheating spouses was Joe's most popular, and least favourite, activity. He had plans to eventually train Chantal and then hand the business over to her. Then he'd retire to the Costa del Sol.

Joe killed a few hours each day playing poker on his laptop. At least, that's what he did while Chantal was on holiday. But she'd be back tomorrow morning and it was her life's mission to keep him from gambling away the business. She couldn't understand that would never happen. He had plenty of money and wasn't gambling more than he could afford to lose. Even though it meant he'd have to stop his daytime poker games, he welcomed the return of the watchdog eyes of his employee. She was good company and always made him laugh.

With a few clicks on the keypad he lost another twenty dollars. He shouted at the monitor and slammed the lid of his laptop shut. "You thieving dickhead bastard." At that exact moment his office door opened, and there stood Chantal, grinning like a Cheshire cat. She was an offbeat looking woman. She had extreme features which she chose to accentuate. She was five foot nothing, hair black as a tinker's pot, recently cut short and choppy. She had a long slender face, with a large Grecian nose that she highlighted by decorating it with various pierced objects. She also had long, large ears that stuck out from her head. Joe guessed that she'd used up all her earrings in her nose, because she'd had the lobes tattooed last month with some ancient Celtic symbols. He tried calling her *Dumbo* once, which resulted in a piece of Boston cream pie sailing through the air and hitting his laptop screen and dribbling down between the keys below. *Prince Charles* got past her radar though. Now he just called her Chuck and she appeared to even prefer it to Chantal.

Her complexion was pale and emphasized by an abundance of eye makeup surrounding her intense catlike eyes and deep crimson lipstick on her full lips which were slightly lopsided. The upshot was that her whole crazy package worked and she turned appreciative heads everywhere she went.

"Hey boss, miss me?" Even though it was hot outside she looked cool and comfortable in a loose black tank top and a flirty little skirt that was a tad shorter than he thought it ought to be. She had an assortment of bracelets on both arms so that she jingled like a Christmas reindeer as she walked further into the office.

"Chantal, what are you doing here? You shouldn't be back till tomorrow."

"Just walking past the office on my way to dinner and saw the *Open* sign still on the door. Thought I'd look in on you." She turned to leave and he grasped he'd hurt her feelings.

"Wait. Don't go. Of course I missed you. How was your holiday?"

"That's more like it," she said, smiling and lowering herself into the chair near his desk. "I just took it easy at home, lazing around the pool. You don't pay me enough to travel anywhere erotic, you know that."

"You mean exotic, Chuck. But yeah, you're right... I don't... I should." Conversing with Chantal was a perpetual English tutorial.

"Exotic, oui. I'm just on my way to dinner. You wanna join me, boss? You can even pay, if you want to."

"Good try. Where you headed? Up to Saint-Catherine?"

"Gonna try that new Spanish Place on de Maisonneuve, near Durocher. They're advertising tepees. You get three tepees and a glass of sangria for $25.00. Wanna go?"

"Tepees? No thanks, hen. I'm gonna make my way home. I'm totally knackered. I'll get a takeaway somewhere, and have an early night of it."

"Any work come in while I've been gone?"

"One job came and went. I'll fill you in tomorrow on all the excitement."

"Tomorrow I'll write up some ads for the Gazette, Le Journal, and the downtown rags. Maybe something will come of it, okay?" She stood up and tried to pull the hemline of her skirt down.

"You're gonna write ad copy? Exciting."

"I can write! In the meantime, quit losing what little dollars we have here on that damn game. I saw you through the window."

Joe nodded as he locked up his desk, turned off the air conditioner, and slid his laptop into the carrying case.

"Go eat, Chuck. Try ordering the tapas, I heard they're great. We'll talk tomorrow." He opened the door, ushering her out onto the sidewalk.

"You got it, Joe. See you tomorrow." She gave him a childlike wave and performed an elegantly choreographed turn.

He watched and listened to her clinking away for a few seconds, before he locked the door, turned in the opposite direction, and headed south to go home.

He stopped at his favourite Indian restaurant—one of the rare mom-and-pop curry houses in the downtown area. Within twenty minutes he had a paper bag full of onion bhajis with mango chutney sauce, a chicken vindaloo that he knew he'd regret eating, a small container of basmati rice, and a naan bread to mop up all the sauce. He stopped again at the corner of Notre-Dame to pick up a six pack.

Arriving at his condo a few minutes later, he emptied his mailbox of the deluge of restaurant menus and realtor brochures, tossing them directly into the green recycle box and stepped into the waiting elevator.

Before he dished out his meal he went to the phone to check his voicemail, but there were no messages. He cracked open a beer and had it emptied before he'd finished scooping all the food onto his plate. He put the plate onto a small tray, and carried it, along with another beer, into the living room.

By the time he had devoured the painfully spicy vindaloo it was just past six o'clock. The central air conditioner was running silently and effectively. He brought the phone into the bathroom, where he could reach it if it rang, and stepped into the shower. The phone was mute throughout, causing him to feel as foolish as a schoolgirl waiting to be asked to the prom. He towelled off as he walked into his bedroom, and chose a pair of khaki shorts and a vintage T-shirt from the 1978 Edinburgh Jazz Festival. Barefoot, he went out to the balcony to lie on the chaise longue, still carrying the silent phone. He resisted the temptation to check if it was working. Two minutes later he verified that there was a dial tone.

He closed his eyes and was asleep within five minutes, but was jerked awake by the ringing of the phone clutched in his hand. He managed to press the talk button just before it switched to voicemail.

"Joe Cameron here."

"Where the hell else would you be?" asked Becky.

"You woke me up. I wasn't sure where I was. What time is it?"

"It's nearly seven o'clock. Andrew and I are at The Donegal. Have you eaten yet?"

"I have, but I could force down a pint or two, if I had to."

"Well, you know where we are now," she replied, and hung up before Joe could say anything. He was discovering that she was a woman of few words and never wasted her time with small talk.

He put away the beer bottles, stopped in the bathroom to wash his face, brush his teeth, gargle twice for the curry, and splash on some Eddie Bauer aftershave. He took the elevator down to the lobby and stepped outside onto Notre-Dame. He considered walking to the corner taxi rank to get up the hill and down Saint-Catherine faster, but worried that it would look too pathetic if he arrived at the pub so soon after her call. So he strolled up Rue de la Montagne.

Reaching Saint-Catherine, he turned left and window shopped all the way to the pub. He opened the door and was met with a refreshing blast of industrial air conditioning. The pub was quiet as the neighbourhood students didn't begin bar-hopping till well past nine o'clock. He spotted Andy and Becky at a small wooden table near the back of the room. Becky's back was facing him, so he waved at Andy and walked over to the bar where Nicola was already pouring him a pint of Guinness.

"Thanks, hen. Run me a tab, would you?"

"You got it, Joe."

He tried to walk over to the table without spilling any of his full pint, but was sadly unsuccessful.

"What took you so bloody long to get here, Joe?" asked Andrew, sliding two five dollar bills from the middle of the table towards Becky. "Forty freakin' minutes! Unbelievable." He shook his head and took a slug from his bottle of Budweiser. "I thought you'd take a cab and be here within ten minutes of the phone call. Rebecca here evidently knows you better."

"I can't believe you two puritans are sitting here gambling. To be honest, I'm shocked to the depth of my soul." He sat down next to Becky, directly in front of Andrew, and slurped at the creamy foam from the top of his glass.

A young aproned girl came out of the kitchen with a tray of food, cutlery, napkins, placemats and condiments. It was Hannah, one of Nicola's daughters. She set down a plate of beer-battered fish, with fries, pickled onions, and tartar sauce, in front of Becky. Andrew had ordered a hamburger steak smothered in caramelized onions, along with fries that were drowning in steaming hot gravy.

Hannah managed a shy whisper of *bon appetit* to the diners before turning on her heels and scurrying back to the safety of her kitchen.

"What did you two get up to today?" Joe asked, tilting his head at Andrew.

"None of your business, Joe. This is a police investigation. Last time I checked, you gave up your badge." He smiled and popped a dangling coppery onion strand into his mouth.

"Give me a break, Andy. I'm not a reporter. Any leads?"

Andrew shook his head. "Nothing earth shattering, no. We still have enquiries to make, but no one has jumped out of the woodwork with a bottle of Special K and given themselves up."

"I might be heading home tomorrow." Becky added this news while intently cutting her fish into perfect rectangular bites.

'Tomorrow? Why?" Joe asked. He was unable to hide the disappointment in his tone or in his face.

"There's a lot more to investigate in Vegas than here. I'll be a lot more useful there than I am here, that's for damn sure." She took a sip of wine, and slipped a ketchup-dunked fry into her mouth.

"But you haven't booked a flight yet, right?" Joe asked hopefully.

"Not yet. Just waiting to hear back from my Captain. When he gives the okay, I'll get the next flight out. I expect he'll want me back soon anyhow. We're coming up to July 4th. Vegas gets super crazy. Even more assholes than normal, if you can believe that."

The table went quiet as Andrew and Becky worked on their meal. Joe went over to the bar and waited while Nicola poured him a half-pint. When he returned to the table, Andrew was already wiping his chin and mouth with a napkin.

"I don't know about you two, but I have to hit the road. The wife is expecting me back at a decent hour tonight. You don't mind, do you?" said Andrew, not waiting for an answer, as he took his wallet out and walked to the bar where Nicola was polishing glasses.

"Night, Andrew. I'll be at the station first thing in the morning," she called out.

"You go right ahead, mate. My best to Lauren," Joe added. He moved over to Andrew's vacated chair, so that he was facing Becky, and pushed the empty plate to one side.

"Will do. See you in the morning, Rebecca," Andy said and left the bar.

Joe knew there was no way Lauren was expecting Andy, well aware that she was in Paris this week. When Lauren wasn't travelling around the world buying fabrics, or locked away in her studio designing a new piece, or overseeing her crew of dressmakers, she was in the shop fussing with the displays. There was only one reason that Andy would take off, and that was to leave Joe and Becky on their own. Joe was damn grateful for the consideration.

"So, any excitement today at all?" Joe asked Becky.

"We haven't found any leads here or in Vegas. There has been absolutely no evidence found at either of the crime scenes. It's as if these two guys just took a bagful of K and drowned themselves. We're just going to have to go over and over the CCTV footage from the casinos and hope we get lucky." She took a large gulp of wine and tamped her lips with her napkin.

Nicola came over to the table to remove the plates and debris. "Sorry to bother you folks, but we have a dart tournament here tonight. It starts in about half an hour, so I'll have to move this table out of the way. Can I set you up somewhere else?" she asked.

"No problem Nic. We'll find a spot," Joe said. He and Becky stood up and began to head over to the bar, when Joe spoke up. "It's going to get awfully noisy, not to mention dangerous, when the dart throwers turn up with their entourage. What about walking the few blocks to my place and having a few drinks on the balcony?"

Becky stared at Joe and took a deep breath. "On one condition. You tell me your story."

"My story?"

"Why you're not in the force anymore. You clammed up about it in Vegas. I'd like to know. I really would." She wasn't taking her eyes off him.

He shrugged and took his wallet out of his back pocket. "Fair enough, if it's that important to you."

Nicola called over that Andy had paid for both meals, so Joe only owed $16.00 for his beer. He put a twenty dollar bill on the bar, bid Nicola a good evening, and they walked out into the street. The sun was nearly set, so the heat wasn't as intense, but the mugginess remained.

They turned off Saint-Catherine to walk south along de la Montagne. Joe pointed out his storefront office and directed her gaze to his condo building standing floors above all the others a few blocks further south. "You can actually see my balcony patio from here. Mine is the one two floors down from the penthouse. See the row of potted evergreen trees?"

Becky nodded and asked about the housing market in Montréal. They chatted about the different neighbourhoods around town until they arrived at his condominium building. They took the elevator up to his floor, in silence. Joe was dreading the upcoming talk and contemplated going a bit light on the details. Becky wasn't even looking at him in the elevator, and he wondered if she was regretting her decision to come over.

Joe unlocked the door and stepped politely back to allow Becky entrance. He had left a table lamp on beside the sofa which spread a warm glow around most of the living room. Montréal's city skyline took centre stage, framed in the floor-to-ceiling windows. Equally spectacular was the rotating four-beam beacon of light slowly revolving atop the forty-seventh floor on the roof of Place Ville

Marie, Montréal's distinctive cruciform office tower. The beacon lit up the night sky like a giant lighthouse.

"Can I get you a beer, or more wine? I also have a few different types of scotch if you're so inclined."

"Wine would be nice. I had a couple glasses at dinner, and I prefer not switching."

"Why don't you go out on the balcony and I'll bring it. We should get a decent breeze off the river now."

Becky slid the patio door open and stepped outside. Joe watched her as she stood at the glass railing and scanned the skyline. He removed the cork on a bottle of reasonably priced pinot noir he had recently discovered, and took two stemless wine glasses down from the cupboard.

He watched Becky walk around inspecting the furniture and glancing through the window to check Joe's progress with the wine. He had taken great pride in decorating his balcony. It was large by most downtown standards, eight feet in depth, and twenty feet long, so he looked on it as being a room in its own right. Patio doors opened off the living room as well as the bedroom. He had covered the grey cement with a Brazilian walnut deck and created two very distinct areas. Outside the living room doors, four cushioned wicker chairs surrounded a teal blue octagonal ceramic table in the centre of which was an outdoor lamp which was solar-powered and motion activated. A large stainless steel barbecue stood nearby against the side railing. In the outer corner was a small gardening table which held a variety of herbs and tools. The scent of basil and mint mingled in the still evening air.

Six terracotta pots held a row of evergreen trees, each about five feet tall, separating the living room space from the area outside the bedroom. On the bedroom side he had two vintage teak lounge chairs which had four inch thick foam cushions covered with black terry cloth. On a warm summer's night they were as comfortable as his bed. Between the lounge chairs was a small teak side table which held another motion detector lamp as well as a pair of high magnification binoculars. When he wasn't using them at work to spy on cheating partners, he left them here to watch cargo ships navigating up and down the St. Lawrence. It reminded him of his childhood, watching boats go up and down the Clyde.

Becky sat down on one of the wicker chairs as Joe arrived with their drinks. He set the two glasses down and poured the wine until they were half full. Becky took a tentative sip and smiled her approval. Joe sat down on the chair closest to her, picked up his glass and downed a much greedier mouthful.

"So…fess up Joe. I want to hear all about why you're a PI and not a cop," ordered Becky. "And I want the truth, not the glossed-over version."

Joe took another swig and refilled his glass, attempting to top up Becky's glass as well, but she covered the opening with the palm of her hand.

"It's complicated, Becky. I went undercover for a year with an east end gang here. You ever go undercover?"

"No, I haven't, and even if I had, this isn't about me. It's about you."

"Well, in order to infiltrate effectively, you have to assimilate, take part…actively. Which I did. Very convincingly, I might add. Too well, some might say." He stopped and took a small sip of wine. He looked at Becky, who was staring intently at him. She nodded encouragingly, and he knew he had to continue. "I bought and sold drugs. Took drugs. Played in high stake backroom poker games. Pimped young girls. Pimped young boys. Shit. You name it,

I probably did it." Joe stared into the night sky watching the revolution of light from Place Ville Marie. He was uneasy about meeting Becky's eyes and seeing her opinion reflected back at him.

"Part of the job, Joe. We can't let ourselves feel guilty about crap like that. We do what we have to. We're in it to make it better … eventually."

Until she spoke he hadn't realized he'd been holding his breath. "I realize all that. It's a job and I did it. But I got *too* involved. There was too much of it that I enjoyed taking part in. The drinking, the poker, the drugs. There was a camaraderie within the gang that I actually embraced. A lot like the force. You'd kill to save a brother, wouldn't you? Well, they would too. They love each other, respect each other. And they party hard while they do it."

"So what happened in the end? Did you take the gang down or not?" Her voice was caring and calm and made it easy for Joe to open up.

"No, that's the point. I was doing a lot of coke and some serious drinking. I was with a couple of my brothers at a brothel in Montréal's east end. We had just parked our bikes and gone in to collect the week's earnings. All of a sudden I couldn't catch my breath and sweat was rolling down my face. Turned out it was a heart attack. One of them carried me out to the street while the other one broke into a car parked right outside the door, and they got me to the Royal Montréal hospital within ten minutes, probably breaking every traffic violation there was. They dumped me at the door to Emergency and left. When I came to, I discovered I would have died if it weren't for them. Next thing I knew I was transferred to another hospital under my real name and when they got me stable, I was sent to a rehab clinic to get off the drugs and sober up."

"Where was your wife at this time?" Becky refilled her wine glass. She put the bottle back on the table without offering him any.

"Anna had left me by this point. Can't blame her really—I was out of control. I only came home sporadically, and when I did, I was either drunk or high or both. It went on for too long and I couldn't live a normal life at the same time as the gang life. After I got cleaned up, she helped me get my shit together, but too much had gone down for us to make a go of it together again."

"And the force—couldn't you have stayed on afterwards?"

"They would have found me a desk job or some crap like that. But they also made the offer of a retirement package. And that's the option I went for. The settlement gave me an opportunity to set myself up in the agency. I had inherited a fair bit of money from my folks as well, years before, so I had enough to live comfortably."

"And now?"

"Now? I drink a little. I gamble a little. No drugs. I never go near any of the places we hung around—too risky. I have to presume they never found out who I was or I'd be fish-food. My death was reported in the newspaper a couple days after they dropped me at the hospital. I guess they bought it."

"Wow, that's more than a story. It's a freakin' made-for-TV movie."

"Sorry you asked?"

"I can't pretend to know what you went through, but you seem to have come out the other side in one piece."

"With a lot of help from friends, believe me. If I hadn't had the support I did, I have no doubt I'd have gone back with my mates in the east end." He couldn't remember ever telling anyone so much of his story, or so truthful a version. She didn't look shocked or judgemental.

"We all need support, Joe. It can't be easy talking about it and I value the fact that you opened up to me about it."

"We can move on then? Nothing else you need to know?" He couldn't have hid the relief in his voice even if he'd tried. He felt better than he had in ages.

"One more question." She smiled and leaned a few inches closer to him. "What's hiding behind the row of trees here on the deck?"

"There's another set of patio doors leading to the bedroom," Joe answered, hoping that Becky couldn't see the flush rising into his face in the evening shadows.

She leaned back in the chair and looked at him questioningly. "I can't get over this place. You did all the decorating yourself? And you're not gay?" She tilted her head and chuckled.

"I'm definitely not gay." He held up the bottle to her and she shook her head. He poured the final dregs into his own glass. "My ex, Anna, helped a lot with the interior. I took charge of this space. There's a great gardening centre around the corner from here, so it wasn't difficult to choose. I wanted this area to be simple and functional."

"Well, I'm impressed. The city is quite beautiful from up here. If we were on a balcony in downtown Vegas, we'd hear music blaring from all the outdoor speakers of the casinos. It bombards the senses there sometimes. Actually, most of the time."

Joe emptied his glass and cradled it in both hands, unconsciously tapping his feet. Becky set her glass down with a loud clink on the ceramic tabletop.

"Maybe you should just kiss me now and we can stop being so damn awkward with each other," Becky said.

Joe's eyes moved slowly up to hers and he replaced the wineglass he'd been holding with her face, and gave her a long slow kiss. She wrapped her arms around his shoulders, responding with a passion that he hadn't expected.

Joe stood, taking both her hands and pulling her up close to him. She pressed her body into his and whispered in his ear, "I haven't been with anyone in years, Joe." He kissed her neck with dozens of little kisses, and led her around the border of trees.

He slid the bedroom door open with one hand, holding her around the waist with his other. There was no light on in the bedroom, but the lights of the city provided a ghostly glow.

Joe guided her to the edge of the bed. Facing her, he slowly unbuttoned her blouse. With each button he leaned down and kissed her exposed skin with increasing urgency. He tossed her blouse onto the floor behind him. Wrapping his arms around her, he undid the clasp of her bra, pulling it towards him and slipping it off her arms.

Becky kicked her sandals off and began to remove her skirt as Joe quickly stripped and threw his clothes on top of her discarded clothing. They stared at each other, smiling, for the briefest of moments, before tumbling onto the bed.

21

The following morning Joe rolled over in bed, expecting to find her warm and frisky body, but finding a note on the pillow next to him instead. He held it above his face to read. *Good morning. Had to leave to get to hotel to check out in case I'm going home today. Call u later. xo*

He looked over at the clock radio, surprised to see the digital red glow of 9:28 a.m., and jumped out of bed. He opened the door to his ensuite bathroom. Becky must have been in there recently. The shower door was dripping wet and the vanity mirror steamed up. He grabbed his still-damp toothbrush, wiped a viewing circle in the mirror, and brushed his teeth. His comb, which was normally propped into the hairbrush, was lying to the side. That she had felt comfortable enough to make herself at home made him smile.

He showered, wrapped a towel around his waist and stepped out onto the balcony. It was still hot, but the mugginess had gone. He went back in and threw on a pair of lightweight cargo shorts and a Celtic T-shirt. He left the air conditioner on so that he could return to a cool home.

He hadn't decided whether to work a full day or not. It was Chantal's first day back from vacation so he'd spend some time filling her in on what she'd missed. He might come back home after that and relax.

He picked up two Danish pastries and an orange juice on his way to the office. He arrived on de la Montagne hot, starving, and dehydrated. He saw the Open sign in his window, which meant that Chantal had arrived and the air conditioner, feeble as it was, would be on high.

Joe was greeted by the lopsided toothy grin that he had missed so much. She reached over to the corner of her desk and turned the volume down on her iPod speaker, which was belting out a tune from her new favourite British indie band, Tankus the Henge.

"Mornin', hen. Brought you a welcome-back-Danish," Joe said, as he removed one of the pastries and with a flourish set it in front of her, on a clean piece of paper which he grabbed from the printer tray on his way to her desk.

"Rather have a welcome-back-Dane, but I thank you nonetheless, Sir," and took a birdlike bite out of it. She stood up, taking her pastry with her, and perched on one corner of his desk. "So what's up, boss? I see absolutely no upcoming appointments in your Daytimer. Are things that friggin slow? Really?"

"Slower. Must be too hot for spouses to fool around." He had a brief flashback to the antics of the previous night and smiled. He filled her in on his trip to Vegas while they ate, after which she returned to her desk. She was determined to write up some print ads for the papers. Joe was delighted she could find something to immerse herself in and was certain he'd be highly entertained by her output. He worked on calculating his Vegas expenses.

Stepping out to the corner store, he bought an assortment of teabags and cookies for the office, much to Chantal's delight. She ripped open the chocolate chip cookies like she hadn't eaten for two weeks. Joe couldn't understand why she wasn't the size of a buffalo.

"See? I can still afford treats. Things aren't so bad around here."

"I know exactly how much money you bring in," she said in her exasperated voice. "Or, should I say, don't bring in?"

"Okay, if it'll make you feel better, I'll move more money into the business account. Beef it up a bit for your peace of mind."

"That's not the point, Doofus. I want to see you earn money, not transfer it."

"Point taken. If I don't get a contract by month's end, I'll hire myself to do something."

Chantal shook her head and went back to work on the ads. The only talking she did over the next hour was over the phone to get prices from various newspapers around town. They reviewed the ads together, later in the morning, and settled on one to run on a months' trial. Joe was quite impressed with her copywriting. It was straightforward and concise.

The only revision he made was the deletion of the cartoon of the James Bondish man waving a spyglass in the top left corner of the ad. He was overjoyed that the gent looked more like Charlie Sheen than Charlie Brown. Chantal often doodled pictures of him, but when she was upset she had the evil habit of adding pounds and subtracting hair and height. She was quite a talented caricaturist and Joe instantly recognized himself so that was a sure sign that he was back in her good books.

"Why am I lifting my right leg in the air with a string connecting my shoe to the sidewalk?" he asked.

"Duh. That's the gum. You're always saying you're a gumshoe guy."

"Right. Nice idea. Let's just go with a print ad. I've finished my Vegas expenses, so you can send an invoice to this address." He handed her Kelly Harper's address along with his expense report. "You can also get some quotes on a new air conditioner. Order one, including installation, if you find a good deal."

"Oui, boss."

Joe returned to his desk and turned off his laptop. "I'm gonna take the rest of the day off, Chuck. You know how to reach me if anything crops up, kiddo. I'll be home in half an hour, gonna stop and pick up some Chinese next door." He slipped his laptop into his backpack.

"Sure thing, boss. Just you go and leave me here on my own with no one to talk to. First day back. I'll be fine. Don't feel guilty."

"Good girl," he smiled, detoured to her desk to give her head a pat, and walked out the door.

22

"Good afternoon. I'm looking for Joe Cameron. Is he here?"

Chantal stared at the elegant woman standing in the doorway of the office. She looked like she had just stepped off a Fifth Avenue runway. Her hair was swept behind her pearl-studded ears, and she was wearing a robin's egg-blue silk sheath dress that hugged every perfect curve. She had ivory skin that looked as if it had never been exposed to the sun's rays.

"I apologize. I'm Kathleen Wentworth. Mr. Cameron came to my office a few days ago with questions about a patient of mine."

"You just missed him by minutes. He's probably still next door getting his lunch," Chantal said, quite sure that Joe wouldn't mind if this woman interrupted his meal. "At Ming's," she added.

"Maybe I should just make an appointment and come back another time. Could I do that with you?" she asked politely.

"Really, Joe won't mind," Chantal assured her. "It's just a couple doors down from here. And for appointments? He knows his schedule better than I do."

"All right, you've persuaded me. I'll check out Ming's. If he's not there, please tell him that I'll call later," she said with a friendly smile, turned around, and left. Chantal could see her standing out on the sidewalk, searching for Ming's sign, and heading in the right direction.

*

The old fashioned brass bell, attached to the door frame, jingled when Kathleen walked through the door, causing Joe to turn his head and step back from the counter. She smiled at him, but it took a few moments for Joe to recognize her.

"Dr. Wentworth? Never expected to run into you here."

"I've never been here before, although from the aromas coming from the kitchen, I might come back. I was at your office, and your secretary seemed confident that you wouldn't mind if I chased you down. I hate to bother you at lunch though," she said as she moved closer.

Ming's was primarily a takeaway restaurant but she had to manoeuvre past two four-seater tables squeezed into the waiting area. "And please ... call me Kathleen."

On the red Formica countertop stood an old fashioned iron cash register, a stack of paper menus, an assortment of Chinese condiments, and a two-foot-tall golden lucky cat with a perpetually waving hand. Louvered swinging wooden doors led to the kitchen where the clanging and clattering of pots and pans was enough to make one think that dozens of people were waiting impatiently for their meals.

"Well, you're no bother at all, Kathleen. Have you remembered something about the Harper boy?" Joe asked.

"This isn't about him. It's a rather delicate matter that I need help with. I've been thinking about getting referrals to a Private Investigator for some time. I noticed, after you left my office the other day, that your business card stated that you're a PI. I had assumed that you were a police detective?" She cocked her head and smiled, but her eyes were sad.

"It wasn't my intention to mislead. Initially, I was hired by Ryan Harper's sister to investigate his death. Now that it's officially a homicide I have no further involvement." He felt like he'd been caught stealing candy from the corner shop. "Kathleen, have you eaten lunch yet?"

"Not yet. I was going to get myself something after stopping by your office. But please, I don't mean to intrude on your plans."

"Let me double this order up. I was going to bring it back home to eat. Please join me. We can talk about whatever is on your mind in complete privacy."

"I couldn't possibly–"

Joe shouted in the direction of the kitchen. "Tommy, another order of everything please." Glancing back at Kathleen, he said "You aren't intolerant of anything? Gluten? Nuts? Dairy? Fortune cookies?"

"No, I'm quite ordinary in the food department."

"Thank God. I'm getting very intolerant of intolerant folk." A few minutes later, Tommy came through the kitchen doors with a large brown paper bag and placed it on the counter. Joe paid the bill and they left.

They walked down the street, chatting like old friends, discussing favourite restaurants, music and markets in town. They arrived at his condo before the food cooled down.

While he prepared plates in the kitchen, Kathleen oohed and aahed over his condo and decor. "As much as I love my house, I've often contemplated moving somewhere modern and easy to maintain like this. I'm not much of a gardener either, so it would be great just to be able to sit out on a balcony like this and watch the world."

"Suits me fine, I must admit. I don't miss the mowing in the summer and shoveling in the winter."

They sat on the bar stools at the kitchen island.

"What am I about to eat? Smells absolutely superb."

"We have Lemon Chicken, Crispy Fried Spinach, Shrimp in Black Bean Sauce, and Steamed Rice. Can I pour you a glass of wine?"

"Lovely. Thank you. This is very kind of you."

Joe had taken a chilled bottle of white chardonnay from the fridge, and removed the cork as Kathleen began opening containers and helping herself to a small portion from each. She took a sip of wine and fiddled with a gold locket hanging from her neck. She took a few bites of food, but most of her effort was spent moving the food around her plate.

"Do you not like it? I can fix you a sandwich or something if you prefer. Don't feel like you have to eat it," Joe said.

"To be truthful, I'm really not very hungry. Must be the heat. It's very good though." She pushed the plate aside and reached for the wine bottle. "Do you mind?" she asked Joe.

"Please, help yourself," Joe said, as she filled her glass nearly to the brim. She stood up, taking her glass with her and walked to the patio doors, staring out at the view. Joe silently watched her as she drained her glass and turned from the window to look at his music collection.

He walked over to her with the wine bottle, and she held her glass out for a refill. "Thank you," was all she said as he returned to the kitchen. She removed the occasional CD, reading the titles, and drinking the wine. Joe realized the bottle was already empty and took another bottle out of the wine cooler.

He walked over to the sofa and placed the new bottle on the coffee table.

"Do you want to sit down and tell me what sort of help you need, Kathleen?"

She put the current CD she was reading back into the rack and came over to the sofa, sitting down and holding out her empty glass simultaneously. "This is harder than I thought it would be. I apologize. I may be wasting your time, Joe."

"Relax, there's no hurry. You don't have to say anything if the time isn't right. Sometimes a client thinks of another way to get answers. Ponder it over for a while. I'm a phone call away if you decide you need help."

"My God, you sound like the shrink here!" she said with a hint of a smile on her lips.

He decided to gently shake the tree and see if an apple fell out. He'd drop it if she didn't respond. "Are you in some sort of trouble, Kathleen?"

"Goodness, no. It's something I've been meaning to deal with for years. I don't really know why I haven't. I suppose I just don't know where or how to begin. But I feel it's time." She held her empty glass out again. Her eyes were avoiding his, and he realized that she was close to tears.

"Maybe you should slow down a bit here with the wine. You hardly ate anything." He sat forward on the sofa hoping she'd look up at him.

Kathleen leaned over and took the wine bottle herself, and poured half a glass. "I want to find my brother," she said softly, gripping the wine glass with both hands and finally looking into Joe's eyes. "Our parents died when we were young. A dreadful car accident. They were at a company Christmas party." The tears began spilling down her face. "My brother and I were put into foster care."

Joe picked up the wine bottle and brought it to the kitchen counter. He retrieved a box of Kleenex from the hall powder room. He checked his cell phone to see if he'd missed a text or call from Becky, but there were no missed notifications. He set it on mute.

As he came back into the living room, Kathleen stood up with her empty glass and walked to the kitchen, stumbling slightly along the way, and plunked herself down on a bar stool. She emptied the bottle into her glass and took a Kleenex from the box Joe put down beside her. She wiped sloppily at the corners of her eyes.

"How old were you, Kathleen?"

"I think I was four and my brother was six. From what little snippets I remember, I had wonderful foster parents, but after a few months I was adopted by a family and moved here to Montréal. I know I was lucky to be adopted. Especially by a good family. You hear such horror stories now, don't you?" He didn't answer and she continued. "I was too young to know what was going on and I don't know what happened to Bobby. I tried a few times to find out what happened to him but it broke my heart more and more each time I hit that brick wall."

"Where were you living when the accident happened?"

"Ottawa. He could be living just two hours away from me, Joe ... and I don't know him." She broke down. Joe moved around to her side of the island, putting his arm around her shoulder.

"Believe me, Kathleen, it doesn't sound like an impossible task. There are plenty of resources available these days. I think we should get together another day and I'll get all the details from you. That might make more sense. I'll call a taxi to take you home now," Joe said.

She stood up and stumbled against him. His arms surrounded her to keep her from falling and she buried her face in his neck. He could feel the warm tears on his skin. She put her arms around his shoulders and clung on to him as if she was drowning. He could feel the tremors of her body through her silk clothing as she tried to catch her breath. He ran his hands up and down her back.

"You have to help me, Joe. I need to find him. I need him in my life so much." She dug her fingers into his neck. Her body pushed against his, and his hands drifted down to her thighs. "I need this...you holding me." Her sobs turned into moans, and she shifted her body back and forth against his. She lowered the straps of her dress and it slid to the floor. She stood naked in front of him. He carried her into the bedroom and lowered her onto the bed. She lay there with her eyes wide and her tears dried, breathless as he tossed his clothes on the floor with hers.

*

Joe woke, in a tangled mess of damp sheets and sweaty body parts, to the ringing of his land-line phone. They had both passed out after passionate and frenzied love-making. Kathleen began to stir without opening her eyes. Still asleep, she threw one of her arms across his chest, pinning him to the bed.

He let the phone go to the answering machine, and could faintly hear Becky's voice from the living room. He could only make out a few words, but he heard enough to hope that Kathleen wasn't conscious enough to hear the message. He didn't want her to think that there was a revolving door on his bedroom. Nothing was further from the truth.

He felt a real bond with Becky, but it was futile to think about trying to maintain a long-distance relationship with her. He wasn't sure what, if anything, would happen in the future with Kathleen, but at least she lived in Montréal.

He craned his neck to see the alarm clock, shocked to see that they had slept the afternoon away and it was 5:10 p.m. He slipped out from under Kathleen's embrace and rolled himself out of bed. He rifled through the clump of clothing at the bottom of the bed, retrieving his boxers, and tiptoed into the living room.

He disconnected the phone. There was no way he could comfortably talk to Becky in front of Kathleen. He returned to the bedroom and put his shorts and a clean tee shirt on. He felt the weight of his cell phone in his pocket, and took it out, seeing a missed voicemail from Becky. He'd listen to it later.

Joe had a maddening post-wine thirst and went to the fridge. He got the carton of pulp-free orange juice out and two glasses. He stood at the counter guzzling one of them down, as a tousled and red-eyed Kathleen appeared in the doorway of the bedroom, looking like Cleopatra in a toga expertly created from the flat sheet.

"Got one of those for me?" she asked hoarsely, and joined him in the kitchen. The mint green colour of the sheet accentuated the emerald green of her eyes.

He poured a glass for her and another one for himself, and said, "Did you sleep alright? I just woke up. Are you hungry? I could make pancakes or French Toast or something." He knew he was talking too much and too fast. He was having difficulty looking her in the eyes.

She kissed him lightly on the cheek. "Like a newborn. If you don't mind though, I'd like to shower and get home. I have some prep work to do for tomorrow's patients. Plus, for some reason, I have a touch of a hangover," she said, with a playful smile.

"You make yourself at home. There's an ensuite off the bedroom, and the white towels on the rack are clean. You should find anything you need in there. If you don't, just call me."

"Don't tempt me, Mr. Cameron," she said with a schoolgirl giggle. She turned away, heading back to the bedroom with her juice, seductively dropping the sheet as she went through the doorway.

As soon as he heard the shower pelting against the glass door, he pulled his cell phone back out and listened to the message.

4:03 p.m. "Joe, I just called your office and was told you had gone home this afternoon. I'm heading home to Vegas tonight. Just wanted to say goodbye and thanks for yesterday. It was fun."

He reconnected the land-line phone and heard the message that had woken him up minutes earlier. "Hi, it's me. Did I totally wear you out last night? Going out for dinner and then I'm off to the airport. If you're ever back in Vegas, my number is 911." He pulled the plug on the phone again. His head was starting to pound, and a sourness was creeping up from his stomach, threatening him with full-on heartburn. He started cleaning up the lunch leftovers and putting the dishes into the washer, when Kathleen appeared in the kitchen, stunningly coiffed and completely dressed.

"I'm sorry, Joe. I really do have to get back. I have hours of work waiting on my desk. I never expected to be out for the entire day. Not that I'm complaining," she added with a wink.

"Understood. I'll walk you to a taxi."

"No need. I want to walk for a while and clear the cobwebs, as they say. I can hail a taxi at some point."

"Can I call you soon? Tomorrow maybe?" Joe asked, walking over to her standing at the front door.

"Of course you can… or I'll call you. I do still want to discuss hiring you to find my brother." She picked her handbag up from the kitchen counter. "I hope you don't think badly of me for today. I drank too much, and emotions got the best of me."

"Please…no apologies. I'm just hoping you don't think I took advantage of you." He opened the door and put his free hand on her shoulder.

"Don't be silly, we're both adults. We knew what we were doing. Maybe get together on the weekend?" she said, pecked him on the cheek and walked out the door.

He reconnected the phone again, retrieved and unmuted his cell, and continued his obsessive wiping down of the countertop.

While he was gathering up the wine bottles and glasses, he started to feel sorry for himself. Two women in 24 hours and neither of them seemed in much of a hurry to see him again.

23

She sat at the bar in the poker room of the Casino Mercier de Montréal. It was horseshoe-shaped, built from slabs of mahogany and fitted with a chrome foot rail. The bar stools were extremely comfortable, upholstered on seat and back with a crimson leather that matched the colour of the felt on the nearby poker tables. The bar could easily accommodate two dozen patrons, but there was no one seated, aside from Lady Macbet.

A few men had approached her since she'd arrived an hour earlier, but she dismissed them all as unsuitable. She knew it wouldn't take long before some miserable young man would arrive for a drink and some solace and she would be available to provide the required comfort. It might not be the ideal situation, luring and trapping a stranger in a busy casino, but she needed someone tonight, and this was the best place to get one. She had thought it through, planned and savoured every imminent moment. This one would be useful as well as fun.

She had dressed with great care tonight. She wore a scooped neck red satin blouse. It was cut deeply enough to advertise the black lace camisole lying beneath. Her flared skirt was black satin and fell mid-thigh. Her stockings were dark grey and her feet were covered in black satin Chinese slippers. She wore red satin gloves.

The outfit was finalized with a black floppy hat, and large dark tinted Hollywood sunglasses.

She sipped slowly on her martini, patiently reading one of the printouts littering the bar. The paper explained the house rules for poker. Ironically, she was reading Rule #9—*profanity is strictly forbidden*—as a young man sat down a few seats away from her and began a tirade directed at no one in particular

"Motherfucker. Pocket Kings. The retard called my bet with fuckin' Ace Queen. And what falls on the river? Motherfuckin' Ace. Every fuckin' time." He had a hint of a French accent but was speaking the world-standard language of poker. He was a scrawny guy—short and bony—and his hair fell like greasy strands of brown yarn down to his shoulders. He was wearing standard poker room issue: jeans, t-shirt, sneakers, hoodie and sunglasses.

The bartender had a tumbler of Glenfiddich poured and sitting on a coaster before the soliloquy was finished. "Tough break, Eric. C'est la vie, mon ami."

Lady Macbet moved two seats closer to Eric, leaving one bar stool between them. She crossed her legs, exposing the top of her silk stockings and the clasp of her garter belt. "Rough night?" she enquired sympathetically, turning her head towards the young man.

"Unfuckinbelievable. Oh shit, excuse-moi. It's just... it does my head in sometimes," he answered as he shot the malt back in one gulp.

"Let me get you another drink. I won a few dollars on the slots tonight, and feel like blowing it."

"Sure, I wouldn't say no to another scotch. Merci."

She lifted her hand, holding up her empty glass, and when the bartender looked over, pointed to Eric's glass as well.

"My name is Suzanne," holding her hand out to him.

He took her hand limply in his and replied, "I'm Eric. Nice to meet you."

She re-crossed her legs, staring ahead into the mirror behind the shelf of bottles. She was instantly gratified to see that Eric's eyes were directed exactly where she had planned. She turned her head back quickly to face him, catching his childish gawk. He looked up at her, a splotchy flush creeping into his cheeks, to meet her amused expression.

Although pleased with his reaction and enjoying his embarrassment, she thought it best to put him at ease again, and knew the best way to do that was to let him talk about himself.

"Have you been playing poker a long time, Eric?"

"Couple years now. I started on-line, but that was shit. I lost a bit of money. I took time to study the game, read some poker strategy books, and began coming here a few months ago."

"And how's that working out for you?"

He picked up his glass and stared into the amber liquid. "I think I'd be better off moving to Las Vegas where people really know how to play. I can't play against these guys who bet with anything. They get so lucky. I need to play against skilled players."

She nodded and tried to look impressed. "Do you work? Or go to university?" she enquired.

"I'm at McGill—the Engineering program. I'm good at math, which is why I'm good at poker. It's all about statistics and probabilities. I've been working on my parents to help me make the move to Vegas. Tuition there is about 20k a year for a non-resident."

"They have a good engineering program there?" she asked incredulously.

"I plan to take a poker dealer training course instead," he said, with a self-satisfied grin. "I could earn some extra money being a dealer at night in one of the smaller casinos and play poker the rest of the time. My parents wouldn't need to know until graduation, and by then I figure I'll be making good money."

"You're very resourceful, Eric." She watched him puff up like a peacock. "I respect someone who knows what he wants and goes out to get it."

"Do you want another drink, Suzanne?" he said.

"I don't usually have an easy time talking to strangers, but you're different. I hope you don't think I'm being too forward, Eric," she replied, shifting slightly in her seat to face him head on. "It's only nine o'clock. Do you have plans for the rest of the evening?" She ignored his offer of a drink.

"The only plan I had was to play poker tonight. I just came over to the bar to calm down. Lucky for us! Fate, huh?" Eric was now looking so self-centred and sure of himself that it took all her willpower not to slap him.

"Fate indeed. I was hoping to have some company to help me celebrate my little win tonight. But if you want to go back to the poker table, I totally understand. Maybe I'll see you another night here." She pouted and put her hand up to the scoop neck of her blouse, running her fingernail along the edge. She opened her purse and took out her wallet to pay the tab.

"Well, hang on. What did you have in mind? You wanted to leave the casino, or what?" Eric asked. His voice was shaking slightly and his eyes darted back and forth from her purse to her face.

"Not leave...not exactly. I have a cooler in my car that just so happens to be holding a bottle of champagne. It's such a beautiful night and I thought I'd sit along the little stream outside and look at the stars. It's a great spot. I love going down there. Very secluded. I'm surprised more people don't go. At this hour you could do absolutely anything there without being seen." Her hand moved down to the hem of her skirt, knowing his eyes would follow and watch her play with the clasp of her garter.

"Sounds interesting." His eyes glazed over as he stared at her hand. His eyes didn't shift from her thigh as he said, "I suppose I could come back here later tonight and play a few hands."

Lady Macbet couldn't believe that he was thinking about coming back to poker after spending time with her. He'd pay for that dearly. "Oh yes, please do. Come outside with me for a while. You'll keep me company, relax, and refuel so later you can take these idiots for all their money."

"I'm convinced. Let's go," he said, jumping off the bar stool like a trained seal.

"Hold on, Eric. It'll take me ten minutes to get to my car and over to the picnic spot. You stay here and have another drink." She put a twenty dollar bill on the bar in front of him. She put another twenty beside her glass. "Do you know where I mean? Just down the slope from the main casino entrance?" she asked as she stood up.

She hugged her large purse close to her body so that there would be no telltale clink of the bottle against glasses. She had swaddled everything in a thin blanket. She didn't want to take any chances of him suspecting that she already had the bottle.

"Oui, I've seen the area. But I could come with you to your car. I don't mind," he replied, eager as a puppy.

"No, definitely not," she said, sternly this time. "Sometimes a woman needs a few minutes to herself before entertaining a man," she added. "Join me there in ten or fifteen minutes. I'll be waiting."

Without waiting for Eric's response, she turned and walked to the escalator. She didn't look back at him once. It was all she could do to restrain herself from running down the moving steps.

She left through the revolving doors of the Casino, as if she was heading to the tourist bus idling outside. She had timed it perfectly; the summer sun had nearly disappeared. She strode past the bus and along the sidewalk until she reached the gravel path which led to the stream below.

Glancing around to ensure that no one was nearby, she stooped to remove her shoes, and walked carefully in stocking feet down the slope. There was a picnic bench which was much too visible by anyone on the walkway above. She followed the stream, passing four benches, until she reached a dense cropping of trees.

Just past the trees was an unruly weeping willow, about eight feet from the water's edge. Between the willow and the water was a gentle incline. There were no overhead light standards this far along. Even if people were looking in this direction from the path, they would only see the drooping feathery limbs of the willow tickling the ground.

She spread the curtain of branches apart, walking into her private den. Removing the blanket from her bag, she unwrapped the bottle and glasses, placing them on the grass.

She spread out the blanket beside a flat topped rock, the perfect table for her liquid feast. Popping the cork as quietly as she could, she filled one glass to the brim and the other half full. She removed the vial from the pouch compartment of her bag and emptied it into the glass, sloshing the contents around for a few seconds, and then topping it up with more champagne.

She sat back on the blanket, using the rock as a backrest. Her heart was pounding with anticipation and she was nearly breathless.

She saw Eric standing near the first picnic table, frantically looking around. He walked along the bank, losing his footing a few times but never falling. Pleased that he was so eager, her entire body began quivering. She stood up and left the comfort of her lair to raise her arm and slowly wave back and forth until he spotted her. She returned to the seclusion of the branches and watched his approach.

He was sprinting toward her along the grass. Just before he reached her, he flicked his cigarette into the stream. She was more excited than she had ever been before. Now that she knew what it was like to watch the spark disappear from someone's eyes, she could better savour the anticipation of it as well.

"Sit down, Eric. I've poured you a drink," she said. He sat cross-legged, like a school boy, on the blanket, constantly revolving the ring on his index finger. He jerked and fidgeted constantly and his eyes never settled on anything for more than a few seconds. She handed him the glass and he took a tentative sip.

"Eric, I don't intimidate you, do I?"

"Not really...no. This is all just unexpected. Not sure what's going on here," he answered, nibbling his lower lip and staring at the rock she was leaning against.

"Alright, then. Relax and drink up. I'm not sure what's going on either." She giggled and placed her hand on his knee. "I suppose it depends how adventurous you want to be," she added provocatively. She undid the buttons of her blouse and eased out of it, exposing her dainty black lace camisole. "It's so hot out here tonight, don't you think?"

Eric merely nodded, his eyes glued to the bulge of her breasts.

"Eric, if you're hot, you could take your shirt off. Or maybe I should put my blouse back on," she said. "Am I being too forward?"

Fumbling with his buttons, he muttered, "No, I'll take this off." His voice wobbled.

Lady Macbet leaned over to push his hands away from his shirt, and began to slowly undo each button, letting her hands linger on his chest between each one, sometimes sliding a finger under his shirt to lightly stroke his chest. His eyes closed as she continued. She finished freeing his buttons.

"Take your shirt off, Eric. You're much too tense, young man. Finish your wine and I'll give you a massage." She clapped her hands together once, like a schoolteacher shushing her students and tilted her head to smile at him. "Let me make you forget about that horrible poker game."

He chugged the entire contents of the glass down his throat.

"Everything goes better with champagne, Eric. You'll see. Lie down on your stomach. I'll do your neck and shoulders. Well, at least, that's what I'll start with." She allowed him to think about that for a few seconds. "We'll see if you're a good boy and do what I say," she added with a giggle.

"I'll be good, I promise." He belly flopped onto the grass, feet pointing towards the stream.

"My first command. Lie horizontal to the water so that I can keep an eye on the pathway. We don't want to be interrupted, do we?" she asked.

He leapt to all fours and turned his body ninety degrees, settling back on top of the blanket. "Should I take my jeans off too?"

"You're eager, aren't you, young man? You'll take your jeans off when I tell you that you can take them off, and not before." She was barely keeping the distaste from her voice. "I think we'll wait a while until we're assured of complete privacy."

He lay prone with his arms down at his side, and his left cheek on the blanket. His eyes were closed. She took his shirt, folded it into a cushion, lifted his head, and placed the pillow under his cheek. "See? I'll take care of you. Is that more comfortable, Eric?" massaging his neck.

"Oui, Madame! Thank you," he murmured.

"Don't be in such a rush, Eric. You should enjoy these few moments with me."

She straddled his torso, and leaned down to whisper in his ear as she continued to squeeze the muscles of his neck and shoulders.

"You must tell me if you get too relaxed, dear boy. You'll want to have some energy left, won't you?" She moved her hands down his back, caressing every inch of his skin. "My, you're strong, aren't you?" He didn't answer. She let her hands sneak under his body to his chest and abdomen, twirling her fingers towards the belt of his jeans.

He began to moan softly. He tried to clear his throat as if he was about to speak. A few faint disjointed words came out. She had to lean with her ear to his mouth to understand him. "Sleepy... please...stop," were the only words she could make out.

"Maybe you're right. We should move this party along, Eric. I certainly wouldn't want you to fall asleep before the end." She was whispering into his ear seductively. "Why don't you turn over onto your back, and let me look after things. Things you can't possibly imagine."

He was straining to try and move.

"Would you like that?"

She stood up, straightening her skirt and putting her blouse back on. She knelt at the side of his head so that he could see her. She saw the confusion in his eyes and his mouth opened a fraction. No sound came out.

"I'll help you, Eric." She put one hand at his left shoulder and the other around his waist, and easily rolled him over onto his back with the aid of the embankment slope. He groaned from somewhere faint and deep inside his throat. She knew his chest would be tightening up soon.

"Eric, I put a special treat in the champagne for you. A favourite little drug of mine. It makes you more obedient. You want to be obedient, don't you?" She rolled him over again. "You don't have to talk for us to have fun. Do you understand?" She rolled him again so that he was facing her. "Eric, are you going to answer when I speak to you?"

*

Eric started to feel a tingling in his groin. He wasn't sure if she was touching him. He couldn't answer. He couldn't move a muscle. He wasn't sure if he was getting hard. He tried to speak. He couldn't. His mind was racing, trying to make sense of it all.

"Eric, it's time for me to have my way with you now. You're ready, aren't you?" She smiled as she leaned in close to his face. "Talk to me, you spoiled little brat," and slapped him across the face. With her gloves on, the noise of the slap was more of a thump. He didn't even flinch. He felt nothing. He was totally mute and couldn't feel his body. His eyes began to glaze over. She rolled him over again … and again.

"Eric, don't worry, you don't have to help me. I can do it all myself," she said petulantly, and rolled him until he was at the very edge of the water, staring up at her. A few minutes earlier he would have felt that coolness of the water surrounding his half naked body.

She leaned down so that her face was an inch away from his. She spoke so quietly that he could barely hear her words. "Eric, one or two more turns should do it. Then you're going to be more relaxed than you could ever imagine." She turned him again and added with the hint of a laugh, "Maybe not right away, but in a few minutes." She turned him again, a full revolution, so that he was facing her, partially submerged. His mouth was open just enough to let the water seep slowly into the corners. There was no longer any possibility of his closing it.

She picked up the nearly full champagne and drained it into the water above his mouth. "No sense wasting it. Enjoy," she whispered. "One more turn should do the trick." She gazed into his eyes and he could see the ecstasy she was in. She gave him one final complete turn. His head was now totally submerged in the shallow stream.

She stared down at him at she folded the blanket and put it back in her purse with the glasses. She propped the empty bottle in the mud beside Eric's head.

The water raced down his throat and nostrils, filling his lungs as his silent screams echoed in his head. He tried to struggle to reach the moonlit air above him. His chest felt like a balloon about to burst. The last thing he saw was her evil smiling face hovering over his as she blew him a kiss and moved out of sight.

24

Hank and Gumbo were in their car, near Nellis Air Force base, driving back to the home of Stephanie Graves. Or Corrigan, as she preferred to be called. For the entire ten minute trip, the car radio was on and blaring country music. Gumbo sang along to most of them as if he was in a karaoke bar.

He was looking forward to Becky coming back to partner up with him. She was a smart detective and ready to work day and night if needed. He missed her fortitude and creativity when working on a case, but most of all he missed her humour. Hank was an okay cop but he was getting world-weary and it showed. Becky was still keen. And not hard on the eyes either.

He knew Hank was feeling more upbeat since he'd received word an hour earlier that he could fly home on the red-eye later that night. Hank had made it pretty clear that he thought all these newfangled ideas and schemes were ridiculous. Gumbo had met cops like him before. They weren't comfortable with the contemporary digital age. They didn't trust some of the modern forensic approaches.

They turned on to her street, driving slowly, as children and pets were running amok everywhere again. There was a street soccer game going on, with goals made of cardboard fridge boxes. Farther along, a hopscotch competition was underway with a queue of girls lined up ready to hop to the top. Skipping was also a popular pastime today. They heard multilingual cheering and singing coming from all directions.

They parked directly in front of her house again. The playpen was still in the front yard, but empty of inmates. The front door was open, but the security grill was closed.

"Ms. Corrigan! Vegas Metro!" Gumbo shouted into the house. "We'd like a word, please!"

From somewhere inside the house, a voice called out: "Fuck's sake! Again? You're bringin' the tone of the place down!" They waited, but there was no sign of her coming to let them in.

"Ms. Corrigan? It's Detectives Thibodeaux and Mason. We need to have another talk, ma'am."

"We've talked already. I've said all I can say. Unless ya'll want me to make shit up for ya'll," she yelled, mimicking Gumbo's southern drawl.

"Okay. Get yourself a sitter for the little'ns, and we'll send a squad car to pick you up and bring you downtown. We'll talk there instead. See you later, ma'am."

A flurry of swearing was followed by thumping footsteps and she appeared at the bars of the security door, tying the sash of the same kimono she had worn the other day. She had no makeup on and her hair was in curlers. She looked prettier and a lot less tough without all the greasepaint.

"Whaddya want today?" she asked, lighting up a cigarette and glaring at them through the bars.

"Invite us in, ma'am. Unless you want all the neighbours to hear your business," Hank said. "Please," he quickly added.

"Oh for chrissake. Come in. And it's Stephanie. Told ya that last time." She unlocked the bars and swung the door open.

"Thank you, ma'am. Very hospitable of you." Gumbo said. The two detectives followed her down the short hallway. The smell of spaghetti sauce and freshly filled diapers hung in the air like a curtain. Both detectives immediately regretted being allowed entry.

"Where are the children?" Hank asked.

"Playing at a neighbour's house, if you must know."

"You going out today, Stephanie?" said Gumbo.

"No business of yours, is it?"

"Just asking. Thought you might be heading downtown." Gumbo pointed at her full head of curlers.

She was silent, leading them into the living room, which transitioned into a dining room at the far end. It was decorated in 1980's Sally Ann except for a state of the art smart television. The only artwork was dozens of crayon drawings applied directly to the wall just above the skirting boards. Like an art gallery for cats and dogs. The only accessories on the coffee and side tables were ashtrays.

She smiled at both in turn and said, "Thought you'd drop by for tea?" She stared pointedly at Gumbo. "Or maybe you were hoping for a small mint julep?" She snickered and plunked herself down on the sofa. She lit another cigarette, reaching into the drawer of the side table for a clean ashtray.

Hank sat down on the other end of the sofa while Gumbo dragged a chair over from the small wooden dining room table. He sat down across from Stephanie, the coffee table between them.

"Let's talk about the night your ex-husband, John Graves, was murdered."

"Alrighty. I never tire of hearing and talking about his death."

"Where were you between midnight and four in the morning that night?"

"Just let me check my social calendar," Stephanie answered, not moving a muscle and not breaking her stare at Gumbo. "I was here, fast asleep," she said after about fifteen seconds.

"Here. Asleep," he repeated. "Where were you, and what were you doing, prior to midnight, then?" he asked.

"Here. Watching TV." She pointed at the fifty inch flat screen perched on a dresser against the opposite wall.

"Here. Watching TV," Gumbo said.

"If you're gonna repeat everything I say, this could take some time." She chuckled and choked on her last puff.

"Stephanie. What if we told you that we spoke to some of your colleagues from that night?" Hank joined in. He was beside her on the sofa, so Stephanie had to turn slightly to look at him.

"Holy kitten crap! Colleagues? I have colleagues?" She widened her stare in simulated surprise.

"What if those colleagues mentioned that they saw you working that night?" Hank continued.

"I'd say they weren't the most trustworthy lot, those colleagues of mine." Her eyes darted between the two men.

"They have no reason to make that up, Stephanie," said Hank.

"Well, I didn't kill the bastard, as much as I'd be proud to take credit for it. So unless you have some sort of evidence, I'll ask you to leave now."

"Don't get your panties in a knot. Why didn't you tell us you work the streets?" Gumbo asked.

"Because I don't. I provide a girlfriend experience," she said with assumed indignation.

"Oh, give us a break, girl. We're not here to pick you up for solicitation. Although we could if we were in the mood. We simply want you to tell us where you were that night. Lying about it doesn't look good. You're smart enough to know that," Gumbo said.

"Okay. Okay. So I was working. No big deal. I knew it wasn't important. That's why I didn't mention it before."

"If you'd said it the first time we were here, then it wouldn't be a big deal, Stephanie. But you didn't, so it is. Understand?" He made no attempt to hide his exasperation.

She jumped up from the sofa, and looked back and forth between the two detectives, like an umpire at Wimbledon, and her voice shook, "So I need a lawyer?"

"Calm yourself, girl. Just tell us where you were from ten o'clock in the evening until morning. Trace your steps for us. And don't lie. We're investigating a homicide, not trying to bust you for making a living, albeit a questionable one," said Hank.

Stephanie took a big deep breath, and sat back down, legs tucked up under her body, and hands in her lap. As she spoke, her eyes and demeanour softened. Now she looked like a teenager who'd been caught breaking curfew.

"I went out that night around eight o'clock."

"Your regular haunt, near downtown?" Hank relaxed into the sofa as Gumbo took over.

"Uh huh. Near the Plaza on Charleston." She nodded and continued. "Business was slow. I remember it was one of those really hot nights. Guys don't seem to like fucking when it's too hot outside. Why is that?" she asked, looking back and forth at the two of them.

Gumbo kept his voice at a soft non-judgemental monotone. "Not a clue, Stephanie. I'll poll the station when I get back. Were there other girls with you?"

"Sure. The regulars. Cindy, Misty, Barbara-Ann. None of us got much work. We hung out most of the time in the burger joint across from the Plaza. Air conditioned. Every so often, Big Rico would come in and give us a pep talk, getting us back out on the street."

"Big Rico. He's your pimp?"

"Supervisor. If I have colleagues, I have a freakin' supervisor."

"Fair enough. He treat you girls okay?" Gumbo asked with some concern.

"Had worse. Takes a bigger cut than most, but he treats us better than most," she answered quietly. "So I didn't get any work 'til the sun went down and it cooled off a bit. Maybe elevenish."

"With a regular?"

"We don't really have regulars so much. Mostly tourist trade. Poor tourists at that." She smiled but it didn't make her face look happy.

"So where did you go with him?"

"Just in his car in the parking lot. Then back to the burger joint. I had a couple more jobs, and then Rico gave me a lift home. I was home before the sun was up, so maybe four or five in the morning."

"Where are your kids when you're out all night like that?" Hank asked.

"Next door. I put them to bed, in sleeping bags, at my neighbours, and she calls me when they wake up in the morning and I go and get them. I pay her twenty bucks a night and she doesn't have to lift a finger," she said defensively.

"Okay, so the girls can vouch for you, off and on. And Rico can verify when he drove you home. Give us phone numbers," Gumbo said.

"You're joking, right?" laughing and clapping her hands. She added, "You wanna talk to the girls or Rico, you'll have to see them at the office." She giggled, really getting into the metaphorical swing of things.

Gumbo stood up and Hank followed his lead. They were both eager to get out of the house and back into the air conditioned car.

"Anything you want to add to your statement, Stephanie?" Gumbo asked as he walked toward the front door.

She didn't answer. She walked behind them. At the door, she looked drained, and older.

"Why don't you get off the street now, while you're young?" Gumbo called from the cracked pavement where he stood. "Get a decent job, bring your kids up proper? We have programs to help, you know?"

"You find me a job that pays anywhere close to the same wage, and I'll put in for a transfer," she answered with a fatalistic shrug.

The two men walked to the car and drove snail-like past the children who were darting in and out from between parked cars. They both looked back at Stephanie as she sat on her front step, removing curler after curler, and chucking them dejectedly into the vacant playpen.

25

I woke up quite late, but that was to be expected. I opened the fridge door, rummaging around for something suitably celebratory and thirst-quenching. I'd had too much alcohol the night before. Two drinks at the casino bar, and then champagne with Eric at our picnic.

I found some lemons in the crisper, so went about making a pitcher of fresh lemonade. I added sugar, a spoonful at a time, and then stirred, and took tiny sips from the spoon until it lost the sourness but wasn't too sweet. Perfect. I poured a tall glass and added a few mint leaves, muddling the drink with a wooden spoon. I tossed two ice cubes in the glass and put the pitcher in the fridge.

I took a small oval platter down from the cupboard, covered the bottom of the plate with tiny blinis, dolloped them with sour cream and sprinkled a spattering of Sevruga black caviar over top. Technically they were eggs and so they qualified as breakfast. They were like little pearls of glistening mercury. Possibly the finest caviar I'd ever had. Well worth buying from that little Russian restaurant. I took the drink and blinis over to the small table at the window. Sinking into the armchair and picking at the food in front of me, I thought back to the events of the previous night.

It hadn't been an ideal plan, but it had to be done. Foolish Eric served a double purpose and really, all in all, the evening had been invigorating and satisfying. In fact, more than I'd hoped, being such a last minute decision. So young but already so callous and bitter. Well, he's been saved from being the disappointment to his parents that he surely would have become.

This was just the right treat for a job well done. Flawless again. I should have bought more caviar. Soon. Very soon.

26

Joe arrived at the office and the red light was flashing on his answering machine. He pushed the answer button, and listened to the message.

"Joe, this is Kathleen. Could we get together soon and talk about finding my brother? I seriously want to get this started. I've put it off for much too long. Call me, please. Thanks." Her voice was shaky but he didn't know whether the tremor was from nervousness, embarrassment, or sadness. The message had been left only twenty minutes earlier, so he hit redial and she answered after two rings.

"Hey Kathleen. It's me, Joe."

"Joe, thanks so much for getting back to me. Could we get together and talk about this? It's eating away at me. I really need to find Robert. Is there any chance we could get together today?" He was relieved to hear her voice sounding composed and unwavering now.

"Absolutely. Anytime today is good with me, so pick a time. Do you want me to come by your office?" Joe asked.

"If you could, that would be great. One o'clock, if that's ok? I'll make something for us for lunch, if you like?"

"Perfect. I'll be there. Have a good morning, Kathleen."

"You too, Joe. Thanks."

They hung up simultaneously. Joe sat back in his chair and put his feet on his desk, thinking about his time with Kathleen two days earlier. And then his mind switched over to Becky the night before that. They were extreme ends of the scale. He felt more of an open connection with Becky, but she lived three thousand miles away. Kathleen was intriguing and he really wanted to get to know her. And the sex. Becky was the girl next door in comparison.

Chantal arrived at work and they settled in to their day. Joe reviewed files while she followed up on accounts payable and receivable. He knew she worried about the business, and he had tried over and over again to put her mind at rest. He could afford to run this place at a loss for the rest of his life. It was a hobby and he was content if he got a case a month. For some reason, she found that hard to believe, and was constantly on a mission to drum up work. And realistically, if he passed over the business to her in a few years' time, she would have to get regular work to make any money.

The morning passed uneventfully and, by noon, Joe was cleaning his desk and about to shut down his laptop. Chantal looked up suspiciously from her keyboard.

"What?" Joe asked.

"Where do you think you're going?"

"I know where I'm going. I have a business meeting. And I may not be back later."

"Who and where? There's nothing written in your colander."

"I agree. It's full of holes." He opened the lid of his laptop and tapped the keys—*12:45-17:00 Business Meeting with a client somewhere*— feeling Chantal's unrelenting glare.

He closed the lid, tucked the laptop under his arm, and strode out the door. As he walked away, he heard the soft thump of a cookie hit the glass of the front door.

*

Joe continued down the street. He waffled about buying a bottle of wine to go with the lunch she was preparing. He didn't want to give the impression that he was after a replay of the other day, although his arm could be twisted—after they discussed her brother of course.

He ducked into the liquor store on Saint-Catherine and picked up a bottle of Brouilly for slightly less than thirty dollars. He'd read a review of it in the weekend paper and wanted to try it. He considered stopping for flowers as well, but that seemed too cliché and desperate.

He hailed a taxi which dropped him off just shy of one o'clock, outside her Grosvenor street home. He began the journey down the walkway to the side office door, when the massive oak front door opened, and Kathleen stood there, looking fresh and lovely in white linen shorts and a black tank top.

Her hair was damp, her skin glistened and she was barefoot. He trotted up the steps, and she gave him a kiss on both cheeks. The fragrance of lemon and grapefruit hung deliciously in the air around her. Grabbing his free hand, she led him into the house.

The entryway was grand—perfectly square in shape—and there was a round centre table topped with a large crystal bowl of exotic looking flowers. The table was anchored by a slightly frayed oriental carpet. Against the far wall stood an antique hallstand, whose seat looked like it would hinge upwards to stow mittens and scarves. The eye-level mirror embedded in the stand was beautifully bevelled, although the rippled reflection was more like that of a funhouse mirror. A pink cashmere sweater hung from one of the four brass hooks. Both pieces were tiger oak, and gleamed with a well-polished shine. Beside the stand was a circular staircase, the treads partially covered with an embroidered oriental runner. It didn't match the floor carpet but the colours were complementary. The walls were covered with a chintz fabric of tiny lily of the valley flowers.

There were two sets of sliding double doors. The ones on the right would lead into the office waiting room that Joe had previously been in with Becky. The doors on the left were open, and he followed Kathleen into a living room which was bright and elegant and suited her perfectly.

She looked all the more spectacular in her simplicity against the backdrop of the ornate room. The walls were papered in a pale blue and ivory stripe. The floors were a dark burgundy hardwood, nearly black, and shone like glass.

She led him to the one modern piece of furniture in the room—a cream coloured sectional sofa. He sunk into the cushion as if it was a marshmallow, as he set his laptop down on the leather-topped coffee table, next to an open bottle of wine and two empty glasses. A platter of cheese, crackers, grapes, and olives sat in the centre of the table. The cheeses were already cut into bite-size pieces.

Joe handed her the wine he had bought. She removed it from the crumpled brown paper bag.

"I love this wine, Joe. Thank you."

"I've never had it, but I've been wanting to try it."

"Well, I've already opened this one so you'll just have to come back," she said with a wink. She reached over and poured them both a glass of wine. Joe opened his laptop and turned it on. He felt his mobile vibrate in his pocket, but ignored it.

"Joe, I have very little for you to go on, I'm afraid."

"Let me ask you some questions, and we'll see where that leads us."

"Fair enough. I'm ready when you are," she said, taking a small sip of wine.

"When were you born?"

"1977. I'm thirty eight. Robert is two years older, born in 1975."

"Exact birthdates?"

"I don't know. I just know how old we were when our parents died. My adoptive parents gave me an honorary birth date of January 1. So I've always used that."

"Fair enough. Full birth names?"

Kathleen took a larger sip of wine.

"I don't know that either. I know my Christian name of Kathleen is right. And Bobby ... Robert. I don't remember my last name. It would probably be easier if I told you what I do remember, instead of you asking me all these questions."

"Go ahead then, tell me what you know." He watched as her eyes glazed over while she looked far into the past.

"I was four. Bobby was six. We lived in Ottawa. I remember it was near a park and near water. There was a large fountain in the park. We used to sit on the outer cement rim and dangle our feet in the cold water, while our mother sat on a park bench a few feet away. She was always reading. I don't know what her name was. She was beautiful though. I have a photograph of her." She pulled out a small frame from the shelf under the coffee table.

"Look," she said. It was a colour photo, but the colours were muted. A crouching woman in the middle, with each arm resting across the shoulders of her two children. The boy was slightly taller than the girl. He held a small truck or train car in his hands. Kathleen cradled a doll in her arms. The woman looked strikingly like Kathleen, although with dark hair. She was frail and delicate and beautiful. The two children were sullen and concentrating intently on the camera. The shot was taken indoors, in front of a large sparsely-decorated Christmas tree. There were a few wrapped gifts beneath the tree. "This is the only picture that I have."

"None of your Dad?"

"No. Maybe my brother will have some." Her voice had become weak as she stared down at the treasured photograph.

They were both quiet, munching on the cheese. Kathleen stared out the window and Joe didn't want to interrupt any memories that might be surfacing. His phone shivered in his pocket again and Joe tried to ignore it.

"I can hear your butt buzzing. Do you want to answer it?"

"I'm sure it's not important." He shook his head slowly. "It'll wait till later. When did your parents die?" Joe asked.

"1981, sometime around Christmas. The Wentworths told me that they went to a company party at my Dad's office, and never came home."

"And you have no paperwork? Birth certificates? Death certificates? Nothing?"

"I have the death certificates of my adoptive parents. That's all. Nothing from before that." Her eyes were flickering and Joe suspected she was holding back a torrent of tears.

"What about your adoption papers?"

"No. No paperwork."

"When did your adoptive parents die?"

"They both died quite a few years ago. My Mom died first, in 2000, and my Dad a year after that. Mom had cancer. It was a long battle; in and out of hospitals for years. Dad had a heart attack in 2001 and died before he even reached the hospital." Kathleen's voice began to crack. "They left everything to me, but there was no paperwork about my adoption. I would have expected some, but I never found any, and I don't understand why."

She stared at the window, trance-like again. She pulled a tissue out of her pocket and dabbed softly at the inside corners of her eyes. Joe rested his hand on her shoulder, giving it a sympathetic squeeze. She shivered and put the tissue back in her pocket. Turning to him, she smiled wistfully and apologized.

Joe asked if she had a photocopy machine in the office so that he could have a copy of the photo. They went through the two sets of sliding doors and Kathleen retrieved a sheet of photo paper from the cabinet beside the copier. Within a minute, Joe had a photo in his hands of equal quality to the original. Back in the living room, they settled onto the sofa again.

"Can you tell me more about your adoptive parents, Kathleen?" he said.

"Well, they were the Wentworths, of course. Jonathan and Eliza. She was French Canadian, born and bred in Montréal. Her maiden name was Benoit. My father was originally from London, England. He immigrated here when he was a young man to study Medicine at McGill. When he graduated, he was immediately offered a position at the Children's Hospital. In the early seventies, he set up a private practice, as a pediatrician, right here in this house, where my office is now. He always remained affiliated with the Children's though."

She stopped and sipped her wine while Joe entered the details into his laptop. He looked up when he realized that she was not continuing. She was holding the family photo, unframed, in both her hands, like it was a delicate piece of parchment.

"Kathleen, I can't promise anything, but I really don't think we'll have a problem tracing your brother."

"I can't tell you what that would mean to me, Joe. I get so frustrated when I try to search for information. I've tried calling adoption agencies and social services. No one can help me. I feel physically sick from it sometimes."

"There are all sorts of government agencies and archives that I can contact on your behalf. You won't have to do a thing. Just leave it with me."

Kathleen fiddled with inserting the family photo back into its frame. "By the way, I've been meaning to ask you if there's any news on Ryan Harper." Her fingers were shaking ever so slightly.

"I haven't heard anything recently. I think it's been a dead end investigation so far. I'll ask the Detective who's on the case and let you know."

She finally managed to slip the photo into the frame and snapped the backing in place. She put it on the coffee table and continued to stare at it. As much as Joe wanted to put his arms around her, he worried how she'd interpret the motion, and when he volunteered to go back to the office and start some enquiries on her behalf, Kathleen immediately stood up and began to walk towards the entry hall. He promised to call her with any news.

Trying to hide his disappointment at not being asked to stay, Joe followed her out, and accepted a friendly kiss on the cheek.

*

He trudged down the sidewalk heading towards downtown and pulled the phone out of his pocket. He slid his finger along the screen and clicked the keypad to access the messages. Both were from Andrew.

U there?

Call me.

Joe texted Andrew that he was on his way to the Donegal if he felt like meeting up. It wasn't even three o'clock yet, but Joe had no interest in going back to the office. He ordered a pint, slumped on his own at a table in the corner, and wrote out possible avenues of research for finding some clues to Kathleen's earlier life. Andrew didn't show up and Joe left at five o'clock.

He walked slowly east along Saint-Catherine, and turned down de la Montagne. Chantal had already closed up the office. He must have missed her by mere minutes. He let himself in and wrote her a note, asking her to open a file for Kathleen Wentworth and start the investigation first thing in the morning. He printed out, from his laptop, the few facts that he had collected. He added a postscript for her not to worry if he was late arriving in the morning.

He wandered into the small basement bar, a couple doors down from the office. The name was simply the Lounge and it was where Chantal had worked as a barmaid after art school. It was the neighbourhood bar which he frequented most often. It personified Joe's definition of a dive. It wasn't a place to hear good music, pick up beautiful women, admire the décor, or take part in stimulating philosophical discussions. It was a fantastic place to drink.

There was the occasional backroom poker game held in the long-condemned kitchen. You could choose to be left alone to drink and stare glassy-eyed at the suspended television, permanently set to the national sports channel, or engage the patrons and bartender in a lively discussion about how old the peanuts were in the vending machine in the corner. It was a perfect spot for a decent liver pummelling.

By the time Joe arrived at his usual bar-stool, stopping to pick up a discarded newspaper on one of the tables, the bartender, Frankie, had a moderately cold bottle of Molson in front of him.

"You want a glass with that, my friend? They're cleanish today," he said.

"As appealing and novel as that sounds, I'll pass."

"Up to you. There's a game going in the back if you want to buy in."

"How much?"

"Minimum buy in is $50. Max is $300. There's five of them back there. Room for a couple more. I may join in when my shift is over at nine o'clock."

"Aye, go ahead, give me $200 in chips then, and another three beers to bring back there with me."

"Lazy bastard," Frankie said, as he handed over a rack of chips and the bottles.

Three hours later, Joe emerged from the back room, handing the empty chip rack over to Frankie with a shrug and a sheepish smile. "I'll settle my tab with you tomorrow," Joe said, and walked out into the cooling evening air.

Before tumbling into bed, he checked his phone which he had forgotten to un-mute after his meeting with Kathleen. He had missed one call from Andy. As he downed a couple aspirin with a few gulps of orange juice, his friend's sombre voice came from the speaker.

"Joe. Couldn't make it to the pub. Busy on another case here. A body was found outside the casino. Just a kid, for fucksake. I'll call you tomorrow."

27

Joe woke up before his alarm went off. He got ready for work and then sat out on the balcony, phone in hand. He pressed Becky's number.

"Newcross," she said. Her voice was groggy.

"Becky. You up and around?" Joe asked.

"Nowhere close. It's not even six in the morning yet. Is there something wrong?"

"Ouch. I forgot about the time difference. Shall I call you back later?"

"No, I'm awake now. Have to get up soon anyhow, so no sense going back to sleep. What's up?"

"I wanted to apologize for not connecting the other day. An emergency came up that I had to take care of. You got home alright?"

"Yes, of course. No worries, Joe. I mean, really, what the hell? We had a good time. Let's leave it at that." Her tone was abrupt. Even if she was sleepy, Joe had hoped for a warmer response. He figured maybe he had some grovelling to do.

"I really did want to see you again, you know. I'm sorry. Honest," he said.

"Sure, if you're ever in this part of the country again, look me up."

"I'd like that."

"It's pretty far to keep a relationship going, Joe. You realize that, right?" Her voice had taken a softer turn.

"Oh, aye, sure. That's what I thought too." He was glad that she couldn't see the colour creeping up his face. He decided to change tracks before he made a total ass of himself.

"Anything new down there with the Graves and Harper cases?" he asked.

"We're just going round in circles here. Graves had no friends. Had no real enemies either. Nobody seemed to know him. Uniforms went door to door all around both crime scenes. They've sat through all of the CCTV footage from the casinos and poker rooms. No leads."

"What about forensics?"

"Hotel rooms are the very worst places to try and get forensic evidence. You know that. There's literally dozens of prints, hair samples, and other much less savoury things. They haven't come up with anything. Whoever killed them knew what they were doing. No traces."

"Are the Buckingham Poker gang still there?" Joe asked.

"No. They're gone now. We've checked each and every one of them, upside down and inside out. Gumbo, my partner, and Hank, the Montréal detective, went through all the CCTV in the casino and there's too many people coming and going to pin down a potential suspect. They tried our facial recognition program to see if there was one person who appeared multiple times within the time period we're interested in. Everyone who turned up more than once had a good reason for being there. Anyhow, enough shop talk. I have to get ready for work."

"Oh, right. You take care, Becky."

"You too, Joe. Keep in touch. Maybe a little later in the day though, if you don't mind?"

"Sorry 'bout th …" He heard the quiet click of her phone.

28

Joe grabbed his laptop and started walking to the office. He stopped to pick up a large coffee and a donut at a new café near the office. While he waited for the order, he texted Andrew.

Donegal? Lunch?

As the server was putting the wax-papered donut into the brown paper bag, Joe asked him to add a second one. He had forgotten Chantal was back, and she would never forgive him for eating a donut in front of her.

It had rained during the night and grey clouds were moving from west to east. Joe could still smell the peculiar metallic odour that sometimes occurs after a lightening storm. The sun was struggling to make an appearance.

Joe arrived at his office, pleased to see that Chantal was already there, sandaled feet parked on her desk, head buried in the morning Gazette. Le Journal was at the corner of her desk and her habit was to read that one during or after lunch. She held her hand out, palm upwards, her bejewelled nose not leaving the news of the day. He dropped the chocolate glazed donut into her open palm, and crossed the few feet back to his desk to eat his donut and wait for his laptop to finish loading. Glancing in Chantal's direction, he noticed the front page headline of her paper.

POKER PLAYER DROWNS OUTSIDE CASINO

Joe tiptoed around his desk and knelt down on the floor, in front of Chantal's, to read the story at eye level.

"That's so totally unnerving, Boss," she said, laying the paper down flat onto her desktop.

"Didn't want to disturb you. I know how you get at this time in the morning."

"You know how *I* get? *Me*? You're the one with the blood shot eyes, and the guilt donut. Rough night!?"

"Dropped by the Lounge for a while after dinner," he said. Chantal was doing the evil shrew impersonation that Joe hated and that always made him feel eight years old.

"After dinner, or for dinner?"

"Why do you sound like you already know the answer, Mom?"

"Because I know the answer, poker putz. I ran into Frankie this morning. You ate peanuts for dinner. Peanuts, Joe. They're antiques."

"Vintage, maybe. Had a big lunch yesterday, and a late one at that. Can I see the front page of your paper? Please?"

Chantal handed over the whole paper and got up to plug the kettle in to make tea.

"I'm finished with it now. Got in early today. What're all these notes you left on my desk?" she asked.

"A case we just got. Woman wants to find her brother. They were separated at a young age. Parents died and they were adopted out to different families. She hasn't had any luck tracing him. I thought it was something you could sink your pearly wee teeth into."

She tossed the last hunk of donut into her mouth, and stared at him suspiciously, until she'd finished chewing. After sucking her fingers clean she said, "This is the hot potato from the other day? She's a client?"

"The potato goes by the name of Kathleen Wentworth and yes, Chuck, she's our newest client. I've written down all the details I know. While I read the paper you can do an initial search with Vital Statistics in Ottawa. And try contacting my pal at Child Services to see if you can find anything there on the adoptions. You know the drill, hen," Joe said.

"Slice of pie, Boss. Slice of pumpkin pie."

29

Andrew stood at the top of the embankment, outside the Montréal casino, surveying the scene.

A perimeter had been cordoned off, yellow police tape wrapped around tree trunks, and tied to the legs of picnic tables that had been moved to the water's edge for that purpose. A bevy of police were pacing slowly, up and down the bank, performing the obligatory and monotonous clue search. They were studying the ground as if they'd all lost their contact lenses.

Less fortunate officers were doing the trickier search of the murky waters where the body had been found. The police photographer was packing up his gear. The body had been removed from the water but was still lying at the water's edge.

A few feet away from the water, on the grass, was a carefully folded shirt, two white sport socks, and a pair of red Vans sneakers. The coroner was sitting at one of the picnic benches. Andrew was happy to see it was Ginette, one of the coroners he had worked dozens of cases with over the years. She was his favourite. Ginette had a passion for details and great instincts that couldn't be taught. She was tapping feverishly on her tablet. Her hair—a rainbow of colours on a base of lemon yellow—was escaping from a ponytail and fluttering around her face in the breeze.

He approached the table and scrunched himself onto the bench across from her.

She continued typing for a minute, and then looked up, lowering her harlequin glasses to the tip of her nose.

"Andrew. It's been a while. How've you been?" Ginette was a francophone Montréaler but perfectly bilingual.

"Good, Ginette. Not too busy. You?"

"I've been on maternity leave for the last few months and I just returned to work last week. This is, in fact, my first case this year. You didn't miss me?" She smiled widely.

"Sorry. Went right out of my head. Little boy, right?"

"Oui. A cutie pie. Except for all the spit and poop. Bugger pissed in my face last night. Ray is taking paternity leave now and I can't wait to see how he manages."

Ray was a coroner as well, and the two of them had worked together for nearly five years before going out on a date. Slow to start a relationship, they got on with it rapidly. They were married within months, and pregnant within a year of that. They were known affectionately as the Odd Couple, for physical reasons as well as their characters. She was a young, hip and wacky woman in her early thirties. Ray was in his forties, and could have passed for an insurance salesman. Nice enough guy but nobody had ever seen him let his hair down. What little of it that there was since he was one step away from a comb-over. Andrew's mother would have labelled Ray as "prim and proper".

"What do we know about the vic, Ginette?"

"Eric something or other. His wallet was in his jeans. There was money in it and plenty of ID. He's 22. Lieutenant Lecavalier can fill you in on all that. If you're looking for him he's set up a room in the casino to interview staff to see if anyone knew the guppy. I overheard him directing his men to get footage from the cameras, inside and out, as well. Your partner, Hank, is up there too. He arrived half an hour ago."

"Cause of death?"

"You know better than to ask that, Andrew. And don't ask me for time of death either. Won't know for sure till I get him back. There's no evidence of a struggle. No bruising. No visible entry wounds. I should know more by the end of the day."

"Who called it in, Ginette?" He looked around and saw Lecavalier crab-walk down the slope and join some of his men at the water's edge.

"A casino security guard. He was doing his rounds. He saw the clothing on the ground, so came down to take a look. Then he saw the body. Swears he didn't touch anything except for one sneaker."

"I'll go talk to Lecavalier. Call me later, yeah?"

"When I know anything."

Andrew watched them bag the body and carry it up to Ginette's van. He walked towards Lecavalier, who was placing the clothes and sneakers into an evidence bag. One of the other officers was retrieving what appeared to be a wine bottle from the water, a few feet from where the body had lain, and was stuffing it into another evidence bag.

Andrew joined Lecavalier as he was speaking to the casino security guard. The guard was an older man, well on his way to becoming bald, with some grey stubble sprouting along his jagged jawline. His belt was cinched tight around his hips and trying its best to support his beer belly. The belly was winning the fight.

"We get a lot of muggings out here if someone has won big and flashes it around. The fact that he has a player's card, well, someone's bound to know the kid."

"You haven't seen him around?" asked Lecavalier, exchanging nods with Andrew.

"Me? No. I'd tell you if I did. But we have a machine in the office… Security Office. We can run his player's card through that and see where and when he played here. Even how much chips he bought and how many he cashed out when he left. That'll give you something to go on, right?"

"Any cameras out here?" Andrew asked, ignoring the guard's question.

"Nothing past the entrance doors, no. But we'll have him everywhere he's been when he was inside." He shook his head slowly back and forth and stared at the bag of clothes that Lecavalier was holding. "There's only been four murders here since we opened nearly thirty years ago. Muggings, yeah…all the time. Suicide…that's popular too. But not murders. Christ. I've found a lot of shit out here in the years I've worked. Five years now. Condoms. Needles. Cell phones. All kinds of clothing. A gun once. I hand everything in, you know? Some knives too. Never a body. I mean, I've found bodies down here but they're alive. You know, doin' stuff? Not dead like this one. Not half-naked and dead."

30

Joe felt his phone vibrating against his thigh. By the time he put his coffee mug down on the desk, contorted enough to retrieve the phone from his front pants pocket, and flick open the screen, he saw Andrew's name as it disappeared. He was contemplating whether or not to call him back when there was a single pulsating burst announcing a text arrival.

Lounge in 1 hour. U free?

Joe shot back a quick affirmation and glanced over at Chantal. "Making any headway with the Wentworth case, Chuck?"

"Nothing yet. Give me some time, Boss. You only gave it to me yesterday for Bob's sake. I've sent off a few emails to Ottawa. No one has responded yet."

"Pete."

"Huh?"

"Pete. It's for Pete's sake. Not Bob's."

"Really? You think so? I was sure it was Bob."

"Why don't you go for lunch now and then I'll go when you get back?"

"Not hungry yet. You go now. I'll go later."

"I have a meeting later. A lunch meeting."

"Nothing in your colander 'bout that." Chantal glided across the pine floor on her rolling office chair, making it all the way to the tea wagon from her desk in one firm push and a few foot scuffles. She refilled her cup and then waved the half full teapot in the air using one finger to point at Joe questioningly. She didn't use the usual index finger.

"Since when do I report to you?" asked Joe. "Go for lunch, Chuck. Be back here in one hour."

"Oh, cripes. Somebody got up on the wrong side of the bed today. Funny, that, considering you have the choice of either side. Or is that the reason you're such a grouchy Grinch?"

Joe walked over to her desk, grabbed her tea cup, and emptied it into his own. "Now you've only got 55 minutes left for lunch."

She opened her bottom drawer. Taking her Roots backpack out and slinging it over her shoulders, she stomped loudly and childlike across the room, flinging the door open and slamming it behind her. Joe watched her prance down the street, wobbling slightly on her heels, towards Boulevard René-Lévesque.

An hour came and went without Chantal returning. Joe waited another few minutes and then switched the window sign to closed and left, locking the door behind him. He hoped she had her set of keys in her backpack.

Turning south on the sidewalk, the same direction as the one Chantal had taken, he arrived 20 seconds later at the door of the Lounge. Opening the door to a blast of cold air and the intricate guitar solo from Stairway to Heaven, Joe spotted Andy, alone in one of the booths, eating a slice of pizza.

The Lounge didn't serve any food—except for the peanuts—but Frankie kept a stash of restaurant menus at the bar so that he and his patrons could have food delivered. Joe slid onto the leatherette bench, facing Andrew, and grabbed a slice of all-dressed from the large open box on the table.

"Frankie! Can I get a beer over here?"

"Do I look like a damn waitress?" Frankie bent down to the fridge, retrieved and twisted the top off of a Molson and set it down with a loud plunk on the bar, returning to the newspaper's daily crossword puzzle.

Joe got up and took the bottle, sliding a glass off the suspended wire rack overhead, and returned to their booth.

"What's up, my boy? News on the Harper kid?"

"You see anything about the casino death?"

"I saw something in the paper about a body found there, yeah. Why? What's the story?"

"A young guy drowned in that little creeky thing right beside the casino. Definitely not a suicide. Face up in a few inches of water. Half-naked."

"Any suspects?"

Andrew ignored the question. "The kid played some blackjack early in the evening. Then poker. Lost a freakin' bundle at both. How the hell do kids afford to do that? How does anyone afford to do that?"

"I don't know, mate. Everybody makes choices."

"Anyhow, Ginette just called me. You remember Ginette? The coroner?" He waited until Joe nodded. "You ready for this? Ketamine in the bloodstream."

"You're not suggesting there's a link to the Vegas killings, are you? That would be odd, to say the least."

"We're not saying anything… yet. There was some other potential evidence left at the scene. It's being analyzed now."

"What sort of evidence?"

"Joe, it may come to nothing. I don't want to speculate. We'll know in a few days." He put his crescent of crust back in the box and took another slice. "Have to run some DNA and see if there's a match in the system."

"Have you talked with anyone in Vegas? Like Becky?"

"The Chief is handling that part of it. We've been told just to concentrate on the vic here for now. I just wanted to give you a heads up. Unofficial. Keep your distance."

"Distance from what?"

"Not from what. From who. Newcross."

"Andrew. What the hell do you mean? What's going on?"

"I don't know what to tell you, man. They're investigating. There's no evidence that any of the deaths were perpetrated by Rebecca. However, there's one glaring fact that nobody can ignore. She was in Vegas for the first two murders. She was here in Montréal for this one at the casino. We have no motive yet, but cause of death seems clearly related. All three involved gambling, drowning, and Ketamine."

"You mentioned a DNA test. What have you got?" Joe dropped the pizza slice back into the box and his hands formed into fists.

"A hair…a blond hair. It was caught on a button of the vic's shirt."

"It still doesn't make sense. C'mon, mate. I've spent time with her. So have you. She's a gentle soul. There's no way she'd do anything like this."

Andrew pried apart another slice of pizza, and Joe waved to Frankie, hoping for a refill, but Frankie simply nonchalantly waved back and returned to his newspaper.

"Joe, I'm lead investigator on this one. I can't just say, "Well folks, me and Joe had a few beers with the chick. Joe even has a crush on her. So she must be cool. Ignore the facts, boys." Chrissake, you know how it works! We haven't had any bloody leads at all. But finally we have a hell of a coincidence. We're gonna look into it, Joe. We'd be insane not to, so there's a background check going on as we speak. We're gonna see what we pull off the cameras at the casino too. If she was there, we'll find her."

Joe slid out of the booth, grabbed his half-eaten slice of pizza, plunked a five dollar bill down on the table and turned towards the door. "Call me when you get leads on the real killer," he shot back, and walked out.

*

He tossed the slice of pizza into a refuse container outside of the Lounge. He reached his office door and saw Chantal through the window, talking on the phone. He opened the door, waved at her and sat behind his desk, opening his laptop to check emails. There were four that had come in while he was with Andy. One from Kathleen. One from Chantal. Two offering to make his willy bigger.

He clicked open the one from Chantal. It just said *Sorry Boss, xox.* He blew a kiss over to her and she appeared to catch it, but dropped her phone in the midst of the highly acrobatic manoeuvre. She didn't seem to understand that the thrown kiss was not a real object. He never tired of it. She scooped up the receiver, saying, "I'll call you back later, Tom," and returned it to the cradle. Joe figured Tom must be her latest conquest and returned to his screen to open the email from Kathleen. Chantal went back to searching the Birth section of the online Canadian Vital Statistics Index.

Dear Joe, Please call me if you get any news regarding my brother. Or for any other reason.

Joe wrote back to her right away. *Hi K, Have begun the investigation. No results yet. Will call you soon. Cheers, J.* He sat back and thought about Becky. He couldn't entertain the idea of her committing these murders. He went over conversations he had had with her, over the past few weeks, looking for some clue or indication that she could be capable of being a killer. A serial killer to boot. Nothing. Sure, she didn't approve of gambling. But that disapproval made up the philosophy of most of the population of America. Nearly everyone he knew thought that gambling was an atrocious illness that was weaned, nurtured and fed by greedy moguls, mafia, and government agencies.

He closed his eyes and listened to the clickety clack of Chantal's pointy little nails hitting the keyboard of her computer. He was about to doze off as the hypnotic clicking stopped.

"Guess how many Roberts were born in Ottawa in the year 1975?"

"No clue." Joe said.

"C'mon, guess."

"24,500."

"Don't be silly! That's such a ridiculous number. That would be like every woman in Ottawa naming their kid Robert."

"So how many were there?"

"31".

"That's not so many then."

"I have to track down 31 people! And probably some of them have moved, you know?"

"Tackle this logically. Go back to the Birth section of the vital statistics register, but for the year 1977. Find a Kathleen born. Find the same last name as one of the 31 Roberts, and Bob's your uncle.

"Steven."

"Pardon me?"

"Mon oncle. Steven is my uncle. My Mom's brother. My Dad didn't have any brothers. He had a couple sisters though. Why are you bringing him up anyhow?"

"Oh, for Pete's sake, woman. Get back to work. Or for Bob's sake. Either one of them. I don't care."

Chantal shook her head like a wet dog and went back to clicking on her keyboard. Joe turned his chair around, put his feet up on the window sill, closed his eyes and tried to work through everything that had gone on since Kelly Harper had walked in his office. When he opened his eyes again, Chantal had disappeared. There was a large pink post it on his computer screen.

Didn't want to disturb your much needed beauty sleep. I have a hot date. Knew you'd understand. You've read about them maybe. See ya tomorrow. Chuck.

He checked his watch to discover it was nearly 7:00 p.m. He thought of calling Becky, but would need to talk to Andrew first. Trouble was, he wasn't in the mood to talk to Andrew again.

He walked over to Chantal's desk to see if she had pulled in any results. There was a print out of all the Roberts but no corresponding list of Kathleens. There was, however, a pad of paper beside the list with a few sketchy pencil portraits of what appeared to be dead fat men at their desks. One had a sword pierced through his head. Another had a dagger protruding from his chest. The third had a phone cord noose spiralling around his neck. Suspiciously, they were all wearing kilts. And, on the off chance he didn't recognize himself, she'd scrawled along the bottom; *My Boss— resting in pieces.*

31

"This is fucking bullshit, Gumbo! The chief has put me on time-out pending Montréal's forensic results. What the crap is that about? They actually could think that I worked all day, and on my way to the airport, dropped by the casino to drown some stupid little poker know-it-all? Fuck this shit!" Her face was as red as the sunburned tourists on the Strip and each expletive was accompanied by her clenched fists hitting her desk.

"Calm down, Becks. You know how this works. Give it a few days. They'll get their results. You'll be clear and back here sweating with the rest of us. You've got a couple days off. I'd trade with you if I could."

Rebecca began throwing things from her desk drawer into her knapsack. She kicked her metal trash can clear across the small office they shared. "I'm so fucking angry I could kill a penguin."

"Nice talk, girl. Go home. Put your feet up and forget about this shit. It's just a formality. Nothing to get so flamin' worked up about. You're carrying on like a piglet in the waiting room of a pork crackling factory."

"The chief, and the bozos from upstairs, interrogated me as if they actually believed I might have done it! I mean, Gumbo, honestly, how could they do that?"

"They have to do it by the book, Becks, you know that. Get yourself home. You'll be cleared as soon as the DNA results come back. That's all they've got."

She glared at him until he bowed his head and began corralling all the paper clips atop his desk. She stuffed her file of the murder investigation into her bag. He was about to warn her about the appropriateness of removing it from the office but thought better of it when he saw the look in her eyes. She was looking for another object to kick and he preferred to not be it. He knew there was no way he could convince her of the recklessness of her decision. He'd probably do the same if he was in her boat.

"That's me. I'm outta here. I'm counting on you to give me a heads up whenever you get any news. Right?" She tossed her laptop and phone into her bag and stood at the door. "Right, Gumbo?"

"Understood, ma'am."

She left, slamming the door behind her. He'd give her a few hours to stew and then drop by on his way home to check up on her. Maybe bring a six-pack over and help her let off steam.

Gumbo went over the files for the umpteenth time. Devil was in the details—he kept repeating to himself like a mantra. Something had to tie these murders together aside from Becky's attendance in both cities. She was like a baby sister to him and he had no doubt that her sole involvement was the investigation of the deaths— certainly not the perpetration of them.

He was in the midst of comparing cell phone records of the two victims found in Vegas. If there were any further correlating factors between the two men, it was in what they didn't have as opposed to what they had. Neither of them had much cellular activity to speak of. It was the same with each of their email accounts. Neither of them maintained any sort of social media account. All they shared, apart from their cause of death, was a lack of friends.

*

Rebecca arrived home, stopping to pick up a bottle of wine from a liquor outlet near the police station and a bucket of four-alarm wings from the BBQ joint at the corner of her street.

She opened the door to her condo, and dumped her packages and knapsack on the kitchen counter. She started up the air conditioner. It wouldn't take more than a few minutes to feel the benefit of the cooled air.

The condo was small, a one bedroom open concept plan in a three story clapboard building at the edge of downtown. It was sparsely, but comfortably, decorated. Leaned more to the shabby side of shabby-chic. She'd bought mostly second hand furniture over her years of being on her own.

Her parents had given her some furniture from her childhood bedroom and a few odds and ends to help her out. They weren't that well-off themselves, retired and living across the border in small town Arizona. They had paid her tuition to attend the police academy, even though they weren't thrilled about her choice of profession.

When she got the job offer a few years ago from Las Vegas, they were heartbroken and extremely vocal about their feelings. Her Dad was terrified she'd be killed in some mafia war. Her Mom thought she'd fall in love with some dashing outlaw and eventually go on the run to Mexico and never be heard from again. She knew that they both secretly hoped that police work was a phase she would outgrow.

She unscrewed the wine and carried the bottle, a glass, the bucket of chicken, and a damp tea towel for her fingers, into the living room, setting it all on the coffee table. Better to switch on the TV remote before her fingers got sticky.

She took a long sip of the cheap California chardonnay and clicked over to the news channel. There was a press conference going on downtown with her Chief, Captain Wellsboro, standing at the podium set up in the station's media room. She missed what the question had been, but Wellsboro looked down at his papers, took a sip of water, and answered, "We have no indications that these two crimes are related. There are similarities but, at this point, we don't want to speculate. We are definitely keeping an open mind, but not ruling out the possibility. We're still examining and analyzing a great deal of forensic evidence and—I must stress—we are optimistic that these results will answer a lot of our own questions and ultimately lead both of these investigations in a more concrete direction. I can assure you that we are extremely confident regarding finding the perpetrator, or perpetrators, of both these crimes. We are following some solid leads and are confident in our team of investigators."

"Fucking asshole!" Rebecca threw a chicken bone at the TV screen, switched the remote off, and topped up her wine.

32

Joe sat on his balcony after finishing off yet another Chinese takeaway meal of Pineapple Chicken, Hoisin Shrimp, and Fried Spinach. He brought the empty containers into the kitchen, leaving them on the counter.

He hadn't felt this confused about so many things since high school exams. He didn't know whether to call Kathleen or wait until he had some news of her brother. He didn't know whether to call Andy after yelling at him over lunch. He didn't know whether to call Becky in case he was all wrong about her. Chantal? She was too daft. That left him with three choices: he could stay at home and drink the few remaining beers in the fridge and stew over all the things making his life topsy-turvy, he could go to the Lounge, be abused by Frankie and maybe watch a baseball game on the bar TV, or he could call his ex-wife who was a great sounding board and would probably give him some advice that he wouldn't take.

She picked up on the second ring.

"Anna, it's me. You busy?"

"I have a few minutes. Heading out soon to see a client with a decorating dilemma. She wants a nursery for a baby but it has to be asexual. The room, not the baby. No pinks. No blues. No wallpaper with ballerinas or trucks. She even asked if I could–"

"Fascinating. But I called to talk about my dilemmas," Joe said.

"Of course you did, darling. I just wanted to see how far I'd get into mine without you interrupting. I'm impressed. Further than usual. I only have two minutes to give you. The client lives here in the building but I don't like being late. You know that. So—this little problem of yours—what's her name?"

"Becky," he said. "And Kathleen," he added while he walked over to the fridge to retrieve a Corona. He tucked the phone between his shoulder and ear as he popped the top and poured it into a glass.

"Drinking alone again?"

"Get yourself a glass of wine if you're feeling righteous." He heard the tell-tale pour of what was probably an exorbitantly priced bottle of Merlot.

"I wouldn't be drinking alone though," she said. "Grant is here with me. So tell me. What have you done?" He could envision Anna settling into her sofa, rolling her eyes at her husband, and taking a delicate sip of wine.

"I met a lovely woman in Las Vegas last week. Becky. Blond. Blue eyes. Funny. Great in bed. She might be a serial killer," taking a slug of beer as he let her digest the news.

"You were in Vegas last week?"

"That's what you got from that? Yes, I was in Vegas last week investigating a suspicious suicide for a client here in Montréal. Which turned out to be a murder."

"Murdered by someone who you then decided to date."

"She's the investigating cop. The bit about her being a murderer is only a theory at the moment. Not my theory, by the by, in any shape or form. Circumstantial evidence stuff. I'm not persuaded.

Far from it, in fact," he said, unfortunately coming across as if he was trying to convince himself as well as Anna.

"And the other one? Kathleen? Arsonist? Armed robber?" she asked.

"Neither that I'm aware of. I just met her as well, last week. She's a psychiatrist here in Montréal. She runs her practice out of her home near Westmount Park. Posh, gorgeous and an animal in bed."

"Offhand I'd say she sounds like the better choice. Having a psychiatrist at your fingertips is a definite bonus."

"That's exactly what Andrew said."

"So what's your problem? Or is this more of a blatant bragging call?"

"Shit, Anna. You know I trust your opinion. I'd like you to meet them. Of course, Becky is back in Vegas right now and possibly soon under custody, but could you invite me and Kathleen over for dinner next week?" Joe asked.

"Still too cheap to take a woman out on a proper dinner date I see," she said.

"There's not a restaurant in Montréal that can hold a candle to your culinary skills. Honestly, I'd like you to meet her."

"I'll check my diary and we'll set something up. Maybe for next weekend. I'll get back to you about it."

"Brilliant. I'll bring wine."

"Yes, you will. I'll let you know what wines to pick up," she said.

"Yessir," he answered. After he hung up the phone, he decided to luge-train on the sofa and watch an old videotape of Celtic winning the European Cup in 1967 in Lisbon. Two hours later he shuffled from the living room to the bedroom, threw his clothes off, and went to bed.

33

Joe woke up to his alarm clock at 8:00 a.m., having slept fitfully on and off all night. After taking a long hot shower, he dressed and stepped out onto the balcony. Judging by the little pools of water on the chair seats, it had rained during the night, but now the sun was up and the temperature felt like perfect mid-twenties. All the humidity had disappeared.

He re-entered the condo through the living room door and went to the kitchen to make toast. He cut a thick slab of sharp cheddar, covered that with Branston chutney, and ate his breakfast sandwich during the uphill walk to work. By the time he turned onto de la Montagne, he had finished it and was busy flicking crumbs off his T-shirt.

Passing the Lounge, which was still three hours away from opening, Joe noticed the morning newspaper resting outside the door. He calmly strolled over to the door, bent down to retrieve the paper, and continued on his way to his own office. It was still early so Chantal hadn't arrived yet. He made a pot of coffee and settled into reading Frankie's Gazette.

Chantal arrived about twenty minutes later and immersed herself back into the hunt for Robert Wentworth.

Shortly before lunchtime, Joe phoned Kathleen to see if she was up to having a proper real date anytime soon—like tonight. The phone went immediately to voicemail so he left a brief message that included an invitation to dinner and drinks and a request for her to get back to him. As he was tidying up his desk, before heading out for lunch, his mobile rang and it was Kathleen.

"Kathleen, cheers for calling back. I was hoping to take you out for dinner. Somewhere posh and overpriced, in Old Montréal. Wine that doesn't come in a box. That sort of place. What do you think?"

"Sounds wonderful, but I have an even better idea. It's such a beautiful day, and the fireworks are on tonight at La Ronde. What do you say to a picnic? My last patient is at 3:00 p.m., so I can pick up the food. You can be in charge of getting champagne. We'll make a night of it."

"Perfect, but it's always so crowded at the Port when the fireworks are on. Where can we meet? Do you know a good spot?"

"You know so little about me, dear man. I have a surprise for you. You mentioned your fondness for watercraft. Well, I happen to own such a thing and it's docked at the Port."

"You have a boat and I'm only hearing about it now? What kind is it, woman?"

"It's what you'd call a cabin cruiser, I suppose. Not large, but certainly comfortable enough for two. It's in the Bassin de l'Horloge. Where the old Clock Tower is. There's a staircase at the eastern tip of Rue Port de Montréal. Turn up at the locked gate there around seven o'clock. I'll keep an eye out for you and come up to get you. Do you know the area well?"

"Of course I do. I stand up there often, drooling down onto the yachts."

Kathleen laughed—a laugh that was full and happy—and that he could listen to for hours. "Will you do something for me?"

"Name it, Skipper. Anything."

"While you're eating and sipping champagne on a boat in the Marina, there are hundreds of tourists gawking over the rail from the boardwalk."

"I know. As I mentioned, I'm normally one of them."

"Yes, the drooler. I thought I had recognized you. Well, my dear, you have a few hours to practice your nonchalant look. You have to look totally disinterested and ever so slightly bored of pouring flutes of champagne day in and day out," she giggled girlishly, yet somehow, at the same time, provocatively.

"It won't be easy, but at least I have some time to work on my world-weary sophisticated look. I'll do my best, but I'll bring a handkerchief just in case some drool leaks out. See you at seven sharp." He hung up the phone and glanced over at Chantal, who was resting her chin in her hands, elbows dug into her desktop, staring at him.

"This sounds good. Your half of the conversation was thrilling. What's up, Boss?"

"Life gets better and better, my little bunny rabbit. She has a freakin' yacht."

"Are you serious? A yacht?"

"Indeedy do, I am. What do you think of this as a blasé done-it-all-before look?" Joe stared up at the ceiling, eyes half closed and lips pursed.

"It's not a look that works well for you. You look constipated." Chantal shook her head slowly back and forth and resumed her search. "Boss, I think I may have found her!"

He jumped up and ran over, pushing his chair along in front him, and plunked himself down beside her. "What did you find?"

"There's a Robert Oxford born at Grace Hospital in Ottawa in 1975. Lo and behold, we have a Kathleen Oxford, also born at Grace, in 1977. There's a couple other name matches, but the years are slightly off. And there's one that's the right years but the baby girl is Catherine. So I've written them down in the file, but I would bet my bottom quarter on these two babies. Wouldn't you?"

"I most certainly would—maybe even a dollar. So try and find a Robert Oxford in all the usual places. If nothing turns up, you could run a search on the deaths of the Oxford couple, around 1981 plus or minus, and see if that gives us any leads."

"Gotcha. I'll work my ass off while you can practice your funny faces."

"Good job, Chuck. I also have to go and buy champagne. I'll go for lunch now and hit up the liquor store. So I may be a bit longer than my usual hour." Joe walked his chair back to his desk, turned his laptop off, and headed out the door, humming the theme from Popeye.

"You've never had a usual hour since I've worked here!" Chantal yelled as the door closed behind him.

34

Joe walked up to Saint-Catherine Street. It was lunchtime and thousands of people were bustling in and out of restaurant doorways. He decided to go to the SAQ first and get the champagne and then he would grab a bite to eat somewhere. Maybe even bring it back to the office to see how Chantal was getting along with the search for Robert. He was excited at the prospect of having some positive results to report to Kathleen tonight.

He arrived at the champagne section of the SAQ and chose a bottle of Bollinger's Brut from the chilled cabinet. Before he got to the cash register, he doubled back and picked up a second bottle. With luck, they might even have something to celebrate. Joe was really looking forward to this. He hadn't been on a boat since his Glasgow days and back then, he was drinking Bovril, not champagne.

He reconsidered working this afternoon. He'd have lunch at the brewpub on the corner, check in at the office to see how Chantal was getting on, and then get home to relax, shower and find something mature and cultured to wear. He could keep the bottles chilled while he got ready.

*

After lunch he got back to the office and realized he'd better stay while Chantal went for lunch or he'd never hear the end of it. She still hadn't found any further vital records of Robert Oxford. He was tempted to have a go at it himself but knew she'd blow her top if he completed what she'd spent days on. So he amused himself playing some on-line poker. By the time Chantal returned, shortly before 2:00 p.m., he had won enough to cover the cost of one of the Bollinger's. He felt his winning boded well.

Chantal was very keen on her investigation. She didn't often get to work on anything more than filing, sending out bills, and banking. But so far there was no sign of Robert on Facebook, LinkedIn, Twitter, or any of the other popular social websites.

Years ago the phone directory used to be a simple method of finding someone. But now, with mobile phones, fewer and fewer people had landlines. There was a real probability that Kathleen's brother had also been adopted and his name changed.

"Chuck, I'm heading home now," Joe said, leaving his laptop on the desk, but taking his phone and retrieving the champagne from the tiny bar fridge under the coffee machine table.

"You go on. I'll check with your pal at Vital whether we can get into adoption records."

"Right. Kathleen might have to request that herself, but give it a shot. Another thing you can do is go online to the Ottawa newspaper archives. Their parents were in some tragic car accident coming home from a Christmas party—that could have made headlines. Check obits as well. We could possibly get names of aunts and uncles, friends, family priest. Who knows? Text me if you find out anything worthwhile."

"Aye-Aye, Captain Crunch. You go have fun. Work on that sexy look a bit more."

"So you admit it was a bit sexy?"

"Sure. In a backwoods trailer-park kind of way. Seriously though. Go. Have fun. I'll keep at it. You'll owe me an arm and a foot in overtime pay. See you tomorrow."

"Thanks, hen. You're doing a grand job. I may just keep you." Joe reached into his top desk drawer, pulled out a little package of Pop Rocks and tossed it across to her desk. It was Chantal's favourite treat and Joe saved packages of them for special occasions. As he closed the door he heard her delighted squeals.

35

Joe arrived home half an hour later. He lay on the sofa and began to watch reruns of his all-time favourite TV show, *Only Fools and Horses*, but he fell asleep at the beginning of the third episode and woke to the closing theme song. He checked his watch and saw it was nearly 5:30 p.m. He just had enough time to shower, change, and walk to the Old Port.

He settled on cream-coloured Dockers, a white T-shirt, and a chocolate brown linen short-sleeved shirt that he left casually unbuttoned. He added a pair of white sneakers that were as close as he had to deck shoes.

After donning a pair of Oakley sunglasses and a vintage Glasgow Celtic baseball cap, he retrieved the chilled champagne bottles, wrapped each of them in a dish towel, carefully slid them into a backpack, and set out for his walk to the marina.

He stopped halfway to buy a bag of ice and a 6-pack of Heineken. He reached Place Jacques Cartier—Montréal's original town square and farmer's market—and stopped at a flower kiosk to buy a bouquet of white freesias. He arrived at his destination five minutes early.

From the top of the stairway leading down to the pier, he saw Kathleen stepping from the pier to the deck of a boat. It seemed as if she had just arrived as well. She was wearing butter-coloured gaucho trousers, a white silk loose-fitting shirt, and a fedora—very Katherine Hepburn. He watched her set down a large straw picnic hamper. Without looking up, she went into the cabin. He had no way of getting through the locked gate so he sat down on a wooden bench to wait.

Within minutes she was back, her eyes scanning the boardwalk overhead. She waved up to him and ascended the stairway, unlocked the metal gate, put her hands on his shoulders and gave him a kiss on the cheek.

"You look spectacular," he said, following behind her on the staircase. She glanced back at him, smiling happily, and gave him an approving once over.

"And you, Sir, are looking very fetching."

They reached the pier and she ran on ahead like a schoolgirl. Joe took a closer look at the boat. He had been too dazzled by Kathleen to take it all in before. She was a vintage Mathis Trumpy yacht, probably built prior to WWII. She was well over 50 feet in length and had a freshly painted ivory-white wooden hull. The cabin was as polished as the Queen's silver and the decks looked like teak. All the fittings, brightwork and railings were glistening brass.

They stepped onto the deck at the aft of the boat and Kathleen offered him the grand tour. They entered the main cabin, which had cushioned bench seating and a bar, before they descended a circular staircase. A heady scent of potpourri hung in the air. There was a galley on the right and a head, nearly as large as his ensuite at home, on the left. Teak stowage cabinets were crammed into every available space.

Kathleen opened a large door past the galley cupboards and they entered a spacious and elegant saloon. There was an emerald-green leather sofa and loveseat and a few vintage teak side tables. Another door opened to a luxurious stateroom where a king size bed was the focal point. Teak cabinetry flanked and surrounded the bed frame. The only light in the room was filtered in through partially closed venetian blinds covering the portholes. She took his hand and pulled him back into the galley.

"I'm impressed. Beyond words," he said. He removed his backpack and handed her the champagne, beer, and flowers.

"Come back up to the deck. We'll open one of these bottles and enjoy what little remains of this glorious sunshine. Or would you prefer one of those beers?" she asked.

"I'll join you in that bottle. We may even have something to celebrate soon," he said. He shoogled the cork back and forth with one hand until it popped. A festive spray of champagne erupted from the neck and she handed him a small towel hanging from the galley cupboard.

"What are we celebrating, Joe? I'm intrigued." They walked back up the steps to the outside and settled into two cushioned teak deck chairs. Joe set the bottle down on a small carved wooden table between the chairs.

"My assistant, Chantal, is chasing down a few leads in finding your brother."

"You're not serious! You've found something? Already? Tell me! This is fantastic." She put her glass down and clapped her hands, leaning forward until they were practically nose to nose. "I can't wait. What have you discovered?"

"Does the surname Oxford mean anything to you?"

Kathleen closed her eyes and lifted her chin up towards the sky. He watched her as she mulled the name over in her head. She was as silent as sleep and didn't move a muscle. Her head gave a little shiver and her eyes opened. "Nothing. Is that definitely my name? It has no effect on me whatsoever. I expected that whenever I heard my name, I'd recognize it."

"I must admit, I thought you would as well, but you were young. We're basing this on the fact that there was a Robert Oxford born in 1975 and a Kathleen Oxford born in 1977, in Ottawa. Chantal is at the office trying to get more details and will text or phone me if she uncovers anything. At this point, it's just the name registration index that she has, and the dates and given names make sense."

"Kathleen and Robert Oxford. It does have a good ring to it though, don't you think?" She sat back on the deck chair, quietly sipping her champagne. "Oh, I forgot the hors d'oeuvres downstairs." She set her glass down on the table. "Refill that for me while I'm gone, will you?" Before leaving she leaned down and gave Joe a soft lingering kiss. It hinted at the near future.

She slowly turned away and went through the cabin door. He could hear the clatter of cutlery. Music drifted up the steps to him. She had turned a radio or iPod on, gentle classical music. He couldn't identify the composer but knew he had heard it before. Joe's phone pinged. There was a message from Chantal.

Bingo. Adoption 1982 Kathleen Oxford to Wentworth. Nada for Robert yet.

Keep trying.

Getting any yet?

Go back 2 work.

Kathleen arrived, tray in hand, as Joe put his phone down on the table between them. "That was Chantal. She confirmed the Oxford name. She obtained an adoption entry for you by the Wentworths."

"And Robert?"

"Nothing's turned up on him yet. Don't worry. We'll get there."

"Oh, Joe. I have to find him. I get this horrible feeling that something is wrong. It's so deep inside of me. I'm worried for him and I can't explain it. You will find him, won't you?"

Instead of sitting on her own deck chair she approached Joe and sat on his lap. She set the tray down on the table. There were three small crystal bowls, filled to the brim with caviar. One black, one red, one green. There was a bone white plate covered with tiny cornmeal pancakes, the size of a nickel. She picked up a pancake, scooped some caviar onto it and guided it to his lips. The flavours burst together in his mouth. "Come downstairs with me. I have a sudden urge to express my gratitude."

36

Chantal finally found an entry in VS for Robert Oxford. But it wasn't an adoption. It was a death. December 20th, 1981. Death by drowning. She didn't know of any way of getting further details without applying for the death certificate and the processing would take a few days. She found the website link for the Canadian Newspaper Archives. A tragic death like this had to have made headlines. It also must have been around the time of the car accident that killed the Oxford parents. So she could hunt for that as well. Joe had said that they were driving home from a company Christmas party.

She opened the archive website and entered *Ottawa Oxford Christmas 1981* into the search engine. There were hundreds of results; everything from an advertisement for a pre-Christmas shoe sale to an article about an Oxford University student visiting his family in Ottawa for the holidays. Chantal continued scrolling down the list until she reached the headline:

Tragedy Strikes Entire Family in Sandy Hill.

She began to read the piece. Before she'd reached the second paragraph she realized she was holding her breath and feeling wobbly. She had trouble swallowing. She tore through the rest of it and reached for her phone.

37

Kathleen slid her arm out from underneath Joe's back. He looked so peaceful, so she decided to go up top, tidy the mess they'd made, and put together another tray to bring out while they watched the fireworks display from the comfort of the boat. There was still half an hour before it would be sufficiently dark for them to begin. They'd be close enough to the exhibition to be able to hear the accompanying music blasting from the powerful outdoor speakers. She'd let Joe nap until then.

The ice cubes in the silver bucket had melted but the water still felt cool when she dipped her finger in, so she dunked the half empty champagne bottle back in. Joe's cell phone was sitting on the table. When she picked it up the screen came to life and she saw he had three text messages and two voicemails—all from Chantal.

The anticipation was too much for her to bear, and she was sure Joe wouldn't mind if she peeked at the texts. He would understand how important any update would be to her. He was a fine man and wanted to please her. She couldn't believe her luck in meeting him. She hadn't ever felt this safe and happy with a man.

She stared down at the tiny screen and read the first message.

Call me now. Big problem.

The second text was directly below the first one.

Call me boss.

The third text said **OPEN ASAP** and had an attachment. Kathleen's hands began to shake. She clicked on it and saw the headline. Her heart fluttered in her chest like a moth trapped in a light fixture. She sat down on the deck chair with the phone cradled in the palm of her hands. Clouds were gusting into her head and her entire body was trembling. She saw the headline and knew in her soul that she didn't want to know what was written there.

She began to read.

38

Chantal phoned Andrew. Joe wasn't responding to text messages and his phone was going directly to voicemail. Andrew's phone also went to voicemail but she knew he was diligent about picking up his messages. She went over to Joe's desk in hopes of finding contact information about Kathleen.

There was a vintage Filofax on his desktop. He didn't write in it but he often inserted and taped business cards into the proper letter of the alphabet. Her fingers flicked their way to *W* and she was immediately rewarded with a pale blue business card. Kathleen Wentworth. There was a phone number but no address. She phoned the number and after one ring a robotic male voice announced the clinic schedule and instructed that all messages would be responded to during regular clinic hours but if there was an emergency to please go to the nearest hospital. There was a further instruction that if you were a patient of Dr. Wentworth's and in urgent need of help, to use the confidential number that had been provided during the first therapy session.

Chantal hunted around Joe's desk to see if she could find any other phone number for the Doctor—nothing. Chantal's phone rang. She ran back to her desk. "Chantal. Andrew here. What the hell is going on, girl?"

"Joe is with that Wentworth bitch."

"I've never heard him refer to her in quite that manner. Explain."

"I'm running a search for her long lost brother, right? Supposedly they were adopted after their parents were killed in a car crash," she said. She tried to get her thoughts in the right order. They were whizzing around her head like Formula One racing cars at the track.

"Right."

"Wrong. I found a newspaper article in the archives. Short story is the father kills the mother and brother. A neighbour hears a young girl screaming and calls the cops."

"Bloody hell. How did he kill them?"

"It doesn't give all the details, but drowning in a bathtub was mentioned," she said. "But Wentworth hired us to find her brother. So she lied to Joe. But why? Je ne comprends pas. This isn't making sense to me."

There was dead silence on the other end of the line. Chantal couldn't even hear Andrew breathing and thought the connection must have broken off. "Andrew, you there?"

"How old was she when it happened?"

"Four."

"She probably doesn't remember, Chantal. That's a severe trauma for a baby. Your mind blocks out memories like that if it can."

"Joe's not answering his cell. He's out with her now."

"Where are they?"

"No idea. Apparently she has some extraordinary boat and they've gone off on that. He left here earlier with champagne." Chantal had trouble catching her breath, she was talking too fast. "I don't know if he was going to her place first or not. I tried calling the number I have for her but it's her office and it's closed. Joe isn't answering his phone. Why would she lie to Joe?"

"Don't worry, sweetie. I doubt if she lied, she just doesn't remember. You can tell him all this tomorrow when you see him. He'll get to the bottom of it."

"Something's not sitting right with me. I swear there's something wrong," she said, her voice shaking.

"I've got another call. Try texting Joe again and I'll call you later."

"You'll call me right back?" Chantal realized that she was talking to dead air.

*

Rebecca inserted the first DVD into her player, a film from the Poker Palace on the evening Ryan Harper was murdered. Gumbo had taken a huge career risk to make copies of the footage for her. Forensics hadn't found anything but she was driven to find a clue connecting the murders. The camera angle was focused on Ryan Harper at a poker table. He was talking to someone out of view.

Suddenly the screen split into two so she could see who he was conversing with. The object of Ryan's anger looked calm and smug but Ryan's face was becoming as red as a fire engine and a manic, desperate glare took over his eyes. He stood up from the table and walked outside the camera's view.

She inserted the second of the three DVDs. The film started up immediately to show two security guards, one on either side of Ryan, arms interlaced, leading him away from the tournament.

The camera changed again to a single screen displaying a corner of the adjacent poker bar. Ryan was sitting there with the female member of the Buckingham Poker organizers. Becky couldn't remember her name. She watched as Ryan's appearance transformed from rage to petulance to forlorn resignation. He could be the poster boy for heartbreak. The Buckingham woman talked to Ryan until he left the bar. There was a final shot of him waiting for the elevator, alone, staring at the carpet, his shoulders slumped over like a man four times his age.

Her last hope lay with the third and final DVD. This would be the second victim, John Graves, playing in the later stages of the same tournament at the same casino, but now there were only a few poker tables of active players left. She went to the kitchen and got a cold beer out of the fridge.

She saw the cardboard box of leftover pizza from the day before. She grabbed the box and went back into the living room. She replaced the Harper DVD with the Graves DVD. She watched impatiently as his table of poker players played hand after hand. The camera angle gave a full view of the table and all the players. They were all men. The dealer was a man as well. There was very little interaction between any of them. The cards were dealt, poker chips were moved into the centre of the table, the flop was dealt, and chips were eventually shipped over to one of the men. There was some smiling and head nodding but no laughter and no anger. Rebecca sat back and nibbled on her pizza and watched hand after hand play out.

She jolted upright as a figure came into view. A woman was walking towards the poker table. The forensics team had tagged this part of the DVD and there were notes inserted on the bottom portion of the screen, indicating an estimated height of 5'9" and weight of 145 pounds.

The woman's features were totally camouflaged by a gigantic sunhat and mammoth sunglasses. She leaned over Graves from behind and whispered into his ear. Before he had time to turn around, the woman had turned away and was striding out of the room. Forensics had also taken the initiative to follow her progress with the eye in the sky camera. They traced her from the poker room, through the bar, and right out the front door. The final shot was of her back leaving the casino. There wasn't one identifiable shot of her face. She had blond hair but they couldn't tell if it was real or a wig. There was a notation on screen that a facial recognition program had been run on her but no positive match came back from it.

Rebecca finished the cold dry pizza. She ejected the DVD and turned off the TV. She went into the kitchen and fought to crumple and fold the pizza box into a small enough parcel to fit into her under-the-sink garbage bin.

She took another beer from the fridge and went out to sit on her small balcony that overlooked the parking lot of a small medical clinic. She watched as cars and people came and went. It was 5:00 p.m. and there was the hustle and bustle of shift change. Something niggled at the back of her mind. She struggled to think what it was that was bothering her. There was something about that last DVD that meant something to her. But what? It had to be that woman. There was something about her that was trying to trigger a memory. She had to relax and let it surface.

She took a long guzzle from the bottle, draining it. She got up to replace it with a full one. At the kitchen she decided to switch to water. She had to remain clearheaded and keep her brain receptive. She opened a bottle of lemon water, filled a tall glass with ice, and went back to the living room. She put the DVD back in and watched the woman walk up to Graves, lean down, turn around, and walk away. That walk, she knew that walk. Ramrod straight. Purposeful. Classy. Shit. She rifled through her purse for her phone.

*

Rebecca sent a text to Gumbo's phone. She was technically off the case and shouldn't even have copies of the DVDs. She'd let Gumbo handle that part of it however he saw fit. He'd gone out on a limb for her.

She made a second call—to Andrew in Montréal—and hoped he'd accept her call. She listened to the ringing at the other end, her whole body shaking.

"Miller."

"Andrew. It's Becky. I just watched the CCTV footage. I know who it is."

39

Andrew called the Port police unit and gave them Wentworth's name. "I don't have the name of the vessel and I don't know whether she docks there or at one of the other yacht clubs around the island." They accessed the computer log and found a boat registered to Wentworth at the exclusive Bassin de l'Horloge in Old Montréal. He explained the urgency and they set off to see if the boat was tied up.

He then called a unit to check on Wentworth's home and office and got in his car to head towards the port. The quay was at the very end of the Rue du Port in Old Montréal.

It seemed like most of the island was taking advantage of the beautiful summer night to take in the firework exhibition so traffic was practically at a standstill. It took him 15 minutes to drive a few dozen blocks. By the time he got to Rue du Port and the marina, he saw the police boat cruising slowly through the aisles of tied up pleasure craft.

Parking his car on the grass, he straddled the fence and took the stairs two at a time, yelling down at his marine colleagues. He ran across the cement pier and onto the wooden walkway where the police boat was idling in front of an empty berth. They reversed in and let him on. As soon as he was seated and jacketed they sped off, winding as quickly as they could through the marina until they reached the rapidly moving waters of the St. Lawrence.

40

Kathleen sat in the chair, eyes tightly closed, clutching the phone. Her knuckles were white and her nails were digging into her palms with such force that tiny drops of blood were forming under her nails. Her knees folded up to reach her chin as she screamed inside and watched the flickering movie on the inside of her eyelids:

Her father's red stubbly face turned away from the tub, looking over at her. His shirt was dripping wet. He was laughing as he stood up and stumbled over to her. The floor of the bathroom was slippery. He stumbled and nearly fell. She was crouching in the corner trying so hard to be invisible. His big rough hands reached down and picked her up under her armpits and slung her over his shoulders like Santa's toy bag. She could see into the tub now. Her Mother was lying straight out. She was naked and her beautiful long hair was floating and swaying back and forth around her head like seaweed in the pond. Her big brother was face down beside her. No part of him was moving.

"You gonna be a good girl now for Daddy? You can play with Bobby and Mommy in the water."

Kathleen's eyes opened wide. She looked down at her hands, still holding Joe's phone, and strode across the deck and down into the cabin. She stared at Joe, fast asleep. She wanted to wake him.

He'd help her understand what it all meant, wouldn't he? He looked so peaceful, lying there, the sheet tangled around his knees. She moved closer to him and noticed he was drooling slightly on the pillow.

My father used to do that. I used to sneak into their room sometimes after all the yelling and crying stopped, just to see if Mommy was alright. There'd be his spit all over her pillow. Sometimes it was pinkish. I detest that. Now there it is, on my pillow. How could he? I'm wrong, they're all the same. Joe won't be any damn different. Look at him. Lying there in his filthy little puddle.

She turned abruptly and went back up on deck, without waking him. She let his phone drop silently into the river. Her body felt as light as a feather. Everything made sense now. It was crystal clear what needed doing. She took the towel from beside the ice bucket, dipped it into the cool melted ice, and cleaned the pinpricks of blood that her nails had made off the palms of her hands.

She secured the bottle of champagne between the back and seat cushion of her chair. She placed two long bench cushions on the forward deck and returned to the wheelhouse, starting up the boat with a slight jerk.

41

When Joe woke up he was lying naked on the bed. He could see through the slats of the porthole blinds that the sky had turned a deep mauve with threads of crimson trailing through it. Kathleen was gone. The music was still playing from an iPod dock. When there was a break in the music, he heard her footsteps padding back and forth on the deck above. There was a deep rumble from underneath the bed and he felt the boat lurch backwards.

*

Kathleen was at the wheel, guiding the boat past the spattering of yachts, sailboats, and dinghies hovering in the water waiting for the fireworks show. She squeezed away the tears that were making an attempt, albeit a feeble one, to ooze their way out of her lustreless eyes. She was totally drained, but determined to reach a spot she remembered, just past the Jacques Cartier bridge, near the abandoned buildings of the old Vickers shipyard. It was far enough away from the action that chances of coming across other boaters would be slim. She was certain that Joe would presume that the desire for privacy had dictated her choice of locale. Seclusion for an entirely different purpose.

*

Joe put his shorts on and shook the grogginess out of his head. The boat was moving faster. He arrived up on deck and stood a few feet behind Kathleen who was steering the boat towards La Ronde. She was wearing a silk dressing gown which was being blown about, exposing her naked ass and legs every few seconds. She looked gorgeous. He came up behind her and his arms encircled her waist. "Where are we going, hen?"

Kathleen leaned back into him. "We'll get closer to the fireworks, love. But far enough away to have some privacy. You go sit down. I've put cushions on the foredeck. I'll stop just off the island near the bridge. We'll be able to lie down and watch the show. Go wait for me." He begrudgingly released her and walked towards the deck. There were long waterproof cushions tied down to form a makeshift bed. He clambered over the rail, and sat down. He continued to admire the occasional exposure of Kathleen's body as the boat began to slow down. She turned the engine off and called over to him. "Joe. Anchor the boat here, will you? I'm going down to get the other bottle of champagne. Or would you prefer a beer now?"

"Whatever you're having. Anything at all."

She returned a few minutes later with a can of beer and a tumbler of champagne. The can was already opened and he took a swig from it. She clinked her glass against his can. "Cheers." She stared at him intently as he sipped on the beer. "Drink up so you can put that can down," Kathleen said. He emptied it with no further encouragement. She took it from him and tossed it in the water. "Lie back, Joe."

"I'm feeling a bit woozy, Kath. I think I'd better get to the aft deck, where it's flat."

Before he could crawl over to the rail, she pressed her palm into his chest and he fell gently onto his back.

"Kath...really...my head...I dunno wha ..." Joe's voice trailed off and he couldn't find any more words.

He heard the music coming from La Ronde amusement park, but it sounded shrill and there was too much echo. He felt like his pulse was pounding in his ears.

She was still staring at him but the stare was intense and quizzical, like she was studying him. It reminded Joe of when his parents had taken him on a picnic near Inverkip and he had caught a tadpole. He'd scooped the wiggly black thing into a jam jar and watched it, in the hopes it would turn into a frog in front of his eyes. But instead he had watched it die.

"I'm sorry, Joe. I feel like I should offer you an explanation. I really meant for us to have a pleasant evening out here, making love and watching the fireworks. I didn't plan for it to end like this."

Joe opened his mouth to question her but only a small grunt passed his lips.

"Although now it feels like an added bonus to the evening. In all fairness, this is your own fault. You're disgusting, Joe. You really are. And I truly had no idea. Well, I suppose I must have known. Deep down."

She stopped talking and looked around as if she had never been on the river before. Her gaze eventually rested on his stare. "You look so confused, my dear. But I'm afraid I have precious little time to explain it all to you. I have to get to that pesky little assistant of yours. Chantal, is it? She found some ridiculous newspaper article about my family. If it's any consolation to you, I wasn't aware what had happened to Bobby and Mum when I gave you this mission, and I was quite prepared to live happily ever after with you. I was even considering not punishing any more stupid boys. Is it dawning on you yet, my sweet?"

*

Joe looked up at her and realized from the tinges of red in her eyes that she'd been crying. Yet now she was smiling. He tried to piece it all together. He came to the startling revelation that he was about to die and, for some reason unbeknownst to him, he was not her first victim. But he still couldn't make sense of it. The front of Kathleen's gown gaped open as she leaned seductively over him. She spoke to him, stroking his face and touching his lips with her own for what seemed like eternity. He felt only a small tingling and then nothing.

She looked up at the night sky and clicked her tongue against the roof of her mouth a few times, as if she was trying to work out a math equation. She lowered her head and smiled at him again, looking like she'd solved it. "You're all the same really. Did you see the state of my linen down below when you got up? You've slobbered all over it. You're quite repulsive."

He stared into her glazed eyes.

"I wish I had more time to tell you everything. But I do have to take care of young Chantal later as well. Busy, busy night for me!" Kathleen's eyes narrowed into razor sharp slits and she grinned at the same time. Her appearance was pure foulness. She rolled him over and over again, effortlessly on the slant of the deck, until he belly flopped into the water.

There was a deafening thunder in his ears and his head pounded. The water burned its way into his nostrils and open mouth. His head and lungs were competing to explode.

The water flooded into his body.

*

The police boat sped through the water, its searchlight alerting all the boaters to an emergency. They knew they were looking for one of the larger boats, which would make it easier. But it was dark and the Wentworth woman could be anchored somewhere with none of the lights on.

One of the officers said it would make sense for her to travel east of the island if she was seeking seclusion. They passed under the Jacques Cartier bridge.

A huge silver fountain of fireworks went off overhead and lit up the sky for a few seconds. Just enough time to see the silhouette of a large yacht a few metres offshore near the old shipyards.

The officer at the wheel, who had been hurriedly introduced as Jean-Pierre, executed a sharp turn in the direction of the yacht.

At that moment, multiple explosions of silver and gold gave them a few precious seconds of visibility and, along with their searchlight, they saw a large object tumbling from the deck of the anchored boat.

42

Joe's first impression on waking was that he was in a crib and his ex-wife was gawking at him from a chair a few feet away against the wall. He assumed he was caught up in some kickass crazy nightmare. His head was pounding harder and more viciously than the worst hangover he'd ever had.

"Joe. Are you awake, you lazy bum? Open your eyes because I'm not going away." Definitely Anna's voice. He clenched his eyelids tighter together.

"C'mon Joe. Open your eyes." Her voice became more concerned. "Do you realize you're in a hospital?"

That explained the crib. He tentatively opened one eye and then the other. He tried to raise his head from the pillow but a jackhammer operator came back on shift. His head toppled back onto the pillow and a searing pain jagged through one eye and out his ear.

When the pain abated he struggled to sit back up. Anna got up from her chair and crossed the few feet to his bed. She reached down and handed him a remote control. Joe pressed the green up arrow and was rewarded with his upper torso and head floating slowly upwards.

"Brilliant. Should get one of these for home," he said. His voice cracked like an old hardwood floor and his hand flew up to his throat. "What happened? Is it my heart again? How did I..?"

Anna handed him a glass of liquid. He took a large swallow of tepid water as a few stray memories crept back into his head. He took another smaller sip and stared down at the glass. Water. Memories were flooding back in like a tidal wave now. He spat out his last sip of water.

"You'll be alright, Joe. You're over the worst of it. Andrew and Chantal stayed at your bedside all night. They're out in the hallway now. Can I let them in?" Not waiting for his answer, she walked over to the door and swung it open.

The duo ran in and surrounded him. Anna took the footboard position and flicked through the chain-attached clipboard. Chantal was on his right and planted a kiss on his forehead. Her eyes were spider-webs of red lines and various coloured tracks of eye makeup ran the length of her face.

"Andrew told me the psychopath gave you a Mickey Mouse and threw you in the water!" Chantal said, holding his two hands in a death-grip. The other three looked at each other, each trying to decipher her words.

Joe finally figured it out and translated for the other two. "Mickey Finn." He grinned at her. "I'll be okay, Chuck." He blew her a kiss, so she released her grasp on him to back up and catch it.

Andy took the other side of the bed. "Good to see you, man. I'll let you visit with these two for a while, and then I'll kick them out and take an official statement from you." He patted Joe's shoulder and left.

43

Chantal and Anna left to pick up some essentials from Joe's condo. Joe was feeling and looking stronger by the minute, but the attending doctor wanted to keep him in a second night.

Andy pulled a chair up close to the bed, turned on his pocket-sized digital recorder, and removed his notepad and pen from his shoulder bag. "So, you know the drill, Joe. What happened yesterday?"

"Kathleen and I made a date. She told me to meet her at the Clock Tower marina. She owns this fancy-schmancy yacht."

"For the record, this wasn't your first date with her, was it?"

"No. We had a couple before this one. For the record, this date was my least favourite."

"Right. Keep going, smartass."

"We had a few drinks. Some food. All very posh. We went below deck for a while. I fell asleep. I was what you might call a satisfied man." He winked and Andy couldn't hold back a smile. "I woke when the engine started up. I don't know what time that was but the sun was down and the fireworks had begun at La Ronde."

He stopped and took a sip of water. "In retrospect the mood had definitely taken a turn. She was a bit on the demanding side. I thought, at the time, we might be playing a game. You know? Some shade of grey or something?" Joe put his clenched hand to his mouth and coughed meaningfully.

"She turned the engine off while I anchored the boat." He took a swallow from his glass, wishing it was beer. He'd had enough water. "She brought me a beer. I drank said beer." He closed his eyes and tried to recall what she had said. "She evidently decided I wasn't for her and, in lieu of a plank to walk, I was rolled off the deck." His head fell back onto the pillow.

"You feeling alright, pal?"

"I'm okay but it's very foggy. I don't remember everything she said to me. I do remember telling her that I was feeling a bit groggy. Then things turned very weird. I knew she was gonna kill me. I knew she'd killed others. She threatened to kill Chuck, I think." Joe shook his head. "I don't know. I think the last thing I said to her was that maybe I just needed a wee something to eat. She stared at me for what seemed like forever and then told me that I didn't need food again. Ever."

"Well, to be honest Joe, you could stand to lose a few pounds."

"I'll ignore your insensitivity for the moment."

Andrew turned the recorder off. "She's made a confession, Joe. I call it that, but it was more like reciting a curriculum vitae in a job interview. Proud as a new Dad as she named her victims. If she'd had cigars I think she would have passed them around at the station last night." He turned the recorder back on. "Keep going. Can you recall anything else that she said?"

"At some point she admitted that she hadn't planned to kill me. But apparently Chantal had discovered something about her so her only choice was to dispose of both of us. I must add that, even though she hadn't planned my death, the idea of killing me didn't seem to overly upset her. As a matter of fact I don't think I've ever seen her more in her element. But how did you guys know I was in trouble and where to look, for that matter?"

"Chantal called me first. She'd found an old newspaper article about the family. Wentworth's father was a piece of work. Drunk gambler with some serious aggression problems. Killed the mother, brother, and was about to kill Kathleen when a neighbour intervened. Made Chantal justifiably uncomfortable. I got off the phone from her to accept a call from your pal in Vegas, Rebecca. She was at home reviewing CCTV footage from the poker tournament and felt damn sure that she recognized the good doctor. She sends her best, by the way. Told me to buy you grapes. So the two phone calls came together like the perfect storm just in time to save your sorry ass. The port police and I were able to witness your graceless dive into the river. Believe me, knowing that it was you being tossed over the side was a shocker!"

"You probably weren't nearly as shocked as I was, mate. I thought I was hallucinating you when I got fished out of the water."

"A squad car went to Wentworth's home, by the way. She has a fascinating collection of smutty clothes, wigs, contact lenses. You remember anything else?"

"I can't think of anything else except it turns out I love caviar."

"She said with the Harper kid she planned to make it look like suicide. She surprised him in Vegas by turning up and pretending she was there to seduce him. She put a paralytic concoction of Remeron and Ketamine in his beer."

"But what about the suicide note? That was his handwriting, wasn't it?"

"That was pretty smart. She told Ryan at his last therapy session to compose and write down what he'd put in a goodbye-to-the-world note. She explained to him that was her method in bringing the reality of such a drastic choice to her patients."

"Shit. Poor kid."

"Then, seeing as how she was in Vegas anyhow with a free night to kill, so to speak, she thought she'd make the most of it. She had been online to monitor Ryan's behaviour and had run across some guy on the chat forum who displayed all the tendencies she detested. Belligerent gambler who treated his wife and kids like crap—Graves. She noticed he was playing in the same tournament, thanks to the player seating chart that Buckingham kept at their desk. So she enticed the man to his death."

"And the third guy, here in Montréal?" Joe asked.

"That was serendipity. She was back home in Montréal and had developed a taste for the kill. Apparently she saw what she assumed was Rebecca's hair in your bathroom hairbrush. She recognized the opportunity to pin the murders on someone who had been in Vegas for the first two crimes, and was now here at the time of the third murder. Planting evidence at the scene provided an added perk of getting you all to herself. Thought she could take down two birds with one stone and planted a single strand of hair where she knew any forensic team worth their salt would find it. She knew that Rebecca's DNA would be on file, because of her being on the force."

"Are you sure these are her only victims?"

Andy switched the recorder off. "Joe, I'm telling you, she's one freaky-as-shit broad. Picture this. We arrive at the side of the boat, right? Before we've even come to a stop one of the marine police dives in the water to fish you out." Andy leans forward like he's telling a bedtime story to a child. "She's sitting on a deckchair sipping champagne, with an amused smile on her face as if we've just arrived a tad late for cocktails. We took her in to the station, she waived rights to a lawyer, and she sat in the interview room for hours proudly sharing her grisly shenanigans. Then she spent a bloody hour psychoanalysing herself for us. It's crazy to see. You should watch the video with me some time. You can buy the popcorn. We finally called in counsel and a doctor for her. She was heading for the rubber room when I came here to interview you."

"So, I repeat, Harper was definitely the first?"

"That's what we figure. I think she would have bragged about any others. She wasn't shy, that one. So, Harper was her patient for years, and she felt his treatment was totally unsuccessful. He exhibited a lot of the traits that her own father had, although she had no recollection of those events from her childhood. She joined the Buckingham Poker website, with the moniker of Lady Macbet, to monitor his actions at the tables and on the bulletin board website. She realized that he was lying to her about the amount of time and money he was spending, as well as hiding the anger that she could see for herself he was exhibiting. When he won the ticket to Vegas she made the decision that it was her responsibility to make the world a better place by removing him from it."

"Jesus. She must have overheard Becky's voicemail to me when I thought she was asleep."

"You've been a busy little boy, haven't you?"

"I'm popular." Joe grinned and sat up to stretch. "Always have been, no doubt always will be. Be as jealous as you like, my good man."

Andy stood up and walked to the door. "I'm hardly jealous of you courting a serial killer, Joe."

Epilogue

I was led to my room by two burly, rather dull-looking, women. They hovered at the doorway, watching me as I set my few belongings down on the grey melamine desk. It was heavily scratched with initials, names, curse words, and poetry—much like desks back in high school.

"Get yourself settled. Lights out in 10 minutes," instructed the larger of the two guards.

"Goodnight ladies," I responded, but they just turned away and the door closed automatically, with a jolting thump, behind them. I heard the clang of the bolt being drawn across the door.

I looked around my room. I refused to call it a cell. A cell is for scruffy, mullet-headed, knuckle tattooed, low-lifes. And, of course, Catholic nuns. I am neither. I'm a woman; brilliant, strong, resourceful.

I changed into the blue polyester pyjamas they'd given me, carefully folding and placing my clothing onto one of the five built-in shelves beside the desk. I inspected the bizarre variety of objects scattered haphazardly on the shelves: a much-thumbed bible, a week-old newspaper, a near-toothless comb, half a roll of toilet paper, a plastic cup, a scratchy white towel, and one dirty white sock.

In the corner, at the end of the adjoining wall, was a toilet and sink. They looked like they'd been rescued from a demolished 1950's motel. There was a bar of yellow soap perched on the lip of the sink, dried up and cracking. The floor was a rusty-red linoleum, and the walls painted Lima Bean green. It was apparent that Martha Stewart never had any influence whatsoever during her time served.

I walked over to the bed and lay down, staring at the ceiling. I suppose the bed should be called a cot. It could only fit one body, and the mattress was thin and lumpy. The pillow was foam rubber and nearly flat. The blanket I was lying on was an itchy grey flannel and brought back a fleeting memory of my childhood.

I rolled over on to my left side, with both hands placed under my cheek to cradle my head. I noticed, on the wall in front of me, but close to the ceiling, a small curtain-free window. The sky was ebony. There were no visible stars, and I suspected that the faint glow I saw wasn't coming from the moon, but from strategically placed spot-lights. There was a large poster-size paper taped to the wall below the window.

The Rules
Bath time is strictly enforced at 6:00 a.m.

A single tear rolled down my cheek and into the palm of my hand. The lights went out.

Thank You for Reading the First Joe Cameron Mystery.

We hope that you enjoyed it.

Stay tuned for more!

ACKNOWLEDGEMENTS

Ian Shaw of Deux Voiliers Publishing. Thank you for taking a chance with this book and for your generous guidance and advice.

Grant Munro. Thank you for the cover artwork. It's so special to me. You're a dear friend.

Ania Szneps, who copy-edited the manuscript. I'm grateful to you for your diligence and meticulousness.

Lori Schubert and Deanna Radford and the Québec Writers Federation. You make the writing community a special place and I'm pleased as punch to be part of it.

Ann Diamond, writer and friend. Thank you for reviewing my first draft and offering such constructive advice. Your honest feedback was essential and taught me so much.

Mike Young, who proofread this before it went to press. Thanks for the time and effort you provided.

My family, friends and writing workshop pals who have read and given me feedback on portions of this book, inspired some parts of it, played poker and drank beer with me. Thanks for making this fun.

Patrick Gillen, my husband. You encouraged me from the start. That evening a few years ago, at the poker table in Vegas, when the fight broke out and you told me I should write about it. Thank you for always believing I could do it.

About the Author

Geri Newell Gillen was born in Ottawa. She grew up in Montréal, on a steady diet of Nancy Drew and Trixie Belden. She was educated in Montréal and held numerous jobs which included Chimpanzee babysitter, program typist for the Festival international du film en 16 mm, and McGill Library shelf-stacker. She finally settled on a career as a Research Technologist for a large manufacturing firm. Following early retirement, she appeased her aspiration of writing by chronicling 200 years of Newell Family History. In researching and writing these genealogical stories, and uncovering a multitude of mysteries along the way, she was drawn to writing a fictional mystery. Combining her love of poker and her quarter-century marriage to an amusing pub-loving Glaswegian, "Quite Perfectly Dead" was born.

Her website is www.gerinewell.com

About Deux Voiliers Publishing

Organized as a writers-plus collective, Deux Voiliers Publishing is a new generation publisher. We focus on emerging Canadian writers. The art of creating new fiction is our driving force.

Other Works of Fiction from Deux Voiliers Publishing

Soldier, Lily, Peace and Pearls by Con Cú (Literary Fiction 2012)

Last of the Ninth by Stephen L. Bennett (Historical Fiction 2012)

Marching to Byzantium by Brendan Ray (Historical Fiction 2012)

Tales of Other Worlds by Chris Turner (Fantasy/Sci-Fiction 2012)

Bidong by Paul Duong (Literary Fiction 2012)

Zaidie and Ferdele by Carol Katz (Children's Fiction 2012)

Sumer Lovin' by Nicole Chardenet (Humour/Fantasy 2013)

Kirk's Landing by Mike Young (Crime/Adventure 2014)

Romulus by Fernand Hibbert and translated by Matthew Robertshaw (Historical Fiction/English Translation 2014)

Palawan Story by Caroline Vu (Literary Fiction 2014)

Cycling to Asylum by Su J. Sokol (Speculative Fiction 2014)

Stage Business by Gerry Fostaty (Crime 2014)

Stark Nakid by Sean McGinnis (Crime/Humour 2014)

Twisted Reasons by Geza Tatrallyay (Crime Thriller 2014)

Four Stones by Norman Hall (Canadian Spy Thriller 2015)

Nothing to Hide by Nick Simon (Dystopian Fiction 2015)

Frack Off by Jason Lawson (Humour/Political Satire 2015)

Wall of Dust by Timothy Niedermann (Literary Fiction 2015)

The Goal by Andrew Caddell (Non-Fiction Short Stories 2015)

Please visit our website for ordering information
www.deuxvoilierspublishing.com